DON'T TOUCH

A Seven Families Novel

LUCY LEROUX

DISCLAIMER

This book is a work of fiction. All of the characters, names, and events portrayed in this novel are products of the author's imagination. Any resemblance to actual events or persons, living or dead, is entirely coincidental.

This eBook is licensed for your personal enjoyment only and may not be re-sold or given away to other people. If you would like to share this book with someone else, please send them to the author's website, where they can find out where to purchase a copy for themselves. Free content can be downloaded at the author's free reads page.

Thank you for respecting the author's work. Enjoy!

TITLES BY LUCY LEROUX

The Singular Obsession Series
Making Her His
Confiscating Charlie, A Singular Obsession Novelette
Calen's Captive
Stolen Angel
The Roman's Woman
Save Me, A Singular Obsession Novella
Take Me, A Singular Obsession Prequel Novella
Trick's Trap
Peyton's Price

The Spellbound Regency Series
The Hex, A Free Spellbound Regency Short
Cursed
Black Widow
Haunted

The Rogues and Rescuers Series
Codename Romeo
The Mercenary Next Door

Knight Takes Queen
The Millionaire's Mechanic
Burned Deep - Coming Soon

Writing As L.B. Gilbert
The Elementals Saga
Discordia, A Free Elementals Story
Fire
Air
Water
Earth

A Shifter's Claim
Kin Selection
Eat You Up
Tooth and Nail
The When Witch and the Wolf

Charmed Legacy Cursed Angel Watchtowers
Forsaken

CREDITS

Cover Design by Robin Harper
   http://www.wickedbydesigncovers.com

Editing by Jason Letts
   https://imbueediting.com/

CHAPTER ONE

Zhi Zheng flipped through the auction catalog with feigned nonchalance. "Which one is it?" he hissed from behind set teeth.

"Hell, if I know," Han muttered. His cousin's placid expression was in direct contrast with his tone. "But judging from this crowd, we were right to drop everything and come here."

Here was the ass end of New York State at the private estate of the recently deceased Llewelyn Montclair. The house was a pretentious Palladian mansion straight out of an English period drama, which fit what he knew about that man. He had never met Montclair in life, but he had seen him from a distance a few times at charity balls and the like. He'd noted him at the time, memorizing his face because of his reputation.

Montclair had been an avid collector of rare and precious antiquities. Normally Zhi didn't give a damn about that sort of thing, but Montclair was one of those who went the extra mile to acquire objects of magical significance. It had been his obsession. He'd traveled the world and learned to speak eight different languages so he could negotiate for his acquisitions without having to go through an interpreter.

And in so doing he had managed to nearly bankrupt himself. Montclair had no children, but he had several nieces and nephews ready to put his collection on the auction block to recoup whatever cash they could, picking over the carcass of his estate. The Marchesi Auction House, the one most favored by the Seven for their expertise in magical artifacts, had been charged with the task of liquidating the assets.

Han leaned forward a bit, his eyes tracking a particularly dangerous witch from the Vakil clan in a form-fitting dress that accentuated every sleek curve.

"I guess the rumors were true. A dangerous artifact must have slipped the Elementals' net. Otherwise, we wouldn't be rubbing elbows with the who's who of the Seven."

The woman they were watching, Danika, paused on the oak chevron-parquet floor to look at him. She inclined her head with a regal nod.

He nodded back. "Any regrets?" his cousin murmured.

His father, Bao, had once considered Danika a possible wife for him, but Zhi had vetoed the plan before the other family caught wind of it.

"No," he murmured. Danika might have been gorgeous, with enough power to guarantee the magic continued to run in their bloodline in the next generation, but he didn't want to spend the rest of his life sleeping with one eye open.

His eidetic memory supplied names to many of the other faces in the room. The more he recognized, the more he retreated behind a wall of icy reserve. *"I see reps from all the seven families here—and not just the lackeys",* he said, switching over to silent communication.

It didn't matter that his cousin didn't share his gift of telepathy. Zhi's power was strong enough to send and receive from anyone. It didn't matter if the person was on the other side of the world. If Zhi had their mental imprint, the strength of his ability meant he could communicate with them as if they were in the next room.

Technically, telepathy wasn't an uncommon ability among witchkind. Many people heard voices in their heads. A few even realized they were other people's thoughts. But of this small subset, a tiny fraction had the strength to focus on an individual voice. Zhi had been born with the ability to do just that, his telepathic touch so precise most people never even realized their innermost thoughts had been heard, while others of his kind were crushed by the wall of sound generated by humans large and small.

But it wasn't that aspect of Zhi's gift that made the members of this jaded and powerful gathering give him a wide berth. He could use his strength to destroy another person's mind, the organic matter crumpling as if it were being squeezed by a physical vice.

To the untrained eye or even a human coroner, the death would appear like a natural, if violently catastrophic, aneurysm. A snapshot of blood and gore flashed through his mind before he could stop it.

"I see two other family heads, not including myself", Zhi continued, not letting the disturbing images of his past show on his face. *"Lots of deadly people in this room."*

"Yeah, and you're one of them", Han said, his inner voice turning decidedly sarcastic. Their telepathic channel was so old and worn that the communication was effortless and crystalline in its clarity. *"The good news is no one is looking at you cross-eyed. You have their respect."*

"I trust your assessment, but it's too soon to say that for certain."

Han smirked. *"Trust me, none of these people want their brains leaking from their ears. As for the crowd, there are several known right-hands and at least one heir, including some shifters I've done business with."* He tilted his head to draw his attention to the dark-garbed man moving with predatory grace on their left.

"Not a wolf or a bear," Zhi replied after a quick assessment. *"Some kind of cat."*

"How do you do that? Hanson still won't tell me what kind he is, and I've known the bastard for years too." Han's lips turned down. *"He's so damn smug about it."*

Zhi lifted a shoulder. *"I can taste his wildness from here."*

What he meant by that was difficult to describe. He had learned how to differentiate the major groups of Supernaturals with his other sense at a very young age. Zhi had always assumed it was an evolutionary response meant to protect him, to show him who his enemies might be so he wouldn't be caught unaware. That thought almost made him laugh aloud.

When you were one of the Seven, that call was usually coming from inside the house.

"It has to be a weapon," he told Han, closing the auction brochure. *"One that every family feels they can't afford to let fall into another family's hands."*

It was the only explanation for the caliber of the crowd here.

"Or it's something that could be weaponized with some tweaking. Otherwise, the Elementals would have descended to take the damn thing. You know they lock up everything truly dangerous in their archive."

The archive's location was a mystery to the Seven. Rumor had it the mythical warrior's supposed impregnable stronghold had been breached recently—an inside job by a close associate. But he didn't believe, as Han had suggested earlier, that they had allowed a potential weapon to slip through their net. If anything, a breach meant that they had doubled or tripled their efforts to secure magical weapons. Nothing would get past them now.

And yet here he was, alongside the other families, each as determined as the other that they get the advantage. Even allies might turn against each other before this day was out.

Zhi raised a brow, looking beyond the auction stage. They were setting up a display table. The antiquities and curiosities that had been Montclair's *raison d'être* were being assembled behind the doors of the ballroom. *"Maybe the Elementals did nab this thing and we don't know it."*

Han's nose wrinkled in response. *"Nah. Too quiet. That girl from the auction house that opened the doors to us would have sounded the alarm. Are you sure you don't want to scan her or the rest of the staff? Might give us an edge. It can at least tell us what we should be bidding on."*

Zhi bristled. *"That would be a violation."*

"Yeah, yeah. I know. You'll only use your powers when the family is threatened. I'm not entirely sure this isn't the case right now."

"I'm aware." And truthfully, he was sorely tempted to violate his own oath. His eyes passed over the crowds again, scanning for threats. *"But there are enough high-level talents who might detect that kind of scan. I'd like to leave this ballroom without having to fight my way out."*

"You are no fun."

Zhi kept scanning. *"I'm aware of that too."*

"All right." Han rubbed his hands. *"Let's go with what we know. Logic dictates the most precious item will be auctioned last—although we should bid on anything this crowd shows an interest in to be safe."*

The fact Han didn't know the nature of the object they were referring to was significant. His cousin's job was to keep his ear to the ground, tracing both hard facts and rumors as unsubstantial as mist with a relentlessness that spoke of his devotion to the family and tenacious nature. His information network was a twisting labyrinth. Han was the Zheng's family bloodhound, while Zhi was its naked blade. A telepath of brutal strength, he had just been made the Zheng family head a mere two months ago.

Three months and he was already swimming with the sharks.

He caught a flash of color. The red-haired junior assistant from Marchesi was pointing out the podium to a balding man in a suit.

The auction was starting.

CHAPTER TWO

Nova Navarro caught herself before she fell flat on her face. Turning, she scowled at the squat, heavy stone totem she'd tripped on.

"Are you all right?" Sandrine, the Marchesi house admin, asked from across the room.

"I'm fine," she said, straightening and smoothing her gloved hands over the front of her satin sheath dress. She couldn't feel the silky smoothness of the fabric with her gloves on, but she liked the sensation of the motion, nonetheless.

The therapist Llewelyn had sent her to had diagnosed this kind of movement as a self-soothing mannerism. The doctor had encouraged her to curtail that kind of behavior, but Llewelyn had argued against it. "Let the girl be. She deserves whatever comfort she can have," he had drawled, waving a hand in a languid gesture she associated with him.

Despite having lived in the Northeast for years, Llewelyn reveled in his image as a Southern gentleman. He still wore seersucker and linen suits despite their unsuitability for the climate. One of his many eccentricities.

A wave of sadness passed over her. Nova would miss Llewelyn Montclair very much.

Blinking rapidly, Nova turned, clearing her throat. "The second item up for auction is ready," she said, pointing to the obsidian figurine set on the table next to the door. The other small auction items were lined up next to it. The larger pieces were scattered around the room. Marchesi had two burly specially trained moving men to take those out to the podium in the ballroom room.

"Please refer to my notes for the recommended starting bid," she said, not for the first time. The Marchesi considered themselves the experts, but no one knew Llewelyn's collection better than she did.

"House Marchesi has already agreed to defer to your expertise," Sandrine said in a surprisingly gentle tone. "Although our in-house appraisers put the value of some of the items below your assessment. This crowd might not pay the higher price tags."

Nova's smile was sad. "They'll pay them."

"You're right." Sandrine paused, biting her lip. "About that last item up for auction...are you certain?"

Nova blinked. Her heart beat a little faster. "Yes, I'm sure," she lied.

Sandrine stared a touch too long, sympathy and pity in her expression. Finally, she nodded, pulling her clipboard a little closer. "Of course. I'll just go to the ballroom to see how the auction is going."

Nova waited until Sandrine had left before sagging where she stood. Her pulse was pounding, and she was starting to sweat. She staggered to the mirror hanging on the wall.

You're doing the right thing, she told her reflection. Only one of the major families would have the resources to protect auction item number thirty.

Or was she shoving her frying pan straight into the flames?

Shaking her head, Nova began her breathing exercises, the ones her therapists had taught her long ago. *You knew the risk. You weighed all your options and did all the research. The course is set.*

In any case, it was far too late to change her mind now.

Sandrine came to the threshold to signal the moving men to bring out the next item. Then another and another.

Nova kept her head down, not caring if Sandrine noticed her

anxiety any longer. As far as Nova was concerned, she was entitled to it.

She waited till the door had closed on that ugly totem that had scuffed her precious vintage T-strap pumps before stopping her exercise to look up and check her flushed complexion.

Nova yelped, startled to find someone standing right behind her.

His face was familiar—he was one of the family heads she had invited personally. The most lethal one, in her opinion.

She swallowed heavily, aware that he could crush her mind with a single thought. "I'm sorry, but you aren't allowed back here." Nova was proud that her voice didn't shake.

Zhi Zheng, head of house Zheng was one scary son of a bitch. But was he the one she needed? The idea of it made her head spin.

Regardless of his suitability, Nova couldn't allow him to win the auction by default.

"Sir, you need to go back to the ballroom. You aren't allowed to examine the items until they take the stage. I'm afraid there is no early buyout option available."

The man smiled. It transformed his face from coldly handsome and forbidding to enticing, like a beautiful flame you wanted to touch. Nova startled, pivoting on her heel to see who Zhi Zheng found so interesting.

But between one blink and the next he had disappeared.

"What the hell?" Nova twisted her head, scanning the room. Except for Marchesi's waiting moving men, she was alone.

Holy crap. Was Zhi Zheng a teleporter? No, all her data told her he was a telepath. He must have hired someone to transport him into the room. But item thirty was still accounted for. What had he come here to find?

Catching her breath, she hurried over to the table to count the labeled antiquities. When none appeared to be missing, she turned and added up the larger objects. Other than the ones that had gone out the door while she did her exercises, nothing was missing.

What had Zhi Zheng wanted?

Just a look at the goods. Nova couldn't decide how she felt about that. Did it mean he was going to bid on thirty or not?

Nova tried to recall the details of his expression. Had that smile been satisfied…or contemptuous? Or did it mean something else entirely? She had no idea.

Fortunately, there were no other incursions by the Seven to the back room. The rest of the families seemed content to let the auction proceed without further interference.

Finally, they were down to the second to last auction item, a rare functional fertility totem that she'd advised Llewelyn not to buy. Not because it didn't work, but because it did. It just wasn't something a confirmed bachelor like Llewelyn would have need of. But it was cut from a rare pink sapphire the size of her fist, so of course he had to have it despite the fact his competitors for it had included more than one infertile couple.

Smoothing her skirt once more, she turned to take a final look in the mirror. But the large oval-looking glass was gone.

Nova frowned. Had one of the auction house's movers picked it up by mistake? Nova hadn't marked it for inclusion in the auction because it was too new, one of the items Llewelyn had neglected to tell her he bought. She hadn't even noticed it until her employer had passed onto his great reward.

Sandrine came into the room just as she was about to go off to find one of the movers to ask. She folded her hands in front of her. "They're ready."

"Oh," she breathed. "Okay."

The mystery of the disappearing mirror would have to wait. It was showtime.

She put her hands to her head, making sure not a single strand of her hair had escaped her careful coiffure. Sandrine waited patiently despite the fact the room next door held some of the most dangerous people in the world.

Remember what Llewelyn always told you. "All the world's a stage, kiddo. If you need the audience to clap at the right moment, then play your part like your life depends on it." Then he would wink and add, "Wearing a fabulous outfit to set the stage never hurts either."

Her final adjustments done, she walked out into the ballroom where the Marchesi house mover was clearing the stage.

I am calm, I am confident, and I am valuable, she told herself, climbing up to the podium.

Once there her eyes nearly crossed in panic, but she did not allow it to show. All the crowd saw was a young woman in a fabulous vintage dress and shoes wearing a serene expression.

"Thank you all for coming to the auction of the world-famous Montclair collection," she said, projecting to the back of the room like Llewelyn had taught her.

She waited until the Marchesi mover had placed the chair in the center of the dais. "It's time to begin bidding for our final item."

Nova walked over and sat down, folding her hands gracefully. She nodded at the auctioneer.

He cleared his throat. "Introducing the Montclair collection item thirty, psychometrist Nova Navarro. Term of service—life."

CHAPTER THREE

Zhi had been at the edge of his seat the entire auction. Some choice antiquities had gone on the auction block, and the avaricious collectors among the Seven had themselves a field day. He bid on nothing, not even the antique Samurai sword imbued with the power of the elite Ishiguro-ke that Han begged him to get.

Tellingly, Naade Gambari and Monira Vakil, the two other family heads present, hadn't bid on anything either.

Finally, it was time for the last item to go up on the block.

Zhi tensed when the chair was placed in the middle of the stage. He ignored the explosion of swear words from Han in his head when the redhead who had met them at the door sat down in it.

"Psychometrist Nova Navarro. Term of service—life."

The words echoed in his mind as the auctioneer raised his voice to be heard over the buzzing crowd. Zhi only processed half of what the man said next, a long list of terms and conditions.

Then the bidding started. It opened at one million dollars and quickly rose to one and a quarter. Then one point five. Then two.

Han's elbow dug into his side. *"You have to bid."*

Zhi's expression remained fixed, but his incredulity was clear in his tone. *"It's a person. I can't buy a person—that's slavery."*

"You weren't paying attention. She's not a slave. You're hiring her."

Zhi threw him a scathing glance. *"For life. An employee who can never quit, that's a slave."*

Han scowled, his eyes going from Naade to Monira. *"Her contract says she can quit if you abuse her—which you would never do! I can't say the same for those two. And both are clearly determined to win. I know you have major reservations about this, but consider the alternative. What will happen to this woman if one of them wins her?"*

It was the right argument to make, but it wasn't the only one. Zhi took a deep breath, studying the back of Naade's head. What did he and Monira know about this girl that they were continuing to bid so damn high?

Psychometrists were rare. Not all had the skill and knowledge to work for a discerning collector like Montclair, let alone be kept on permanent retainer by him. The few who did typically worked for exclusive auction houses like Marchesi, but they did outside contract work for the Seven on a regular basis. You didn't *buy* them or force them into contracts of lifetime servitude.

There was something else going on. Nova was more than she appeared, and the other family heads knew it.

"Fuck," he swore to Han. *"I can't believe I'm doing this."*

Zhi raised his hand and joined the bidding war. He won it less than ten minutes later.

The price was one hundred million dollars.

THE MINUTE the auction was over, Zhi and Han were ushered out of the ballroom to a small salon. He was handed a thick stack of papers in a leather folio by a Marchesi employee who introduced herself as Sandrine.

His recent acquisition was nowhere in sight.

"This is Nova Navarro's contract," Sandrine explained when he asked what it was. "The sale is not final until it is signed with all the stipulations agreed to. No exceptions can be made for a particular clause. You must agree to all of them, but I can assure you that each is quite reasonable."

He opened the folio, flipping through the thick sheets. He could barely process the words, so he signaled Han and handed them to him. His cousin's law degree an asset once again.

Sandrine excused herself with a murmur, but he stopped her at the door. "Where is the girl?"

The woman turned, her sheath dress so similar to the redhead's that he wondered if they shopped together. *But the other one was wearing gloves*, he reminded himself. The mark of a psychometrist.

"I believe she is packing."

"So Navarro lived here with Montclair?" Han asked.

Sandrine folded her hands in front of her. "Yes, for many years. She was already a part of his staff when I joined Marchesi. As you can probably guess, Mr. Montclair did a great deal of business with us. It was a great privilege to handle the liquidation of his collection."

"We thought Miss Navarro worked for Marchesi when she met us at the door."

"Oh, no." Sandrine shook her head. "We would love to have her of course, had she been free to seek employment outside of the Seven."

A knock on the door interrupted before he could ask what she meant by that. One of the other assistants whispered something to her. She nodded to them and made a move to excuse herself.

"Again, congratulations on the winning bid. Marchesi house thanks you for your business. If you'll excuse me, I'm going to help facilitate the transfer of the other auction items."

Han waited till she was gone to smirk. "More like go and make sure an all-out war doesn't break out among the losers. Did you see the look Naade gave you when you threw down that final bid?"

"I did," he acknowledged with an inclination of his head. "But I think there was resignation in that too."

Naade wouldn't resort to violence. Despite the other man's greater age and experience, he knew in a one-to-one fight he couldn't take Zhi.

"Well, obviously. Monira was more sanguine. She clearly wasn't willing to shell out a cool hundred mil for the girl, but she also didn't want Naade to get her. I think she was almost relieved when you won."

"Which was interesting, don't you think? House Gambari and

House Vakil are supposed to be allies. There's even talk of a marriage alliance between them."

"Yeah. Which means we have to figure out why this girl is so damn special they'd risk jeopardizing their good relations."

"Hmm," Han grunted, flipping through the contract. "Some of that may be partially explained here."

He stood up to join him. "What are we looking at?"

Han flipped the sheets at the back of the pile. "In addition to the contract, there's a long list of items Nova Navarro has authenticated. Both famous *and* infamous stuff. Her skill is good enough to pinpoint the exact age and provenance of an object—any object."

Zhi snorted. "No psychometrist is that sensitive. Their gifts are too murky. Even the best can only go back a few centuries. And most can't handle objects associated with violence."

From the little he knew, the talent appeared hardwired in people with gentle and thoughtful natures. Touching objects with bloody histories generally went badly for their kind.

"Ah." Han flipped back to the front of the pile. "That explains this line in the contract: a single assessment is enough to determine the provenance of an object. Employee will not be asked for multiple readings of the same item, particularly those associated with violence regardless of age. Requests for repeat readings are grounds for termination of the contract."

Zhi raised a brow. "In other words, we can't torture her by making her touch murder weapons or instruments of war."

"Not more than once anyway," Han muttered.

Suddenly Zhi was angry. "That she's willing to do it even once does not speak well of Montclair."

Han handed him the contract. "The fact that she's able to do it at all puts her head and shoulders above any other psychometrist I've ever met."

"*Have* you met any?" Han was his right hand. If he'd met a psychometrist in person, then chances were Zhi would have been there too.

Han tilted his head. "Come to think of it, no. Pretty sure I haven't. But they're around. Every major auction house has one. Or contracts one. They must fade into the woodwork or only socialize when needed."

That last was more likely to be true. Someone this sensitive wouldn't be able to handle life in the outside world.

His cousin raised a brow. "What do you think the family is going to say when they find out you spent that much on a *woman*?"

They exchanged a loaded glance. Zhi was not looking forward to that conversation. Of course, the same could be said for resuming the business he'd left unfinished in order to fly out here.

"We'll deal with that later," he sighed.

Han shrugged philosophically. "Well, at least we won't be cheated on any future art acquisitions. Remember that forged Dalí I insisted on buying when we were thirteen?"

Zhi smacked his lips. "You have a point. Both our mothers were furious over being cheated. Especially considering that was supposed to be a reputable art dealer."

"Which is why your mom never told your father what I did, a detail I will forever be grateful for," Han added.

"What did you do with that piece anyway? I seem to remember mother telling you to throw it away in case Bao saw it somewhere in your house."

Han grinned unexpectedly. "I gave it pride of place—in my bathroom. Where it is to this day."

He fished a pen out of the holder in the folio. "But enough chitchat. We better get cracking on this contract. Something tells me we want this deal done sooner rather than later."

CHAPTER FOUR

Nova introduced herself to her intimidating new employer and his cousin in the grand foyer where she waited with all her belongings.

Zhi Zheng was taller than she thought, at least six-foot-two. His sculpted features were attractive in an ascetic and rather forbidding way, his face and form a blend of his Chinese father and his half-Russian, half-Scandinavian mother.

That was the way of the Seven. They freely mixed across race and cultural lines in a way similarly wealthy and old human families did not, because it wasn't money or racial purity that motivated them. To the Seven, magic was the first and last criteria when negotiating a marriage contract, the goal to produce progeny with the same or greater facility for magic than the generation before. Intelligence and pleasing physical attributes were close secondary considerations, because beauty frequently opened doors magic would otherwise have to force.

Each of these goals had been met and surpassed in Zhi. What she hadn't expected was her visceral reaction to those coal-black eyes. Or was it the remarkably broad shoulders? Zhi's features were both perfect and cold, a masculine beauty so severe it did not invite touch.

He was a long, sleek blade set against his cousin's shorter, squatter battle-axe.

It had taken her a moment to recognize Han Zheng despite the fact he was in the background of the few photographs she'd found of Zhi. They didn't resemble each other beyond a similarity in coloring, but Nova hadn't gone into this blind. She'd done her research on the Seven. For the past few weeks, she had divided her time between settling several outstanding matters with Llewelyn's estate, arranging the auction, and researching her potential employers.

Which was how she knew Han was Zhi's right hand. When Zhi went off to conduct business that represented his family, Han was always there. Most of the Seven gossip blogs confirmed this, the conjecture being that Zhi's cousin served as his personal bodyguard as well as the family attorney. However, the commenters hadn't known what Zhi's talent was. A bodyguard was redundant when you could cause aneurysms with a single thought.

Thanks to Llewelyn, she knew exactly what Zhi could do. And that knowledge sat like a boulder in her gut. Her new employer could crush the average witch like a bug. He could have easily compromised the minds of most of the people in the ballroom. Only the strongest witches in the room would have survived the assault.

Nova was not one of them.

Sweat trickled down her back despite the coolness of the room. She thought she had been prepared for this, but there were so many factors in play, so much unknown. And this man was so dangerous.

Never let them see you sweat, kiddo, Llewelyn's voice said in her head. There was no turning back now. With that, she squared her shoulders and waited for them to speak.

Han studied her vintage trunks. "Why does it look like you are preparing for a voyage on the Titanic?"

"My luggage was a gift from my former employer. And in a way, I am preparing for a life-altering voyage," she added with a smile.

Zhi narrowed his eyes on her face. "Let us hope this one ends more auspiciously, for both our sakes."

Her smile dimmed at the coldness in his voice. *He's a family head and the world's most dangerous telepath,* she reminded herself. The Seven were not known for their warmth. But it was fine, appropriate even. He was supposed to be terrifying.

This was what she had signed up for.

"I'm afraid we don't have room in our car for all of your trunks," Han said, his tone distinctly lighter than the man he accompanied, a trace apologetic as well.

She turned to him, glad to be on familiar ground. "The Marchesi auction house is charged with transferring my belongings to your home."

"So you intend to live with us?" Zhi asked, lifting one eyebrow imperiously.

Nova blinked in surprise. "I need to...in order to serve you at full capacity."

He took two steps forward, invading her personal space. "Why are you for sale?" he asked in a soft voice.

Nova swallowed. Zhi was so tall that the closer proximity forced her to tilt her head at an unnatural angle to meet his eyes. Coal black and ice cold at the same time, they were studying her with disturbing intensity.

He leaned closer, forcing her to take a step back.

The subtle change in his expression seemed to indicate that he found her retreat satisfying.

Ugh. He was going to be one of those.

Thankfully he stopped backing her into a corner, tilting his head in seemingly never-ending scrutiny.

"You could have gone to work at Marchesi," he continued. "Any of the major auction houses would have been happy to have you. What did you do for Montclair that made every major house so eager to win you?"

Nova's lips parted. It was starting to dawn on her that this man had spent a fortune on her without an understanding of what he'd bought. It had been a staggering sum too.

"My apologies, I thought you had been briefed on my function."

She folded one hand over the other, retreating behind her mask of cool professionalism. This was her purpose, and she took pride in her work. "I served as Llewelyn Montclair's factotum. I was his personal assistant, oversaw all his travel arrangements, and ran his household in addition to my duties appraising the art he wished to purchase. I also accompanied him on his trips and attended many business dinners of... shall we say, a sensitive nature."

Han made a face. "How sensitive?"

Nova sensed these men preferred plain speaking. "These were meetings where it would have been more expedient for the broker to poison us both and take the cash or object we were trading for theirs from us. Not all the people we did business with were willing to accept a wire transfer. My presence negated this threat."

Zhi's tone became downright frigid. "Did Montclair use you as a food taster?"

"Not precisely." Nova held out her gloved hands, turning them palm up. "My psychometry is of a rare class. My sensitivity is so high that I can often ascertain the composition of a thing without touching it."

Zhi frowned. "Care to elaborate?"

She put her hands out, imitating hovering them over a plate. "It means that I can detect poisons without having to ingest the food."

"*What?*" Han's mouth gaped at the same time Zhi's pressed firmly shut. The timing of it was so flawlessly in sync Nova was tempted to smile. The cousins' connection was very strong.

She pivoted on her heel to face Zhi, using the motion to subtly take one more step back. "Llewelyn and I did quite a bit of experimentation to determine the range of my abilities on this front. I have conducted successful trials against all the major domestic human poisons as well as several hundred magical ones. In fact, the more potent the poison or curse, the easier it is for me to detect."

Nova had Zhi's full attention now. "Did you say *curse?*"

She nodded. "Yes. Specifically, the kind transferred via an object a client may touch or ingest through food or drink—methods relying on subterfuge to infect the host. I can't, for example, prevent a client from being infected by a curse hurled by a witch. But then, the latter is a method where the intent is obvious."

Zhi stared at her for a very long moment as if he did not quite believe her.

She tilted her head a fraction. "You appear skeptical. Would you like to scan me with your telepathy to assess my veracity?"

Zhi's pupils flared, the first sign of life that wasn't intimidating or scary as hell. Han's mouth had also dropped open. Both men appeared shocked by her offer.

"You would submit to a scan?" Han didn't bother to hide his incredulity.

"Of course." Nova's brow puckered. "Why wouldn't I?"

She was afraid of Zhi, but not because he could read her mind. No, her fear was more practical. She liked her brains in her head, thank you very much.

One of the men scoffed, but they were so still she was unsure which one of them it had been.

"Because most people object to having their brains invaded and their memories riffled through." Han's tone was flat and dry.

Nova understood their reactions now.

"Oh, I've been scanned before. Several times during particularly fraught negotiations. I'm not certain the telepaths in question were as strong as Mr. Zheng here," she added, indicating Zhi with a tilt of her head, "but as long as I'm telling the truth there is no need for concern. Is there?"

They just stared at her.

"All right." Han snorted, turning to his cousin. "I think we know why the other families were willing to pay such a high price tag."

Zhi appeared to come to a decision. "Let's get the hell out of here before one of the others decides the advantage she presents is worth a war with our family."

He reached for her, but she shied away, following when he indicated she should follow.

She picked up her small folio and attempted to fall in step behind them. There was an awkward moment when both men stopped. Nova hesitated, confused when Han waved her forward, insisting she walk with them.

Her discomfort increased when they stepped outside. There were only a few cars left parked out on the circular gravel drive. Most were sleek sports cars, the kind with only two seats.

"I trust you have a vehicle that will accommodate all of us," she asked but without much hope. According to her research, Zhi was very fond of sports cars.

Zhi muttered something, while Han waved. A long, dark limousine pulled in front of them. Relieved, she beamed at them. "Oh, good."

A driver stepped out, opening the door. One glance from Zhi and she climbed inside, sitting in her usual spot when she traveled with Llewelyn, directly behind the driver to leave the front-facing seats to her new employers.

The driver started the car, getting underway. Nova sidled closer to the window, taking a lingering last look at her former home.

There were too many emotions assailing her to dissect any single one. She just watched, conscious of a slight tightness in her throat.

"How long did you live here?" Han asked.

Turning, Nova refocused on him. "Sixteen years."

Zhi scowled at her. He was starting to do that a lot. "How old are you?"

"Twenty-four."

"You lived here with Llewelyn Montclair since you were eight years old?" he asked slowly. "As a servant?"

"Well, not at first," she laughed. "Obviously."

He and Han exchanged another glance. She could tell from the compression of Zhi's lips that his estimation of Llewelyn was plummeting.

Her deeply ingrained sense of loyalty came to the fore. "I know what you're thinking, but Llewelyn was very good to me. He was the first to recognize my potential. He gave me a home and saw to my education. I'd still be in the institution if it weren't for him."

Zhi's lashes flickered. Han leaned forward. "The what?"

Damn it. Nova hadn't meant to mention the hospital.

She took a deep breath, considering both men. This was fine. They were going to investigate her background sooner or later. Like her and Llewelyn, they were gifted. But unlike her, they had been born into a family that recognized magic. They wouldn't hold her origins against her. And if they did, it would be most unfair of them.

"Greenpark," she said after a short pause. "It's a human-run state facility that has a children's ward. That is where I used to live before Llewelyn came and got me."

This was not enough explanation for Zhi. "Was Montclair a relative?"

"No. I don't have any of those," Nova said lightly. Her earliest memories were of the hospital. She didn't like dwelling on her time there, preferring to remember what came after.

"Montclair showed up one day and took you? Did he adopt you?" Zhi still looked handsome, despite his expression souring. Life was so unfair.

"No, of course not." Nova hadn't expected anything like that. She hadn't even known about mothers and fathers back then.

Most of the children at Greenpark had been orphans or like her. The few who did have parents had been long abandoned by them, even if the state said otherwise.

"Llewelyn filled out some papers, so everything was above board and official." What those papers were, she didn't know. Nova hadn't been able to read at the time.

"Uh-huh," Zhi murmured. "I take it you were institutionalized because your psychometry made it difficult to cope with the outside world. Humans wouldn't have known what was really going on. How did Montclair learn about you?"

She lifted a shoulder. "I believe one of the orderlies, an older man named Samson, knew him. They came together one day."

Zhi and Han looked at each other again, long enough for her to assume they were speaking telepathically.

"So, this Samson," Zhi began after they stopped their private convo. "Was he the first person to recognize you had genuine magic and weren't mentally ill?"

"He and another nurse." She could suddenly smell Marta's perfume, the sense memory sharp enough to invade the back of the limousine. The day Nurse Marta had handed her a series of objects, family heirlooms, was one of her few pleasant memories of Greenpark. It was the day Nova had learned that she wasn't crazy, that the things she saw and felt when she touched things weren't a product of a broken or diseased mind.

"I had been misdiagnosed as a schizophrenic. I left Greenpark shortly after with Llewelyn. He couldn't send me to school," she said, holding up her gloves by way of explanation. "But he hired tutors of all kinds. I also had free reign of the library. Several of them. As I said, we traveled a great deal on collecting and research trips."

"Uh-huh." Zhi appeared fond of this phrase. "And that was good enough for you?"

Nova's smile slipped. Funny how Zhi Zheng could knock it right off her face.

Han leaned forward, elbowing his cousin in the process. "It was more like you were a surrogate daughter, right?"

Nova hesitated and shook her head. "While there was a paternal aspect to our relationship, I never thought of Llewelyn as a father."

Zhi grunted. "That's because you always knew you were destined for a life of service, like a sl—"

Han elbowed Zhi again, harder this time.

Glaring, Zhi rubbed his ribs. "I guess that's true," he growled, answering a question she hadn't heard Han ask. "And you're right. We do have a more pressing concern."

Nova's brow creased as the cousins resumed their silent conversation. She did not know them well, but they had a tense, watchful air about them.

As if on cue, Han turned to look back through the rear windshield while Zhi began texting. But neither seemed inclined to enlighten her.

"May I ask what that pressing concern might be?"

Han blinked and focused on her. The certainty that she was interrupting their conversation came too late.

She was going to have to pay closer attention to their body language to avoid that.

"Oh, it's nothing to worry about." Han waved dismissively. "We're just being followed."

CHAPTER FIVE

Zhi shouldn't have been surprised when Nova accepted the fact they were being tailed in stride, hustling up the stairs of the family's private jet without help and only mild concern on her face. And even that melted away once they were safely on the plane.

Knowing Montclair's reputation, she was probably used to making quick getaways.

Once inside, Nova took stock of the plane's luxurious surroundings with a quietly pleased air. She excused herself and prepared for the flight by stowing her suitcase and fastening her seat belt, choosing a seat in the last row. She left the open communal space and couches to him and Han.

They were in the air soon after. The minute the pilot announced they were free to move about the cabin, she unclipped her seatbelt, stretched out, and fell asleep.

"Well, she certainly took the fact we were being chased well," Han thought to him, noting Nova's relaxed form.

"It's okay," he said aloud. "She's out." And if she wasn't, the engine noise would muffle their speech.

Also, the speed with which Nova had dropped off suggested several sleepless nights. Clearly, she wasn't as relaxed as she would have them believe.

"Understandable," Han said, getting up to pour them both drinks. He sat down, his eyes fixed on Nova. "Even professionals get stressed. And she's had a doozy of a day, hasn't she? One that you seemed determined to make even more stressful for some reason. Still, your rude ass aside, she was remarkably composed considering..."

"Considering the fact we bought her like chattel?" Zhi growled.

"You know that's not what happened." Han sighed, pulling out the contract from his case and waving it at him. "Clearly she needs us. She's got skills that make the predators of our world sit up and pant like dogs. Only one of the Seven could protect her. That's probably why she went along with Montclair's scheme to include her in the auction. He must have convinced her she was better off throwing in her lot with one of the major houses."

He began to flip through the papers of the contract, speed-reading, a skill he'd taught himself in high school. "*Aha*. I knew it," he said a few minutes later.

"What?"

Han looked up with a satisfied expression. "The principal beneficiary of the money we just paid isn't the Montclair estate. They only get a small percentage—the same cut as the auction house."

"Then who gets the rest of the money?"

Han jerked a thumb at Nova. "She does. It's being put in a trust for her."

He grimaced, scanning the paper again. "Except it looks like she doesn't have access to the cash. Not directly. It says here there's some law firm panel installed as oversight for any major disbursements. This must be something Montclair set up."

Han kept reading. "Yeah, it was him—this trust has been in place since Nova was sixteen, the age when she officially started working for him as an art appraiser. She gets an allowance from it. The good news is that allowance is in lieu of salary."

"How is that good news?" Not being able to pay the woman just made all of this more suspicious, not less.

Han ignored this, too intent on reading.

"Remind me of that later. I want to look into that oversight panel," Zhi said. He'd prefer his winning bid didn't line the coffers of some random law firm. "And what's with the way she kept recoiling back? Does she have problems with human touch? Is it part of the psychometry thing?"

His cousin flipped back to the front of the contract. "That'll be a hell yeah. No touching. Not ever."

Shit. Zhi had to stop and absorb that for a minute. His telepathic power was off the charts strong. Had he been born outside the Seven, he would have ended up a pariah. And that was a best-case scenario. Without the powerful Zheng clan to shield him, he wouldn't have made it to adulthood.

Even some of the members of his own family treaded warily around him. But there were enough like Han, family members gifted in their own right, who had no fear of him. They'd grown up with him and were used to his ability. Moreover, they treated him like everybody else. Someone normal.

Nova didn't have that. She'd never had it.

"I guess her inability to bear touch makes sense. Especially if her gift is sensitive enough to detect curses and poisons without physical contact."

Han's chin wrinkled, but he didn't lift his head. "You know, the curse detection part, I get it. They say the Elementals are hardwired to sense magic, even curses that self-protect to evade detection. Supposedly, some high-level witches can do it too. So that part I do understand. There's precedence in the universal genetic code. But doesn't the fact she can detect normal everyday poison seem weird?"

Zhi chewed his lip, considering the question. "Maybe. Maybe not. Poison disrupts life. It's a violent release of energy. Perhaps Nova's psychometry reads the potential for release as well as the actual. Like it's mixed in with precognition somehow."

"Interesting hypothesis. Do you—*hell*."

He sat up straighter. "What?

Han sighed, passing a hand over his face. "I just read what happens if you make and sustain skin contact. She has a seizure."

Zhi leaned forward, lips parting. "Her gift is that extreme?"

Han nodded. "Risk of permanent brain damage. She'll basically stroke out."

He stared at his cousin, aghast. "Are you serious?"

Han waved the contract at him. "That's what it says here in black and white."

"That explains why she gave us such a wide berth every time we encroached on her personal space."

"What the hell do you mean *we?*" Han snorted.

"I wanted to test her limits, to gauge where her line is."

His cousin harrumphed skeptically.

"It was necessary," Zhi insisted.

Han smacked his lips. "Nice to know you weren't being a dick for dick's sake." He looked past him to Nova and shook his head before draining his glass and getting up for a refill. "Some gift. More like a curse if you ask me."

"Yeah. No kidding."

They didn't resume their conversation until they had both finished their drinks and Han remembered their hasty exit. "I almost forgot to ask—who was following us? One of Naade's lackeys or one of the Burgess kids?" he asked, naming the two parties who'd seemed most annoyed to lose the bid.

"Neither."

"Then who was it?"

"I can't be sure. My attempts to probe kept sliding off their minds, and I didn't want to force the issue."

Han frowned. He knew there was only one group who had a partial immunity to his talent. Partial because if Zhi pushed, their minds would give eventually, although with significant brain damage.

"Huh. I knew they bid, but I don't know why they would want her that bad."

Zhi shrugged. "Who knows why shifters do anything?"

••••••••••••••••••••••••••••••

CHAPTER SIX

••••••••••••••••••••••••••••••

Nova woke up groggily when her phone's alarm went off. She felt hungover, the feel of her silk sheets the only familiar thing about her surroundings. Turning it off, she forced herself to get up and take stock.

They arrived at the Zheng mansion late last night. Located on the coast west of Portland, the sprawling eighty-eight-room mansion was nestled at the edge of a bluff overlooking the Pacific.

She'd had a very brief look at the foyer before being ushered up the grand staircase and escorted down a few similarly opulent hallways to a bedroom in the east wing.

Her bedroom was large, bigger than most of the hotel rooms she had been in. It was furnished with dark mahogany furniture, classic pieces she knew she'd have to touch-test sooner rather than later.

The bed itself was a blessing. It was a large and modern sleigh bed made of the same dark wood as the bureau and the vanity. It had a brand-new mattress that had likely been delivered only moments before their arrival. The plastic was still on it.

She cut the plastic off herself, eschewing the still-sealed package of sheets on top of it in favor of her own. Nova always traveled with a set of silk sheets in her carry-on. They were far too small for the king-sized bed of course, but that was why she'd sewn buttons onto them, turning the set into a makeshift sleeping bag she could use anywhere.

But after getting her bed ready, she had no more energy to explore her surroundings. She hadn't even looked in the restroom. Now she contemplated the bathroom door with trepidation.

Best to get it over with. Sucking in a deep breath, Nova slipped on the gloves she'd left waiting on the bedside table. She waved her hands over the doorknob, hoping to pick up the spore of violence before touching it.

The heavy thick weave on the gloves was excellent protection. They insulated her ability to a fair degree. But not a hundred percent, more like seventy-five.

She got nothing from the doorknob, even after grasping it firmly with her gloves. Letting out a sigh of relief, she pushed the door open and proceeded to go over the sink, commode, and bath stall with hovering hands.

No alarm bells rang in her brain. Nova removed her gloves brusquely, touching everything again with her bare hands with light, tentative brushes of her fingers.

Normally she wouldn't do this so soon in a new environment, but this was going to be her living space. If there was a ticking time bomb here, she needed to know as quickly as possible.

A blur of images filtered through her mind, faces of guests who had stayed there, all the way back to the men who had installed the tub and shower stall combo.

She started laughing when she realized the toilet seat was new, saving her the trouble of digging her own out of the box in her trunks.

Perhaps she had underestimated her employer. If Zhi Zheng could see to her comfort to this degree, then he might not be so bad. But then maybe it had been Han who'd seen to these details, trying to make her comfortable. Nevertheless, she decided to take it as a good sign. Perhaps she hadn't made a terrible mistake yesterday.

Feeling a tad more optimistic than before, she finished making herself presentable. She was about to leave the room to find her employer when there was a knock at the door.

She opened it to a trio of uniformed servants. One man, the

largest, was holding a small wooden table, the second a matching chair that still had the plastic on the back and seat. The last servant was a sturdy female who introduced herself as Wen. She held a covered tray.

"Master Zhi thought you might be hungry," she said in lightly accented English, setting the tray down once the men had arranged the table in front of the window. "And while you are welcome to join the family in the dining room whenever you wish, he has already broken his fast."

"So early?" Nova checked her watch. It was half-past seven in the morning.

Wen's smile was not unfriendly. "When his mother and sister are not in residence, Master Zhi eats early. Master Han has a tray delivered to his desk in the west wing around nine. Master Zhi has requested you meet him in his office when you are ready."

"Oh, I see." Nova stepped back to the table. She gestured for the woman to stay when she attempted to leave. "May I ask you a few questions?"

Wen looked a little surprised but nodded, dismissing the other men with a hand wave.

"How large is the staff?" she asked, taking her seat and uncovering the dishes. It was a standard continental breakfast, Seven-family style. The still-warm croissant was liberally lashed chocolate, and the fruit was tropical and perfectly ripe. A serving of Greek yogurt with home-made granola and delicate little quail eggs were served in separate little bowls as well as a delicate China cup for her choice of coffee or tea in their own individual pots.

"There are over two dozen, including the gardeners and security personnel," Wen replied, rattling a list of names that proved the racial composition of the staff reflected that of the Seven—mixed.

"And how much of that is in the kitchen?"

Wen appeared pleasantly surprised by her interest. "Four, including Chef Sam." Wen continued to answer her questions, giving Nova a sense of the large house's rhythms and routines.

Nova was adept at reading between the lines, so she paid attention to what Wen did not say with as much attention as what she did.

The picture she got was of a well-run, if somewhat formal, household. Both Han and Zhi were seen as hardworking, although it was clear from Wen's words and intonation that Zhi was the pride of the family, a tireless and dedicated first son.

More importantly, Nova didn't detect any fear or hesitation when Wen spoke of Zhi. Relieved, she nodded and smiled when Wen finally excused herself.

Once she was gone, Nova finished her breakfast quickly, leaving the tray on the table as instructed. She brushed her teeth and descended to the ground floor.

Zhi's office was located off the main foyer next to the library, its double doors open to reveal an extensive collection of leather-bound volumes. She peeked inside, hoping she would be allowed to take books to her room.

Wiping her hands, she finally went to the door Wen had indicated was Zhi's office.

"Come in."

Nova startled. That clear, crisp voice had been in her head. Though she had been scanned before, none of the telepaths had spoken to her in such a fashion, perhaps because they didn't have the ability.

Nova rolled her shoulders, shaking off that singular sensation before opening the door and stepping inside.

CHAPTER SEVEN

Nova had a brief impression of an opulent room done up in varying shades of black, green, and gold before focusing on Zhi Zheng. Once she did, it was impossible to turn away.

The boss was wearing a crisp white button-down shirt with the sleeves rolled up, the well-defined forearms worthy of a master sculptor's attention.

He was sitting in a leather chair behind a massive wooden desk elaborately carved with dragons and other Eastern motifs. Unlike the vases and object d'art on display around the room, the furniture wasn't antique. Like the embroidered covered panels, shelves, and chairs, the expertly crafted pieces were a modern update that paid homage to the long history of the Zheng family while maintaining the comfort and utility found in modern furniture.

Zhi was engrossed in the file he was reading, a lock of his hair rebelling against the otherwise cool perfection of his three-hundred-dollar haircut. The blue-black lock contrasted with the sun-kissed gold of his skin.

It took several moments for Zhi to look up at Nova. When he did, his pupils flared as if he was surprised.

She tilted her head to the side. "Sorry, were you expecting someone else? Your cousin?"

"No. Han never knocks," he replied, leaning back in his seat. His expression had defaulted to its normal inscrutableness. "I thought you were one of the staff."

"Well, technically I am," Nova replied, her smile bright. She motioned to one of the chairs set in front of the desk. "Are you free to discuss my duties now, or should I come back later?"

Zhi ran a hand through his dark hair, the gesture surprisingly boyish for such an intimidating-looking man. "Now is fine. Please sit."

Nodding, she sat down, smoothing her skirt with her gloved hands. "I hope you don't mind, but I took the liberty of speaking with Wen, who confirmed you don't have a social secretary."

He frowned. "I have a PA. She works out of ZZ8 headquarters in down-town Seattle. She handles logistics when Han can't. Or I do it myself."

ZZ8 was a multinational conglomerate controlled by the Zheng family. Her research hadn't been too in-depth on its various business interests or how many people it employed. All she knew was that it made a lot of money and was virtually unknown in wider business circles, a common tactic for the Seven. Though there were exceptions to the rule. The magical elite preferred to be shadow power players with fingers in every pie.

"I see." Nova stifled a sigh. "And it's not inconvenient having her operating from a distance? Or do you normally work from the city?"

He pursed his lips. "I work from here half the time while Patricia holds down the fort in town. The rest is divided between Seattle or travel to cities where our partners have offices."

"Are most of those in China?" she asked, aware the American branch kept close ties with the Zheng clan in the homeland.

"Only one or two," he said. "I spend more time in New York and London. Sometimes Sydney."

She didn't say anything, crossing her legs and waiting.

He closed his eyes briefly. "I suppose it would make sense for someone to take over logistics and travel arrangements. But..."

The corner of her mouth lifted. "But you like that it's just you and

Han deciding on the when and where of your business dealings, because the more people involved the less secure things are. More points of vulnerability, as it were."

He raised one very black eyebrow. "Are you about to point out that the very high price tag I paid guarantees your loyalty?"

"The contract you signed does explicitly detail my part in protecting my employer's interests." Nova leaned forward a touch. "And you are of course welcome to scan me at any time to confirm my sincerity should you have any doubts."

Zhi's dark eyes narrowed on her face. "You know most people find the possibility of being brain scanned, on a regular basis no less, alarming."

"So you said yesterday, but I don't mind. It really doesn't feel like anything," she added, raising her hands and gesturing to her head.

"What you just experienced was a short-range broadcast. If I were speaking directly to you, it might be different—high-end magic users such as yourself tend to interpret it differently. The experience varies."

Oh. This was interesting. "There are different types of telepathy?"

"Yes. There is one that everyone in a predefined range can hear. The kind I employ with Han and other family members is a private one-to-one communication. According to Han, it does engender a physical sensation. Han says it's like his brain hears static for a sec, almost as if it were an open phone line. But my mother describes it as being aware of door opening a room away." He shrugged. "It all depends on how your mind chooses to interpret it."

She leaned forward, fascinated. "Can you demonstrate?"

He stared at her for a long moment then inclined his head a fraction. "*Very well*."

Nova twitched in her seat. Now that *had* felt different. She sat in her seat, trying not to show how surprised she was.

His telepathic voice was just as clear as before, but he had been honest that this direct mind-to-mind communication was different. It was almost like fur had brushed her, but for the life of her she couldn't pinpoint where because she had felt it everywhere. And it didn't hurt. For someone who could not bear skin-to-skin contact, that might have been the most jarring detail.

Zhi leaned back in his chair, those intense eyes darkening with an emotion she couldn't identify. "Now you know why people generally want to avoid this kind of direct communication with me."

He'd misread her shock for consternation.

"Oh, it's not a problem for me," she assured him, glossing over her desire to unpack the sensation his telepathy had engendered. This meeting was about information. She would need as much as she could get to prepare for her role in serving this family. "Really it was just the novelty of the sensation. I'm curious, can you throttle that down if you're just eavesdropping and not speaking?"

He didn't reply.

Nova folded her hands in front of her. "Again, I would never disclose any of the information you shared with me to a third party. My confidentiality has been assured from the moment you signed the contract to employ me. Also—bonus—I can't be tortured for information because I can't be touched. I go straight to seizure and brain death."

One of his dark brows raised. "I don't consider that a bonus. As of yesterday, you are House Zheng's most valuable asset."

"Thank you," she laughed. "I'll try to live up to that assessment."

Zhi drummed his fingers on the table. "As for your question, listening and speaking are two very different telepathic modes. One can be done...shall we say, more discreetly than the other."

Her eyes widened. "Even with the high-end magic users?" she asked, borrowing his term.

He shook his head, a rueful exasperation creeping into his expression. "No comment."

She lifted a shoulder. Nova should have been more concerned about annoying him, but this was her permanent home now. It was best to begin as she meant to go along, with perfect candor. "Can you do group conferences, like a mental Zoom call?"

His dark lashes fluttered, and he made a small, rough sound in his throat that might have been the start of a laugh. "In a manner of speaking."

"Handy in emergencies," she said. "You could warn everyone in a burning building to get out."

The suggestion of a smile ghosted across his face. "Except then they'd all think they experienced a psychotic break."

She grinned at him. "Or a religious experience."

This time his lip definitely twitched. "I'll keep that in mind. Should the occasion arise, I'll try and sound suitably angelic."

Don't laugh, she ordered herself. Her boss was a terrifying telepath, the scourge of the Seven, and he was not making a joke. Probably not anyway.

"But to get back to your duties—I have no pressing engagements on the horizon that would require you to travel with me. Not in the near future."

"Not even to Seattle?"

"Perhaps," he acknowledged. "But I don't really plan those trips. However, in the interest of keeping you in the loop, the next meeting of significance will happen here at the house. Negotiations are still underway. A date has not been set."

She waited, but he did not elaborate. Nova made a mental note to ask Han about this meeting. Zhi wasn't likely to tell her why he sounded like he'd rather get a root canal. Or a colonoscopy.

"That's perfect. It will give me a chance to take a complete inventory of the house, starting with the kitchens."

"The kitchens?" He blinked. "Not the art gallery?"

She shook her head. "The kitchen is more of an immediate concern."

All traces of amusement bled out of his expression. "Is that so?"

She held up a hand. "Don't get me wrong. I have full confidence in Chef Sam and his crew and whoever else you employ, especially if you scan them on a regular basis."

He frowned. "I don't do that. But security is not really an issue. Han vets all the staff, and he's very good at his job. Not to mention that most of our retainers are second or third-generation employees of my family."

Nova hadn't anticipated that Zhi would hold back with his telepathy. The few who she had met had seemed to revel in using their ability. But she had never met a telepath of Zhi's strength before. Experience must have taught him to use it sparingly.

Llewelyn would never have left such an advantage on the table.

"I'm sure Han is thorough," she said. "But unless the estate is also a working farm, the kitchen gets its ingredients from commercial sources. No matter how careful one is, that will always be a point of vulnerability. Regular screening of the incoming groceries and goods will go a long way to closing any loopholes."

She waved this off as inconsequential. "I can set this up with the staff without your input. The only thing I need is any inventory you have of your art collection—if there is one and if you wish for your existing holdings to be authenticated."

His head tilted a fraction. "Isn't that your *raison d'etre?*"

"Forgeries are rife in the art world," she replied slowly, choosing her words with care. "To be honest, sometimes it's better not to disclose that a particular acquisition isn't authentic to all parties. Also, I should add that there aren't many people who are foolhardy enough to attempt to cross a member of the Seven. But there's always the odd forger who can't seem to resist the challenge."

Zhi templed his hands like a Bond supervillain. "And what would you say if your inspection discovers a recent forgery, something from a dealer you have done business with? Would you stop me from seeking retribution?"

The hair on the back of her neck stood up despite having been asked this question in various forms before. "I would never presume to tell you what to do. But I would like to say that Llewelyn found some rather ingenious uses for some of the forgers I uncovered. Uses that did not involve bloodshed."

"Hmm." He put his hands down. "An interesting suggestion. But as you say, there aren't many who would dare cheat a member of the Seven."

A sudden grin transformed his face, the warmth in it making the coldly handsome visage downright devastating. Had she been standing, her knees would have buckled. "When they don't know who they're dealing with, that is. Make a note to ask Han about his Dalí."

"Okay, I will," she said with a weak chuckle. It was a good thing he didn't appear to smile very often.

The warmth dropped away as if it had never existed. He drummed his fingers on the table as he looked at her in silent appraisal. "I know Marchesi made you an offer of employment. I'm sure they would have accommodated your every need. Tell me, why did you throw in your lot with the Seven?"

Nova smoothed her skirt. She liked it when he stuck to the script, asking questions she had prepared answers for.

"Llewelyn felt that only the Seven can make full use of my abilities. And even established Houses like Marchesi contract out a great deal. He also did not wish an itinerant life for me, going from deal to deal, constantly surrounded by strangers. A position within one of the major houses is more stable. Though every position a psychometrist will find requires some travel, working for a family enables you to have a home base, making the travel part much easier to bear."

"If traveling is hard on you, then why not make staying in one place a condition of your employment?"

"Because that would be so boring." She laughed and then held up her gloves. "Besides, I've learned to cope. Silk affords me some protection. Having newly manufactured clothing and toiletries also ameliorates the effects of my talent. The fewer human hands handling my personal belongings, the better."

"But the dress you're wearing today and the one you wore yesterday are vintage."

His attention to detail was startling. She nodded. "Yes, that's true. Good eye."

"How can you..." He trailed off, waving to encompass her outfit.

Her hand moved to the bodice of her dress. "This was owned by a single woman before me. Her family donated it after her death."

A line creased his forehead. "Was she famous?"

"No. I don't even know her name. But I can sense her as an echo in the fibers. She was, in a word, formidable. And satisfied with who she was."

He inclined his head in understanding. "It gives you confidence."

Nova shrugged. "A small boost. It helps that the impressions are shallow. Deeper would be distracting."

The previous owner had only worn the dress on special occasions, parties where she had donned the gown like armor and fought polite social battles where she'd come out on top. Nova liked having the boost on days like today.

It helped that the former owner had been human as well. Had the woman been a magic user, the dress would have been intolerable against her skin.

Zhi palmed a pen, rolling it on his blotter. "So you can tolerate touching things but not people?"

She shook her head. "I'm afraid not. As for the objects, it all depends on the strength of the impressions left behind on them. I don't know many other psychometrists because there's not that many of us, but those few have been very open with their knowledge. I can say with some confidence that the modern age of manufacturing has been a boon for all of us. A psychometrist with my degree of sensitivity probably would have died quite young a century ago."

He scowled. "And yet most of the things you have worn so far tend to expose some skin."

Of course, he would ask. She smoothed her skirt again, very conscious of where her stockinged legs were in relation to the chair she was sitting in. "I've learned the hard way that covering up from head to toe merely encourages people around me to be lax about proximity and accidental contact. Also, there is no fabric that can insulate me against the burn of a significantly charged artifact. Or even a moderately charged one, to be honest."

He absorbed this for a moment. "Han will get you the inventory you've asked for. According to him, it's a few decades out of date, so you'll be busy."

She beamed in genuine pleasure. "My favorite way to be. I take it you had a private chat with Han while we were speaking?" She tapped her temple.

"A quick one," he acknowledged.

"You must be an excellent multi-tasker." Unlike their convo in the car, she hadn't noticed Zhi's attention was split.

Her compliment appeared to surprise him. "Juggling multiple streams of thought while having active conversations was something I had to learn to do as a child."

His mind was remarkable. Brilliant and cold like a diamond, but remarkable. "Does Han have an office on this floor?"

"No. He prefers to use a third-floor room in the west wing. He likes the view from up there but still gripes about all the stairs. There is no elevator in the house."

"It is a very large house to be without one," she said. "Does it really have eighty-eight rooms?" That was a frequently cited detail about the house, meant to bless the inhabitants with good luck, according to Chinese numerology.

He gave her another one of those half smiles that felt like a whole one. "It does, however having that many would make each room claustrophobically small, so the architect wisely relegated many to the basement. It features many closet-sized storage rooms."

"Ah. An expedient solution." She rose to her feet. "If there's nothing else, I will go find Han's office before I speak to the chef."

"There is one thing." His gaze became sardonic. "You smiled when I mentioned your high price tag. Are you pleased with the amount you fetched?"

"Oh." Nova could feel her face heat. "Well, I suppose I was," she admitted, her tone riding the line between humble and confident.

It was imperative that Zhi believed she was worth every penny. Anything else would spell disaster. "I went for more than *Rideau, Cruchon et Compotier* by Cézanne but less than *Bassin aux Nympheas* by Monet, two pieces I authenticated once."

He huffed lightly. "Then I guess this was meant to be."

Nova chose to ignore the hint of sarcasm in his statement, excusing herself to go and find Han. Then she continued to the kitchens, officially beginning her term of service to the Zheng family.

CHAPTER EIGHT

Two Months Later

Zimo, the broker, wiped his mouth with an elegant gesture. He set the napkin on the table and rose, bowing to Zhi and Han, just deep enough for it to appear genuine but shallow enough for them to know he was just observing the formalities. Behind him, the skyline of downtown Seattle was a carpet of lights against a dark blue-velvet backdrop.

"I am very glad we were able to come to an agreement." He slid his cashmere coat over his tight designer suit.

"As am I," Zhi lied.

Zimo tossed a silk scarf around his neck with an understated flourish. "Excellent. I'll be in touch as soon as the family confirms these dates."

"Always a pleasure," Han added, lifting his glass. He sounded as if he meant it. Zimo wasn't fooled, but he was amused. A moment later the man walked out the door, leaving them alone.

Han threw back what was left of the cognac he'd ordered as an after-dinner aperitif. "I wish the Zhous had chosen another marriage broker. This one is worse than the last one. What was her name?

"Stanasha." Zhi craned his neck to look behind him at the door, but Nova didn't come through it, likely because Han had joined him.

His newest employee had accompanied him to Seattle half a dozen times now for dinner meetings with ZZ8 clients. Most of the time he introduced her as his assistant. She would sit unobtrusively at the table across from him and the client, making sure the waitstaff passed the plates and their drink over her shoulder. That was near enough for her to scan them for poisons.

However, Han had forewarned her that this meeting was sensitive in nature. She'd opted to sit outside, inspecting the dishes before they entered the private dining room.

Zhi should have made sure they put a small table nearby instead so she would be served a plate, but his head had been elsewhere.

"What the hell kind of a name was Stanasha?" Han groused.

He had no clue. "I prefer this broker. Stanasha was...irritating."

"You mean her pit-bull negotiating skills or the fact she tossed in sex with her as a signing bonus?"

He flicked his eyes at Han. "That was unprofessional. At least Zimo is straightforward on the family's expectations."

"And he's straightforwardly trying to gouge us on the marriage settlements. Han looked at him over the rim of his glass. "Are you sure you want to do this now? Getting wifed up can wait. You're not even thirty yet."

Zhi grunted. Despite a long sexual drought, he was not particularly eager to end his bachelor state. Marriage could wait, as far as he was concerned, but his mother strongly disagreed. Ever since his father had died, she had picked up the gauntlet he'd dropped, making it her mission in life to see him wed to a fertile wife who'd ensure the line of succession. However, he and his surviving parent had wildly differing opinions on what qualities to look for in a bride.

Both his father and now his mother were only concerned with the superficial—looks and money. Well, that wasn't strictly true. They also had to have some brains and enough magical talent to ensure his children inherited lots of both. But his father had wanted a cipher, someone who never argued and wouldn't make waves.

His mother was selfish enough to agree. She didn't want anyone who threatened her position as the matriarch of House Zheng—a short-sided viewpoint, in his opinion. His wife needed to be strong if she was going to sit at his side in the years to come.

Zhi didn't want a broodmare with the right bloodlines. He wanted a partner.

"You know how long these things take. Even if we meet now, the actual wedding wouldn't happen till next year or the one after," he said, his eyes on the skyline but not seeing it.

"Hey, it wasn't your fault the negotiations fell apart with the Rochas. Your dad was the one who scuppered that deal."

Zhi frowned at his cousin before remembering his last girlfriend had been a sailing enthusiast. Han had even bought a boat despite knowing next to nothing about sailing. Thankfully he'd come to his senses and sold the boat as soon as the girl dumped him.

"I know. But I should have tried harder to salvage matters. It will take years for our relationships in South America to recover."

Han snorted. "You know you'd rather eat glass than get married. Even dealing with the Brazilians' bullshit is preferable to shackling yourself for life to a stranger. At least poke around the dating pool first."

Zhi suppressed a sigh. He and Han had a version of this conversation at least once a week. "Most marriages in the Seven are arranged. It's better that way—everyone knows what they're in for. Besides, we can't put this off any longer. Dad's official mourning period has come and gone. If we don't respond to this overture now, the Zhou family will take offense. Larissa is the pride of their house. I need to see and talk to the woman myself so I know I'm not wasting our time."

He broke off and looked over Han's shoulder at the door. "Did Nova eat?"

His cousin shrugged. "I'm sure they gave her a plate or something to take away."

"Make sure, will you?" Zhi asked, taking out his phone when a familiar ringtone alerted him to a new text. "She's liable to skip or wait till we get home to raid the fridge."

"Okay," Han muttered, giving him a bit of side-eye as he stood but doing as he asked.

Nova had become a fixture at their dinner table and meetings, fitting in so seamlessly that her absence today had been felt by both of them.

Integration into House Zheng should not have been that easy. Unless it was a formal meeting, his family did not have guests for dinner. Only close relatives broke bread with them, and even they knew to announce their intention to stop by when business brought them to the states.

But his newest employee possessed a skill Zhi had never mastered —she could fit in anywhere.

Nova was well-read and knowledgeable on a wide range of subjects beyond art and antiquities. Her conversation was charming and informed. She could speak eloquently on history to politics all the way to the latest *on dits* in pop culture. She also knew finance well enough to have valuable insights on his ongoing business dealings, from green energy to high-end electronics manufacturing. Whatever she didn't know she asked about, her curiosity genuine and endless.

She was also diplomatic and self-effacing. He'd learned this on day one when he'd sent Han down to the kitchens so his cousin could run interference between the psychometrist and Samuel, his brilliant but temperamental chef.

Han had been as surprised as he was.

"I can't believe it, but there are no fireworks," his cousin had said, gesticulating to the floor to indicate the lack of drama he found in the kitchen. "I walked in there expecting to find Sam waving his knives around threateningly the way he does when we ask him to change the menu. Instead, he's quizzing Nova on her favorite restaurants and the most exciting meals she's had while she went through the cupboards."

Somehow Nova had charmed Samuel into cooperating with a full inventory. And he meant *full*. Nova had passed her gloved hands over every canned and tinned item before tackling the raw ingredients in the pantry.

"She even handled all the frozen stuff," Han had told him. "Although I'm pretty sure those gloves were worthless for that. Wet silk can't protect you from frostbitten fingers."

But Nova hadn't complained. Nor did she balk at cleaning their antiquities, preferring to do it herself instead of the maid assigned to the task. Since it had made Jane sweat profusely every time she had to dust a Ming vase, Zhi had allowed the transfer of duties.

It was an easy decision given that Nova was a qualified art restorer with multiple big-name references under her belt. He wouldn't soon forget the image of her crawling on all fours around their fifteenth-century jade carving of the Chinese Imperial palace. She'd been wearing kneepads over a disposable oversized hazmat suit, the kind used in clean rooms. The white suit was covered in grime by the time she was done. But the carving had never looked better.

Zhi appreciated that kind of work ethic. What he did not appreciate was his mother blowing up his phone to find out how this dinner had gone. A second distinctive chime joined in the fun. His sister was as eager as his mother to find out when the Zhous would descend on them.

Resigned, he opened his cell to their group chat, giving them a concise summary and a short list of the concessions made. It was nothing unexpected. They had planned to make bigger ones, but naturally neither was satisfied.

He put away his phone with a grunt, walking out of the private dining room to find Han and Nova chatting amiably. She had a square takeout container in her hands. The white Styrofoam looked so out of place against the elegant backdrop of the *De Coeur a Coeur* restaurant that he strongly suspected the staff had to run out and buy or borrow it. This was not the kind of restaurant that gave doggie bags.

Capturing their attention he herded them to the door, thanking the maître d' for his personal attention on his way out.

He touched base with Nova on the elevator, making silent small talk while Han took out his phone, quickly becoming engrossed. But his cousin broke his reverie to eyeball him when Nova giggled suddenly, smiling at Zhi quickly as if to say "good one" before turning to face the elevator doors.

The crisp night air was welcome. Rolling his neck as the driver pulled up, he took a deep cleansing breath before opening the door to let Nova enter first.

"I think I'm going to stay and hit a few clubs," Han said, hanging back as she got settled. "Want to join? Marcus can drop Nova at the house. We can make our own way back."

Zhi hesitated. "No thanks. I think I just want to go home and shower. Did you want us to drop you off?"

Han got a funny little smile on his face. He shook his head. "Nah, I'm good."

He left with a wave, whistling as he crossed the parking lot. Zhi watched his cousin turn onto the sidewalk, melting into the late-night crowds of young people.

Zhi almost snorted. He wasn't even thirty and was already referring to people his age as "young people."

He slipped into the car, wondering if he was going to start yelling at the neighbor kids to get off his lawn. Except that wasn't an issue. Their closest neighbors were a good five or six miles away.

"Is something wrong?" Nova noticed his distraction.

It spoke to his level of comfort with her that he didn't hesitate to be honest. "Just feeling ancient."

Nova leaned forward in the seat across from him. "You should go out with Han. And by all means, take the car. I can order a ride. Go have some fun—you work so hard."

Zhi chuckled. She was one to talk.

In the few short weeks since she'd started working for them, Nova had done her best to make herself indispensable. In addition to her work with the art and in the kitchen, she coordinated with Patricia and Han, taking over the management of his social calendar.

The first thing she'd done was redirect the bulk of his non-priority calls to herself. Between the three of them, they established an efficient system of vetting his calls and the other demands on his time that came through other channels—usually from his extended family. She streamlined access to him in a way he hadn't realized was possible. And she did it without pissing off his relatives.

That alone may have been worth her contract fee.

"I'm not actually a fan of nightclubs."

Zhi had developed diamond-hard mental shields as a child. He'd had to, otherwise the combined weight of the world's thoughts would have crushed his mind. Nevertheless, clubs were full of people broadcasting their thoughts and emotions. The alcohol and recreational drugs they consumed in such spaces only exacerbated the effect. And if he drank, a little leakage was inevitable. And he could forget about recreational drugs. That was a recipe for disaster.

Which meant the real issue was him. Call it temptation or recklessness, but he'd learned the hard way that clubs were not places where he could kick back and relax.

He looked at Nova. It was tempting to say they had a lot in common, but his issues were nowhere near as extreme as hers.

"Hey, I have a better idea," he said, thinking of an item he'd caught in one of Han's detailed information briefs. "Want to make an unscheduled stop?"

CHAPTER NINE

Nova's neck was starting to hurt, but she couldn't stop marveling at the tree affixed to the ceiling of the Seattle Art Museum.

Just how much power did Zhi Zheng wield? He'd gotten them after-hours access to the museum with a *text* and only twenty minutes' notice. Not only that, but the head curator herself was here to greet them. It was great but also disconcerting...for a variety of reasons, one of which was professional.

Nova braced herself, waiting for the light of recognition to dawn in the other woman's eyes. But the curator barely glanced at her. She was too busy giving Zhi the kind of greeting reserved for heads of state. Or big-ass donors.

Zhi turned, broadcasting his intention to introduce her. Nova bit her lip and took one step back, gesturing a subtle no behind the woman's eye-line.

He caught himself so seamlessly there was no interruption or hesitation. "Thank you again for accommodating us on such short notice," Zhi said in clear dismissal.

"Of course." The woman waved off his gratitude, visibly disappointed that she wasn't going to have the opportunity to conduct a guided tour. "It was my pleasure. And please, if you have any questions about any of the pieces you see, don't hesitate to ask."

And still the woman lingered, waiting for Zhi to take the bait. Nova wasn't sure if it was because the Zhengs were prominent donors or because Zhi's cheekbones were the stuff fantasies were made of.

The cheekbones. Definitely the cheekbones.

After an awkward silence, the woman gave up, the click-clack of sensible heels signaling her departure. Zhi gestured for her to follow him through the empty corridors that had been lit just for them.

"Any reason you didn't want me to introduce you?"

She glanced behind them with a sheepish grin. Thankfully, the woman was gone. "I was worried she'd recognize my name."

Dark eyes flicked at her as they continued through a gallery featuring Islamic art. "Why is that a problem? I thought you would appreciate a little professional quid pro quo. Aren't these your people?"

She tilted her head. "In a way. I have certainly spent a lot of time in museums." Her heels were slightly louder on the polished wooden floors than the curators. "But it's a singular experience walking into one and not being herded into a back room."

"Is that where you do your authentications?"

She nodded. "More often than not it's a mixed crowd of magically capable and normals, so I do a little song and dance examining brush-strokes and taking the occasional scraping to analyze paint composition. But I can almost tell if a piece is the real thing or not at a glance."

Zhi stopped halfway through the Islamic art gallery, his eyes lighting with interest. He jerked his thumb at an exquisite handblown perfume bottle in its own display case. "So..."

Nova walked around the bottle before coming to stand next to him. "It's exactly what the label claims it is, but the painting over there is a fake, albeit it an excellent one."

Snickering Zhi stepped up to the painting she pointed out, a replica of a sixteenth-century Persian hunting scene. "Interesting. Very interesting."

He spun on his heel and gestured to the room at large. There was a devilish gleam in his eye. "How many?"

Biting her lip to keep from laughing, Nova cleared her throat and composed her features before walking a circuit around the room. "Not as many as you'd expect. I'd say thirty percent of the works on display are fabrications."

"Thirty percent?" he laughed. His eyebrows shot up. "You don't consider that a lot? This is a major museum."

"It would be much higher in the European gallery," she warned him. "On average, you can expect twenty-five to forty percent of all paintings to be fabrications."

He laughed out loud then wiped the amusement from his face.

"Better not have too much fun in case they are watching us through the security cams," he explained. "And it's now very clear why you wouldn't want a curator to know who you are and what you can do. They'd have a meltdown if you told them how many things are fakes."

"Exactly." She paused to admire a particularly fine Madonna and child, gesturing as if she was pointing out something in the brush-strokes. "This, for example, is meant to be eighteenth-century Italian, but the pigments are modern. Also, the chiaroscuro is deeper and richer than it should be. All in all, a masterful execution. Better than the original, in my opinion."

"But not what the museum acquisitions department paid for."

"I'm afraid not." She gave him a coy look over her shoulder. "I had the pleasure of viewing the original a few years ago in a Saudi prince's secret collection."

The look on his face was priceless. He was like a kid who'd overheard a juicy secret and reveled in it.

"Okay," he whispered, signaling for her to continue moving down the gallery. "Point them all out."

Maintaining a serious expression, she walked at his side, launching into a running commentary punctuated with an occasional nod or hand gesture to indicate a specific piece.

By the time they hit the European art gallery, he'd made a game of it. Zhi guessed which were fakes and which were real at least eight out of ten times.

"Are you reading my mind?" She made sure to smile so he'd know she didn't mind. "Because you are way too good at this."

"I'm not, I assure you." Zhi put his hands behind his back.

Nova stopped, her mouth dropping open at the smug tinge in his expression.

"You think I have a tell." She put her hands on her hips. "That is patently untrue. Llewelyn trained me himself. I'm not giving the game away here."

He pressed his lips together but couldn't entirely suppress the smile. "I'm afraid you are."

Her mouth dropped open in indignation, resisting the urge to poke him. Even gloved, contact with a magic user of Zhi's strength was unwise.

He covered his face, hiding the fact he was laughing at her.

She crossed her arms. "Fine," she said, suddenly serious. "What am I doing wrong?"

Zhi put his hand down, seeming to understand her concern. If she was transmitting the answers, she was a liability. He could never allow her in the room in sensitive negotiations.

"It's not a tell in the traditional sense. I'm just very good at reading people—even without telepathy. I've made a study of people and can read micro expressions. Every time you spot a good fake, there is a glint in your eye. You *want* me to spot the fake, and so I do."

She hummed, considering. "I will have to work on that. But I doubt anyone negotiating against you would be paying much attention to me."

Pivoting on her heel, she waved to encompass all of him. "In such instances, it's unwise to take your eyes off the biggest predator in the room."

He acknowledged this with a bow of his head. "*Touché*. But I should add it's highly unlikely you'll find contract negotiations quite this fun, so I doubt we have much to worry about."

Zhi gestured to the next gallery, and they continued the game, but it wasn't until they reached the far wall of the Post-Impressionist room that she learned why they were really there.

Her grin stretched her mouth so wide it almost hurt. "*Rideau, Cruchon et Compotier.*"

The Cézanne had pride of place. The painting was hung alone on a large empty stretch of wall with only a discreet plaque underneath it.

"It seems the owner has generously arranged for a country-wide tour of the piece. It arrived here in town yesterday. I thought you might enjoy seeing it again."

Touched that he'd given her desires any consideration, she stepped closer to the painting. Her breath caught, sensation building in her chest and filling her to bursting.

Turning her head with as much nonchalance as she could muster, she noted the placement of discreetly sized security cameras before taking a step closer to Zhi. She angled her body so her mouth wouldn't be captured by any of the lenses trained in their direction.

"This isn't the real Cezanne," she whispered.

Zhi did a double take, his head going from the painting to her face and back again. "But it hasn't changed hands since your appraisal. I checked. Was it stolen earlier in the tour? Should we alert the museum?"

She grimaced, showing her teeth. "Somehow I doubt the current owner would appreciate that."

Zhi's expression morphed to sardonic amusement. He snickered lightly. "You think he had a fake made for the tour."

Nova pressed her lips together then made a zipping motion with her hand. But she unzipped it because this knowledge might be relevant to him someday. Also, it was too juicy to keep to herself.

"Honestly, the only times I've seen someone go to the trouble of making a fake this well-executed and detailed is when they are planning on passing it off as the original to another buyer." She straightened the jacket of her blazer with a pull. "Not that I'm suggesting that's what is happening here of course. There could be any number of reasons for not choosing to display the real painting."

Zhi tilted his head to the side. "But you think a future sale is likely."

She smacked her lips lightly. "I wouldn't want to speculate."

He turned back to the still-life, contemplating the colorful assemblage. "I bet he plans on selling. Why else would he send this version out on tour? Chances are he's inviting lesser art authenticators out to view it. That way when he sells the fake he can bring one of them in to verify it. And lo and behold the brushstrokes will match." He rocked on his heels. "Meanwhile, the real Cezanne is probably in a private vault in his house."

"Again, I wouldn't want to speculate...but I've witnessed that exact scenario before. More than once," she added delicately.

He raised his brows. "What if I told you I might use this information?"

"As leverage?"

The owner of record was an old-money conservative federal judge angling for a spot on the Supreme Court. She hadn't heard of Zhi Zheng being active in politics, but information was currency in the circles she traveled in.

"I take it that it would be a conflict of interest—your former employer and your current one?"

She put her hands behind her back. "Actually, my authentication of the painting was done under the purview of the Louvre at the previous owner's request before sale to the judge—that and the old coot is a complete misogynist turd. There is no conflict."

Zhi's expression sharpened to one of feral amusement. "Excellent."

They exchanged conspiratorial looks. By mutual silent agreement, they turned to leave, dodging the curator on the way out.

CHAPTER TEN

Zhi made a detour into his office to shoot Patricia a quick email asking her to look into the honorable Judge Francis when Han spun the black-leather chair placed behind his desk around like the villain in a Bond movie.

"I can't believe you carried that all the way from your office." Zhi's plush and non-swiveling chair was sitting at the other end of the room behind the couch where he wouldn't notice it right away.

Han grunted. "You're supposed to be startled and caught off guard."

As if anyone could sneak up on a telepath. "Why do you keep trying?"

Han was well aware Zhi could sense a mind from a hundred paces, no matter how well-hidden. The scan ran constantly in the back of his mind. He'd been born doing it and could even tell a comatose mind from an active healthy one.

What very few people knew was that with a little effort he could push his telepathic range from a few hundred meters to a few miles, detecting each mind in that range with pinpoint accuracy. Not that he made it a habit to do that. Keeping it up for more than a few minutes gave him a headache.

"Well," his cousin sniffed, "I thought I might have a chance of bypassing the great ZZ Top since he was preoccupied with nookie that can never be."

Zhi yanked off his coat. "First off, I've told you to never call me that and second—what the hell are you talking about? What nookie?"

"I'm talking about Nova."

Zhi rolled his eyes and headed for the sideboard to pour himself a drink, adding a few spheres of ice from the freezer hidden in the cabinet.

"Okay, how much did you have to drink?" Because that was the most preposterous thing Han had ever said. And Han had once tried to convince him that his dad was a closeted BTS fan.

He stopped to take a big swig of his fifty-four-year-old Bowmore scotch. "Seriously, do I need to tell you that there's nothing going on there?"

"Oh, I know that." Han snorted. "But only because it's physically impossible."

Zhi wanted to go to bed but knew that wasn't going to happen when Han got up to pour his own drink. His cousin was his best friend, and they were tight. They rarely disagreed, but when they did Han was as relentless as a tick. And he meant that literally. Zhi would have to cut off his head to get him to stop.

Han would block the damn door if he didn't let him say his piece.

Zhi plopped himself in one of the armchairs and waited in silence until Han took the other one.

"Why are you home so early?" he asked. "I thought you'd be out till the small hours."

His cousin gave him a sour look. "And I thought you were coming straight back, not taking off with Nova to parts unknown."

"What is this?" Zhi rolled his shoulders, trying to work out the tension building in his neck. "You ran home to bust me?"

"I actually came home early to tell you some news, but this is more important. You can't mess around with Nova."

What the hell was this? "I couldn't if I tried."

"Except in a way you are." Han's expression morphed from irritation to concern. "I get why you're excited about her. She's not anything you've ever experienced before—a smart, funny, beautiful woman who accepts your telepathy like it's a normal thing. She even encourages you to use it. To her, it's no different from her ability, and telling you not to use it would be like asking her to strip off her skin so she couldn't get readings from every damn thing."

He started to interrupt, but Han held up a hand. "Nova asks you to treat her like you treat me, something an outsider has never done before. I get how rare and amazing that is, I really do. You've never had that kind of acceptance outside the family. But it can't happen."

"You say that like I don't know all of this."

"I know you know." Han waved his glass too hard, splashing a little. He licked the whiskey from his fingers before sighing. "But do you *know* know?"

"This is ridiculous."

Han leaned forward in his seat. "Look, I really like Nova. She's a good kid who was dealt a really shitty hand in life and is making the best of it. Not only that, she didn't let it make her bitter or jaded. Despite having what most people in our circles would consider a monstrous handicap, Nova enjoys her life. She appreciates the little pleasures—good food, beautiful art, catchy music. But what you're doing is going to screw all that up for her."

He frowned. Shit, Han was serious. "*How?*"

His cousin stared at him with uncharacteristic gravity. "By making her want more."

Zhi looked away, his fingertips growing a little numb around his glass. He forced himself to relax his hold.

"That little moment in the elevator is not the first time you and Nova shared a private joke," Han continued. "You've been doing it for weeks now."

"And how the hell do you know that?" Zhi narrowed his eyes at Han. "Have you been spying on her?"

"No, jerk off," he said in exasperation. "But I do check in with her. I wanted to make sure she was settling in, and since we both work for the family we do have to coordinate our schedules—and yours. It now takes both of us to get you from point A to point B. I have reason to see her everyday. We do it for you, you defensive ass."

Zhi held up a hand to cut him off mid-rant. "Okay, fine. But I have reason to touch base with her just as often. Nova is part of our household now. Am I supposed to treat her like a serf or a slave? Hell, you were the one who insisted she share meals with us. So what if I make the occasional joke?"

Han snorted. "Because you don't have a sense of humor, buttmunch. Are you looking up jokes online?"

"I can be funny," he said indignantly.

Han's head drew back so far he gave himself a double chin. "Sure you can. Did you hire a comedy writer on the sly to come up with material?"

His cousin lapsed into silence, letting it stretch until Zhi closed his eyes, giving up. He was suddenly very tired. "Fine. I like her."

"I know, man." Han's sympathy was grating. But Zhi knew where it was coming from. His cousin would take a bullet for him and vice versa. "But you two can't get more emotionally involved. You gotta walk this back before she falls for you too."

"What makes you think that's going to happen?" Nova did laugh at his jokes, but she did it because they *were* funny. She got his dry and slightly cerebral sense of humor. "Ultimately she doesn't treat me any different than she does you."

He knew this because he'd analyzed and dissected everything Nova said and did. He just couldn't help himself. But he'd seen enough to say for certain. Nova was just as cheerful and bright around Han, Wen, and everyone else she met. Even temperamental Chef Samuel got his share of that indefatigable bright light.

It made Zhi want to snatch her up and take her to the woods so he could hoard the sunshine for himself.

"It's not exactly the same," Han said after a long silence. His gimlet stare dared Zhi to ask.

"Spit it out, you smug bastard."

Gloating, Han slowly finished his drink before replying. "She jumps."

"What?"

"When you contact her mind to mind from another part of the

house, she sometimes jumps...or twitches. And it's not because she's surprised."

Han sat back in his seat, pulling up his pant leg so he could cross it comfortably. "The first time I saw her do it, I thought you'd caught her off guard. But that wasn't it. She said you *buzzed* her. I thought she was telling me you were summoning her to your office. Turns out she meant literally. It's like you tap her on the shoulder, except it's her brain."

Zhi's brow puckered. "She feels it when I telepath her? As touch?"

Nova told you that. In his office on her first day, she said, "I felt that." He thought she'd meant it figuratively. No one else had ever described his telepathy as having a tactile component. That was why it was so insidious. He could just pop into almost anyone's mind and delve through their thoughts and memories without any of them being the wiser. The only exceptions were those with superb mental shields like shifters or those with a great deal of magic, which Nova had in spades.

He stilled, the glass in his hand forgotten. "Something about Nova's ability is interpreting my telepathy as physical sensation."

Han shook his head. "Or as close to it as she can get. Think about what it must be like for her. You're the only person in the world who can touch her, even in this phantom half-assed way."

He shut up then, letting his words sink in.

"It's not enough," Zhi muttered after a long pause.

Han threw up his hands. "Hallelujah. He finally gets it. But the more you carry on trying to be charming, trying to make her laugh, the more chance she'll latch onto it. Make more of it than what it is. Because it's all she can have. And you—we're shopping for a wife for you. Imagine if Nova felt for you what you are starting to feel for her. Now throw a wife into that mix. It's a recipe for disaster on the level of a Shakespearean tragedy."

The wind grew solid in the ensuing silence. Zhi lifted his head to the window as the first fat drops began to pelt it. "You've made your point."

"Good." Han made no motion to get up. "I wish things were different. I certainly like Nova a lot better than your prospective bride-to-be."

"You've never met Larissa." Neither had he.

Han stuck his hand out. "A thousand dollars I'm right."

Zhi sipped his whiskey. "I'm not drunk enough to take that bet."

Because the chances were better than good that neither of them would like Larissa more than Nova. It was impossible.

Han straightened in his chair. "Does Nova know?"

"Does she know what?"

"What tonight's dinner was about? That we're arranging your marriage?"

"Of course." Then he paled. "You told her, right?"

"No." Han looked away as if searching his memories. "I don't think I did. Didn't you? You two are so chummy these days."

Zhi lifted a shoulder. "We haven't discussed it."

"I wonder why that is," Han deadpanned.

"Someone has to tell her."

"Yeah, you, dipshit."

Zhi switched his empty glass to his other hand and pushed himself to his feet. As much as he wanted to shove this responsibility on someone else, he knew he had to take care of this himself.

"I'll do it tomorrow."

CHAPTER ELEVEN

Zhi sat bolt upright in bed, his barely conscious brain blaring an alert, one that was far too late to be useful. Not only had he overslept, but the house had two more occupants now.

He grabbed his alarm clock and shook it. It had been set to go off over an hour ago, but the screen was dark despite being plugged in. *"Damn it, Jinx."*

His older sister, known to the rest of the world as Jing Vladlena Zhen, chortled in his head.

"What?" his sister replied. *"I was just giving you a chance to sleep in. Han said you had a late night. Which is good in my opinion. I'm glad you realized you need to live a little, although I do think you left it a bit late. But I get it. Squeeze in all the partying you can before you get shackled."*

Zhi sighed and collapsed back on the bed. Like him, his older sister had power above and beyond the usual practitioner complement. In her case, it was a certain facility with electronics. His mother had discovered it after Jinx turned three when her Russian-language soap opera would spontaneously change to Sesame Street. Jinx's electro-kinetic ability wasn't very strong as a child, a blessing considering how much they traveled on airplanes.

But Jinx's ability had always been precise, giving her the ability to short out the electronic device of her choosing. When he was young, it had been his Nintendo or his cell phone whenever she thought he wasn't paying sufficient attention to one of her lectures. It had been annoying, but at least she had always been sorry afterward.

Jinx's sense of remorse was a thing of the past. She'd outgrown it along with her red glitter-covered Mary Jane shoes. But he still got the lectures. Jinx would never outgrow those.

It was too late to warn Nova about his mother and sister's arrival. She was no doubt aware. And he trusted that she'd done her homework on them as thoroughly as she'd researched him and Han. That hadn't stopped when he won the auction. No one could truly prepare for the reality of Elizaveta and Jinx, but Nova might come close.

That didn't mean he wasn't going to shower at the speed of light and get out there.

Ten minutes later, he found Nova in deep conversation with his sister in the main hall. Zhi stopped on the stairs to listen for a minute before closing his eyes, praying for patience, and then joining them.

"*Jinx*," he growled, interrupting his sister's selfish request. "Nova does not do Starbucks' runs."

His sister pivoted on her Louis Vuitton high-heeled boots. She was wearing a cashmere sweater dress of the purest white, which contrasted with the black dress and gloves Nova was wearing. His heart did a quick dip when he realized she was wearing her confidence-boosting dress.

"It's not Starbucks," Jinx chided. "This is special Mexican coffee, and it is worth the trip downtown. And I'm still on Paris time, so I need something special to help me stay awake. Now come here and greet me properly."

Suppressing an eye roll, he dutifully embraced his older sister, bussing her cheek. "Do not take this hug as agreement. Nova doesn't run errands."

"I can Postmate your coffee for you," Nova offered helpfully as he stepped back.

Zhi held up a hand. "No, you will not. The kitchen has a commercial-grade espresso maker we paid a premium for and the staff trained to use it. Jinx will get her coffee from them and leave you to continue your work."

At the moment that included a battered Renoir in mid-restoration. The painting was set on a special easel in the middle of the art gallery, with some paintbrushes and assorted cleaning supplies neatly laid out on the table next to it.

His sister opened her mouth to argue with him, but Nova forestalled her. "I am familiar with the best coffee roaster in Seattle. Their premium teaberry beans are sourced from a grower on Mount Kilimanjaro and are reserved months in advance, but I have an in with them. If you like, I can order those for the house."

Jinx closed her mouth, shooting Nova an approving look. "That sounds good. Check and see if they have anything from Mexico as well."

Nova nodded, a warm expression lighting her face. "Will do."

His sister rounded on him, hip-checking him in the process. "In the meantime, I will make do with what's in the kitchen. But Nova, I would like to meet with you later to discuss some purchases I intend to make. Welcome to the household."

She walked off with a wave, her heels clicking on the marble floor.

"Nova is a million-dollar asset," he called after the bane of his existence. "You will treat her as such."

"I'm glad you realize this." His mother's clipped voice came from the staircase behind him.

Turning around, he walked over to greet her, giving her the same cheek kiss he'd given Jinx. Only this one hovered a millimeter over Elizaveta's cheek.

His mother had never liked it when he messed up her make-up.

"Hello Mother, how was your flight?"

"Long," his mother answered, her steel-gray eyes on Nova. She was looking at her up and down in blatant assessment.

It felt like a very long time passed before she smoothed her hands over the front of her heavily embroidered skirt. His mother preferred her clothing to have such intricate detail. "You know I've never questioned any of your financial decisions. You've always steered the family right in that respect. However, this is an investment that may take years to pay off, especially in light of the fact you're not even utilizing it yet."

"*Her,* Mother. Not *it.*" He bit back a second scathing comment, making an effort to compose himself. "And just what do you mean by that?"

Nova was working her butt off.

Damn it, there he went thinking about a body part he had no right to think about.

His mother gave him that half-supercilious, half-impatient mother look she had perfected in his teens. "I mean that we now possess the world's most sought-after art and artifact authenticator. But so far you haven't made a move to put her to work."

"She does nothing but work," he protested, making Nova smile.

Elizaveta held up a flawlessly manicured finger. "I mean on outside contracts the way she did for Montclair, making him money."

Good grief. The woman couldn't tolerate touch, and he was supposed to send her out to God knows where *on her own* to make money they didn't even need? "Nova is still busy working on our collection in addition to her other duties—which apparently includes shopping for Jinx now."

His mother tapped her Louis Vuitton on the marble floor. "But you *are* planning on sending her out to do authentications?"

Zhi turned to Nova, who had been standing there holding her tablet in preparation to carry out a set of new orders. Or make a new list. She was always making lists.

"We'll discuss it after she's done dealing with the family's holdings."

The entire family, he added silently. His sprawling network of relatives would keep Nova occupied for *years*, long enough for him to get used to the idea of her working for other people.

"All items here have been authenticated, but I am still working on restoring some of the older more fragile pieces," Nova said when Elizaveta turned to her.

His mother tsked but relented. "Very well. Out of curiosity, did you find any fakes in our collection?"

Nova beamed. "Only two."

Zhi held up a hand. "The Dali and the Strum necklet," he said, naming a famous diamond and ruby choker that had been presented to one of his great-uncles over a century ago as a gift from a trusted ally.

Unfortunately for his uncle, Jun Hie, that ally had been turned and was conspiring against their family. The historically famous necklet had been marked with a powerful curse, one that nearly killed his ancestor.

But Jun Hie had survived. His wife had given the necklet a place in their art gallery, displaying it behind a thick layer of protective glass—a lesson to future generations that there was no such thing as a trustworthy ally. Loyalty only existed within the family.

And sometimes not even then...

"The Strum?" his mother asked, raising her brows.

"It's hardly a surprise the necklace itself was fake," he said. "Why bother cursing the real one when a close imitation achieves its goal— to kill the person touching it."

"But the stones are genuine," Nova added. "Also, two is a very small number of fakes for a collection of this size."

"She means it," he said at his mother's skeptical look. "We've fared better than most museums and the other members of the Seven Nova has done work for."

The woman in question clutched her tablet to her chest with a bright smile. "No doubt due to your family's formidable reputation."

"Hmm, well that is something." His mother gave Nova a small but genuine smile, proving once again that Nova could win anyone over. God knew his mother was a hard case. "We should meet soon to discuss welcome gifts for the Zhou family."

Govno. Zhi's mind had clearly been elsewhere. He should have anticipated this. Dozens of half-formed explanations were evaluated and discarded as he stood there like a jackass.

"Ah yes, that," he said lamely when his mother noticed his consternation, her upper lip pulling back into a frown.

"*Syn,* I know you think there's plenty of time, but you're not getting any younger. It's high time you were married. As for your bride, trust your mother will do a better job than your father's miserable attempt at selecting the right one."

"We'll see." He glanced at Nova to see how she was taking this development.

Her open eager-to-please expression hadn't budged. Instead, she held up her tablet. "I have a list of suggestions appropriate for the head of household and the prospective bride."

He blinked. "You do?"

"At least one of you is prepared." Elizaveta leaned over and pecked his cheek, no doubt leaving a smear of burgundy lipstick. "I look forward to looking over this list. Please print out a copy and leave it in my sitting room."

Nova nodded. "I'll drop it off in a few minutes before resuming work on the Renoir."

Elizaveta bestowed another benevolent nod upon her and left in a swish of expensive fabric. Then they were alone.

He stared at her long enough for her to grow visibly confused. *Say something, idiot.* "I hope Han gave you sufficient time to find those gifts."

And that clinched it. He was a total *mudak*.

Nova's puckered brow cleared. "Oh, don't worry. I had plenty of warning."

"Oh." He put his hands in his pockets. Had Han warned her after all? From what he'd said last night, he assumed he wasn't relishing the task any more than Zhi was.

Nova's face was politely blank with no hint of her mischievous sparkle. "Chef Sam has been planning the menu for the Zhous' visit for weeks."

"Ah." Of course he had.

She leaned forward a fraction. "I take it the previous attempt to negotiate a bride didn't go well?"

And there was the sparkle. Only a glimmer of it. "Err, no. It did not."

"May I ask what happened?" She shifted her weight from one kitten heel to the other—her version of practical at-home shoes. "The information might help prevent a similar unfortunate outcome."

That made sense. She'd want to know so she could help smooth over any bumps. Anticipate. She was good at that. Too good. And lucky him, she'd use those skills to help win him a bride.

Perfect.

He cleared his throat. "There's not much to tell. My father chose Melissa Rocha. I and the other members of my family assumed that meant he approved of her."

Her eyes widened. "Uh oh."

He sighed. "Exactly."

"What did he do?"

"What didn't he do?" Zhi passed a hand over his face. "A week into the visit, she got tired of being harangued and running Bao's gauntlet. She called the whole thing off and bolted. Her parents were horrified. They were determined to seal the deal. Apparently allowing your daughter to be emotionally tortured by her future in-laws is acceptable in some circles.

"They would have forced her back had I not let it be known I also found her unsuitable." He lifted a shoulder. "I hear she married into one of the other Brazilian clans."

She raised her brows. "Another member of the Seven?"

"No, but she nabbed the heir's brother. My father found that satisfying."

"Because he was able to look down on them both?"

He cocked his head at her. "You would have handled my father well."

Like she did everyone else. Probably even his future wife.

"I'm sorry he ruined your first engagement."

"It hadn't gotten to the point of a formal arrangement," he corrected. "And honestly, I wasn't upset. She put up a good front, but she was very uncomfortable with the idea of marrying a telepath. And who could blame her?" His laugh was a touch bitter. "Hello, I'm Zhi, and I can read your mind. Want to spend the rest of your life with me?"

Nova winced, and Zhi realized she was confused. Or was it wistfulness?

This was bitterly ironic. The only woman he'd met without qualms about his ability was the only one he couldn't have.

"Whoever marries me will always wonder if I am reading their mind. They'd second-guess everything they said to me."

The little pucker between her brows remained. "But you don't scan people. Not really."

He shook his head. "Doesn't matter. All that matters is that I could."

Melissa Rocha had started out strong. But her flawless manners had crumpled after a few days. He didn't understand why until she confessed that she didn't want to be caught in a lie. He'd tried to reassure her that he wasn't reading her mind, but she hadn't believed him. Melissa had overcompensated by holding her tongue whenever he was around. By the end of that fateful week she had been incapable of uttering a word in his presence.

"Well, I'm sure things will go better this time," Nova said in a determinedly upbeat tone. "Would you also like a copy of my curated list of suggested gifts? Larissa would no doubt appreciate the personal touch from a prospective husband." She paused. "Unless you already had a gift in mind?"

"No. Mother chose the gift the last time."

Nova pulled her shoulders back. "In that case, it would be good if you chose something from my list. If you are hoping for a different outcome, that is."

No comment. "I guess you're right."

She wrinkled her nose impishly. "I am."

"Except for one thing. I don't know what Larissa would like."

"What are her interests? Hobbies?"

He shook his head. "I've never met her. That's what the upcoming visit will be about. To see if we suit each other."

"Oh," she said, nonplussed. But she was quick to recover, waving as if to dismiss this inconsequential detail. "Not to worry. Any item on my list would make an appropriate gift for a young woman of this station."

"Even you?"

The second he said it he wanted to take it back. Because while she did a good job of hiding the flash of hurt the flitted across her face, he still saw it. And it felt like a literal punch to the gut.

She took a step back and smiled. "I did say any woman."

But it was too late. He'd seen beneath the armor of professionalism she wrapped around herself like a coat. The uber-professional armor had faltered only for a moment, but it was too late. He'd seen beneath it.

Han was right. He had to stop this. Zhi would not be the reason Nova was hurt. He couldn't bear that.

Meanwhile, she had recovered her composure, looking behind her to the staircase as if she'd heard someone calling for her. "I should run that list up to your mother. I assume you want an electronic copy."

"Yes, email it to me," he said in a low voice.

"Will do." She gave him a playful salute and walked away, leaving him to be slowly digested by his stomach acid.

CHAPTER TWELVE

Don't worry. This is temporary.

Nova glanced over at her boss, trying to think of something to say that was light and funny. But Zhi's forbidding expression kept her silent. He kept staring out the rain-streaked windows of the limo, the harshly carved planes of his face a flawless masterpiece made of ice.

He'd been like this for days, ever since his mother and sister had come home. Nova would have liked to believe that this was the reason for his withdrawal, but she knew better. He actually seemed to get on well with his mother and sister despite the two women's colorfully forthright attitudes.

Both kept Nova at a distance, treating her more like a servant than either Zhi or Han, but that attitude didn't worry her. She took comfort in Elizaveta's vocal appreciation of her skills and the way she kept pushing for Zhi to let her take out contract work outside the family.

Meanwhile Jing was using her as a personal shopper. Had she been an average socialite, this might have been annoying. But Jing was a princess among the Seven and was used to only the very best. Nova enjoyed finding her the most exclusive clothing designers and bespoke jewelry.

Nova was happy when she was useful. Or at least she used to be. Before Zhi got weird about his own wedding.

She supposed that was to be expected. Marriage in the Seven was a delicate proposition involving months of careful negotiations, dowries, and the occasional bribe or violent altercation.

So, yes, she understood his preoccupation and tension. But it left her in the unenviable position of having to accompany him and feeling like an intruder. Nova was in a constant state of discomfort and awkwardness.

And she wasn't even wearing a pretty dress to cheer herself up. Today she was garbed in a pantsuit and specially made faux-leather gloves, the ones with special conductive fingertips, because she was working on the Zheng family collection inventory. The bulk of the work was done, but she was adding a few appraisal notes so future generations would be able to assign a monetary value to the item in question.

She peeked at Zhi, who hadn't moved in all this time.

This was the longest stretch of time she'd been alone with him since that moment in the foyer. He'd stopped touching base with her as often. No more casual conversations in her head. No more surprisingly nerdy jokes. His subsequent withdrawal was far more noticeable without Han around or his other family members around.

Zhi was different. Remote. This was the Seven family head she had expected to work for that day he won the auction.

It's for the best, she thought, grateful for the fact that she wasn't a crier. Her pre-Llewelyn Montclair life had taught her tears were a weakness. A carefully crafted facade of imperturbable professionalism, on the other hand, was the machete required to hack your way through life.

However, her coping mechanisms were failing her now. Until she realized she was the only one experiencing this as a painful silence. Zhi was entitled to his thoughts. He was probably contemplating life with his future bride. And she had work to do.

A few minutes later, she realized they'd turned off the highway. "Are we making an unscheduled stop?"

Zhi blinked at her with the air of a man who'd forgotten he wasn't alone. *Ouch.*

"Er, yes." He straightened in his seat. "My apologies. I forgot to mention it this morning."

"No, problem." She set her tablet down. "Is it another client meeting?"

They had spent the morning in the ZZ8 building in back-to-back appointments. In the space of five hours, Zhi had negotiated importing rights to the UK for one of his electronic subsidiaries, signed a new beverage distributor for another, and had gotten in-person reports from half a dozen department heads.

"Actually, no. It's a standing appointment." Zhi hesitated. "Maybe I should send you home and have Jaxson come back for me. This visit is sensitive."

That well-practiced poker face really came in handy as hurt feelings welled.

"A private meeting is not an issue. I can stay in the car." She picked up the tablet. "I have plenty of work to keep me occupied."

"It's not private. But I am used to going alone for...reasons." Zhi made a rough sound in the back of his throat. "I'm going to visit a relative."

Nova blinked. "Really? I had no idea a member of the extended family lived so close by."

Other members of the Zheng family had come and gone to visit since her tenure began. Only the privileged few stayed with the family at the house, the rest choosing to stay at five-star hotels in Seattle. But they had all come from other cities, flying in for business or pleasure, or to pay homage to the de facto leader of the family.

"This is awkward." Zhi gestured to the road. "But I don't think the car will be far enough. Jaxson drops me off and then gets out of range."

Out of range? "I don't understand."

"My standing appointment is with another telepath," Zhi explained.

"*Oh.*" Nova didn't hide her surprise. "I didn't realize there was another one."

This must not be publicly available information, or else she would have come across it in her research.

"Andre is a second cousin on my mother's side of the family," he explained. "He's fifteen years older than me. For the first twenty or so years of his life, he was institutionalized at a special facility in the outskirts of Mordovia. An isolated location."

Her lips parted in sympathy. "I see." She flicked her fingers at her own head. "He can't filter like you can."

Zhi shook his head. "He was born without mental shields."

That must have been devastating. "I had no idea telepathy was a common gift in your mother's family."

"It runs in both, but I wouldn't call it common—maybe once every two or three generations for the Zhengs. There's a slightly higher incidence in the matrilineal line. That's one of the reasons my father selected my mother as a bride. They birth a telepath at least once a generation. But on rare occasions it sometimes goes wrong, and the telepath is born without the ability to shield. We're working on it, but it's very difficult for him."

A million thoughts ran through Nova's mind, but what she blurted out was something envious she should have kept to herself.

"That's terrible he has to be so isolated. But at least he has you. It must be very useful to have such detailed knowledge of your family history."

Zhi frowned. "Don't you know your people?"

He assumed she was an orphan. Most people did. "No."

"And you never attempted to trace your family?"

Nova shook her head, regretting the impulse to blurt out her every thought around him. Her family was dead. At least that was what she told herself, because the alternative was too depressing to contemplate.

"Your relative, Andrei—does he still live in a mental institution?"

Nova had intended on changing the subject, but her tone came out rough and slightly strangled.

"*No*." Zhi leaned forward. "Don't worry. We're not headed to one of those places."

Nova let out a pent-up breath she hadn't been aware of holding. She leaned back in her seat, surreptitiously rubbing her gloves on her skirt half a dozen times. "Oh, good—not out of any personal concern, mind you. I barely remember Greenpark. But I imagine such a place would be unhealthy for someone who heard other people's thoughts."

"Yes, it would be," he said slowly, those dark eyes scanning her face. Penetrating too deep without the aid of telepathy. "However, Andrei has his own place, a house in the woods several dozen miles away from his nearest neighbors."

Zhi checked the view out the window as if trying to see how far their destination remained. "I should warn you that because of Andrei's condition I usually only bring Han out. Mother and Jing visit less frequently. Once a week, a caretaker comes to clean, do laundry, and prepare meals he can reheat. Andrei chooses this time to go on a long hike. No one else comes by. The only exception is a semi-annual medical exam where I bring out the family's private physician."

She nodded. "For his comfort. I completely understand. Would distance help? I can take a walk. I can try and get as far as possible from his mind. If you like you can pick me up on the road away from his place."

"Ah, no." Zhi appeared uncomfortable. "You see, during my non-solo visits I shield the person with me. It helps keep Andrei focused as we practice building his own."

Her brow puckered. "You can do that? Block another's mind from other telepaths?"

"Yes, but this is where the warning part comes in. Being shielded is not like having a conversation with me. Han and the others don't like it."

"Why not?"

Zhi lifted a shoulder. "Han said it's like having a blanket tossed over his head...or rather his brain. Jing says it makes her mind duller, her reactions slower, but only for the first few minutes. She grows accustomed to it over time but doesn't pretend to enjoy it."

"And your mother? How does she experience being shielded?"

He smiled suddenly. "For her, it's like flying in an airplane, how the body adjusts to the difference in air pressure as a plane climbs to a higher altitude. She's fine after her ears pop. The experience varies for each person, but none have called it comfortable. I'm not sure how you will experience it, which is why I think you should stay with Jaxson. I'm sorry I didn't think to warn you earlier."

"I see..." Nova thought quickly. Her body did appear to interpret Zhi's telepathy differently. It stood to reason that she'd feel this more viscerally.

This could be a slippery slope. Part of her thought Zhi was right to maintain the distance between them, but he was also wrong. "I think I should stay."

She crossed her legs, which must have surprised Zhi, because his eyes flicked to her silk stockings with a jerk. "I haven't experienced an adverse effect from your telepathy before, and this shielding is an extension of it. It's better to try it in this context."

"I can't imagine there would be another."

"I disagree. Though most are not as strong as you, you're not the only telepath in the world. There may come a time when we face one in a negotiation, making shielding me a necessity. Let's get it out of the way and figure out how I'll react."

She hesitated. "Unless it makes you uncomfortable. How do you experience shielding? Is it..."

Nova trailed off, unable to ask if he would feel her more viscerally too.

He regarded her steadily, but she had the sense she had surprised him. "It's not a problem for me."

"All right then." She folded her hands and smiled. "Then by all means let's proceed."

"Once we get there," he said with all the enthusiasm of an executioner.

"Okay," she agreed, settling back to wait.

Nova wasn't sure what she expected the home of a shut-in forced to live in isolation would look like, but it wasn't a modern two-story glass and steel structure in the constructivist style with all the hallmarks of green architecture. It was even outfitted with a large array of solar panels on the roof. She had momentarily forgotten what family she was dealing with.

Nova waited until Zhi had exited the vehicle to step out—a little extra insurance to avoid brushing up against him. "This is spectacular."

He looked at the building as if seeing it for the first time. "I didn't think you'd like modern architecture."

"It's a work of art. I like all art—well not plastination of the human body." She shuddered. "Displaying the dissected human form is not art to me. I find it hideous and macabre. That sort of thing should be the purview of medical students and no one else. But modern architecture's great."

Many museums were designed in modern styles, as if in counterpoint to their contents.

Zhi's cheek twitched, but he didn't otherwise react to the random detour she took in conversation. "I would have to agree about the body dissection. What is your favorite type of art?"

Nova pushed the door of the limo closed. "It's more of a specific subgenre of still-life. I love paintings where cats are stealing food. They just tickle me."

He burst out laughing before sobering, twisting his head to the house as if someone had called out to him. "Andrei is intrigued. Which means he's liable to start riffling through your mind any minute now. It's time to shield you."

She walked around the car, standing in front of him. "Is there anything I should do?"

"No." Then he cut her knees out from under her even as he protected her mind, because being shielded *was* like having a warm blanket thrown over her, one that smelled of Zhi and tasted like she imagined he did.

She was for all intents and purposes covered in Zhi...

CHAPTER THIRTEEN

Zhi had to physically check the impulse to catch Nova in his arms as she staggered on her feet. But he jerked his hands back, clenching his jaw as she tried to straighten. Her face was flushed, and she was breathing fast, trying to catch her breath.

She wasn't the only one.

Nova was *in* him. He could feel her on his skin and smell her scent in his lungs. He was drawing her in deeper with every breath.

The impact was like a punch to the gut. His relatives had never reacted like this. Shielding had *never* been like this.

Zhi took a deep breath and focused, pushing that peculiar sensation of familiar otherness back, forcing it to retreat until if felt more like Nova was curled in a ball against him. As if he'd tucked her under his arm instead of having her naked body pressed to his.

"Oh, that's, um, that's interesting." Nova blinked several times, shaking her head as if to clear it.

She looked intoxicated—not quite drunk but something like it. Nova never indulged in alcohol. With her ability, she had to be on guard at all times. Who would put her to bed when she had one too many?

"Are you all right?" he asked, trying not to picture her in his arms.

It could never happen. What he was experiencing now was as close as they would ever get.

"Good." She gave him a bracing smile that told him without words that she was lying. "I'm good."

"You're sure?" he asked skeptically as she weaved to the door.

"Of course."

The door swung open. Andrei stood in the opening wearing what he called his "good" track suit. He looked at him and Nova with unholy glee.

"Intriguing. Very intriguing," his oldest cousin said.

ZHI GRABBED Andre by the arm when the older man attempted to embrace Nova.

"Sorry, I'm a hugger." He looked at Nova as if she was the most delicious confection. Kara-Kum or that clumsy bear chocolate he loved so much.

"She can't tolerate touch," he said, adding silently. "*It hurts her very badly, so please give her a wide berth.*"

Andrei was shocked, his gaze bobbing between him and Nova. "No touch at all?"

"No." He narrowed his eyes on Andrei's bearded face. "*And she probably doesn't appreciate being eye-banged either, so cut that out.*"

"This is Nova," he said aloud. "She's my new assistant and our resident psychometrist."

Andrei's eyes nearly bugged out of his head. "The one from the auction? I've never met anyone worth so many millions before. Not even this one," he added, nudging Zhi.

"It's a pleasure to meet you, Andrei." Nova appeared equally fascinated by his big bear of a cousin. He would bet she hadn't been this close to anyone in a track suit in her entire life.

"I take it touch does not heighten your telepathy," she said, stepping carefully to one side.

"No. Touching makes no difference." Andrei gestured to the woods beyond the threshold before closing the door. "Everyone who gets within range is like a radio channel I can't turn off. But someday I will learn to shield the way this *Perhot'-podzalupnaya* does. Then I too am going to get a woman and just go to town—"

"Stop." Zhi held up a hand before passing it over his face. *"Nova is an employee. Try to keep it PG."*

That earned him an eye roll, but having a female visitor who wasn't a relative was making his excitable cousin downright giddy.

"How about a tour?" he offered, clapping his hands and gesturing like an amiable host of a home improvement show during the reveal part.

Nova beamed, a warmth in her expression that had been sadly lacking around him lately. "That would be lovely," she said.

Zhi fought back the urge to smack Andrei for no reason. He was *not* jealous of his unkempt hermit of a cousin.

These inappropriate thoughts would go away. If his bride-to-be was even a tenth as perfect as his mother claimed, then these feelings would melt away into the aether once she arrived.

Grinning back at her, Andrei walked backward, gesturing all around him. "This is the living room, also known as my man-cave."

Zhi smacked a hand over his eyes, wishing he could do the same for Nova. "And the tour is over."

Andrei jerked his eyes back to him. "What? Why?"

"Why, he asks." Zhi pointed at the couch. "That's why. For fuck's sake Andre, put it away."

His cousin scowled, stepped back, and put his hand on the shoulder of the life-size sex doll propped up on the couch. "Nadia is perfectly presentable."

And indeed, the sex doll was dressed in an emerald green cocktail dress he'd give his eyeteeth to see Nova wearing.

"Andrei." This time his tone held an unmistakable warning.

"I cannot move her." Andrei pointed to the braided cable running from the back of the doll to the ethernet port in the wall. "Nadia is updating her firmware. It's still downloading."

Zhi's face was going to stay stuck in a perma-scowl if this kept up much longer. "She's internet-enabled?"

"Of course. Nadia is the latest model. I could do the update over Wi-Fi, but that would take all night."

"Is Nadia a companion?" Nova asked, her tone flawlessly polite, as if conversing with a technologically advanced sex doll in the room was commonplace.

"Yes." Andrei rewarded her with a too-familiar smile, pushing aside the many gaming controllers he had piled next to the doll as if inviting Nova to sit with her. "Nadia is the best. And she is very advanced, the latest model with three motorized—"

"Okay, enough," Zhi interrupted. Clearly he should have spoken to Andrei and warned him to be on his best behavior before bringing a young and attractive single woman into his orbit.

Although for Andrei this was likely the best he was capable of. His cousin had never gotten the chance to socialize outside of a medical facility.

"We need to begin your shield practice. Nova, why don't you wait in…" He trailed off, turning to glare at his cousin. "How many of these do you have?"

Because he was almost positive the other doll he'd seen in previous visits had been a different model.

"Well, I didn't have the heart to throw out the earlier models, so Sasha and Vera sometimes join us for dinner—"

"There are three?" For crying out loud. "What room is safe?"

Andrei drew himself up, offended. "They're not weapons."

"Andrei, so help me God…"

His cousin sniffed. "The dining room is out. Sasha and Vera are heavy, so I just leave them there."

Nova waved her tablet. "On the contrary, the dining room is fine. I'm happy to sit with your former companions while I go over some work."

Andrei pivoted, scanning her face to see if she was being sarcastic. When he saw only genuine earnestness, he began to cry.

It was like watching a wall being knocked down from the other side, only to realize the seemingly solid structure had been made of Halva the whole time. The bigger man folded into his arms like an accordion and proceeded to sob with the high-volume drama Zhi had come to expect from his mother's side of the family.

Nova jerked her eyes to his, startled. "Did I say something wrong?"

"No. He's fine." Zhi patted Andrei awkwardly on the back. "Why don't you go into the kitchen to work? Feel free to grab anything you want to eat or drink."

He knew for a fact Andrei never took his companions into the kitchen. Not after streaming the Melanie Griffith cult classic *Cherry 2000*, in which an amorous dishwashing scene had destroyed the titular character—a sex doll.

Nova excused herself with a murmur while Zhi continued to whack Andrei on the back until he'd cried himself out.

"Maybe you should drop into your chat room after this, talk to your friends."

Sex doll preoccupation aside, modern technology had done wonders for Andrei, improving his quality of life in a way Zhi hadn't anticipated. It had to do with a fundamental difference in their telepathy.

Zhi's range was several orders of magnitude larger than his cousin's. However, the drawback to that was that his brain tended to latch onto those he forged bonds with. It didn't matter where they were in the world. He could talk to them anywhere.

Andrei was wired differently. As long as they were outside his range, he was safe from their thoughts, which meant his cousin could develop friendships if they were remote.

Some, like his sister, argued that friends you never got to see in real life didn't count. But Zhi disagreed. It was the age of the internet. Having online-only friends wasn't unusual these days. Andrei's chat room buddies were scattered all over the world.

The small storm over, Andrei wiped his cheeks. "I will learn to shield," he said solely. "Then I'm going to have a real-life girlfriend just like Nova."

Zhi didn't have the heart to tell him the bad news. There was no one else like Nova. But why do that to the guy? Andrei had it bad enough.

"Are you trying to make Nadia jealous?"

Andrei appeared to consider that. "I guess you're right. Nadia has been known to make catty remarks about her predecessors."

Zhi suppressed a wince, wondering if he should have visited more than twice a month.

But his cousin just laughed at his expression. "Relax. I haven't lost touch with reality. I told you Nadia is Wi-Fi enabled. For a small fee you can connect her to a highly rated phone-sex service."

"Ah." Zhi blinked, trying to think of what to say. He eventually settled on "That's very...handy."

"It's *zamechatel'no*." Andrei clapped him on the back. "Thanks for paying for it."

"You're welcome," he said in a tone as dry as his mother's favorite wine. "Why don't we go to the office for our session?"

An hour later, he and Nova climbed back into the limo. He settled in, closing his eyes and rubbing his temples. When he was done, Nova offered him a bottle of iced coffee from the mini fridge.

"Would you prefer something without caffeine?" she asked when he didn't accept it.

"No, this is good." He took the coffee, taking care not to touch her despite her gloves.

"It must be draining, working with Andrei while shielding someone else."

"I'm fine."

She paused, studying his closed features. "How is Andrei doing?"

"While his shields are still inadequate for what he needs, they've grown since the last time we met. A bit anyway. He can also maintain them a touch longer. Not enough to rejoin mainstream society, but enough to make the occasional visit to the nearby grocery store. Or a Starbuck's run."

Zhi had been doing these sessions with Andrei since he turned ten, a few years after he'd learned of Andrei's existence. His great uncle Yosef, Andrei's father, had discarded his telepath son when the boy was seven after giving up hope that the flaw in his telepathy would sort itself out.

It had been Elizaveta who'd plucked Andrei from the institution where he'd been left to rot, much to Yosef's disgust.

The bastard was a subscriber of a survival of the fittest mentality that was so pervasive among the Seven. Zhi didn't agree, but he made exceptions. Like when Yosef had gotten so drunk he'd wandered onto a main thoroughfare and had been killed after being struck by not one but *two* different taxi cabs taking other drunks home. That had been a classic case proving the theory as far as he was concerned.

Sometimes karma worked exactly the way you wanted it to.

"Can you make a note to contact the ZZ8 internal security team? I'm going to need one of them to look into that sex doll's internet security protocols," he said, explaining how the new companion was Wi-Fi enabled.

"Andrei can have a real person log in and talk through the doll?"

"It's part of the premium service I am apparently paying for."

Nova bit her lip. "And you're worried Nadia might have a virus," she began in a suspiciously bland tone. "Like an electronic STD?"

You will not laugh. But the continuing spark of deviltry in her eyes made him want to hold her in real life, not just in his mind via the shielding.

Speaking of... The twisted pine he used as a landmark was just up ahead. He waited a beat.

"That's the end of Andrei's range. I can stop shielding you now."

She straightened in her seat. "Okay, I'm ready."

"I'll try and slide it off slower, in case that helps."

"Sure." Nova braced her gloved hands on either side of her lap. She gave him a nod to go ahead.

He began to withdraw, slower and more carefully than he'd used earlier in an effort to minimize the impact. But he stopped in the middle when her lips parted and her breath shortened.

"Nova," he asked alarmed. "Am I hurting you?"

Nova's head tilted, features slack. Her eyes were clouded. As he watched her give herself a hard shake, the glazed look in her eyes retreated until only alarm remained.

"I think..." She stopped to clear her throat. "I think it's best you pull the shield away fast."

His stomach dropped to his feet, but not before an invisible gremlin unwound his intestines and tossed it like a lasso around his neck.

"I *did* hurt you."

"*No.*" Her tone was firm, but Nova wouldn't look at him. Cheeks blazing, she kept her head turned to the window.

Zhi scooted down the seat until he was opposite her. "If I've harmed you in any way, I need to know."

"I said it didn't hurt." Her voice was strained.

"Then why won't you look at me?"

"It—" She stopped and cleared her throat. "It was..."

The reason for her blush suddenly became clear.

"Oh." Zhi froze, heat rising unbidden until he was sitting there, burning. "Can I help?"

He could barely make out the shake of her head. "Nova, have you considered that I could..."

With a languid movement, Nova turned her head to look at him. "If you could what?"

His eyes skated over the delicate curves and planes of her face. "The brain governs sensation."

"What?"

"I can do it. It won't be actual touch, but it would feel like it."

She stared at him, a line appearing between her fine brows.

"Think about it," he pressed. Zhi knew he should stop, but he couldn't stop himself. "Why do soldiers still feel limbs they've lost? It's because their mind tells them it's still there. The brain can be tricked."

Nova's mouth pressed into a line. "It wouldn't be real."

He leaned forward in his seat, unable to stop staring at her lips. Painted a dark, rich red, they were lush and perfectly formed. "Does that matter?"

Nova gasped. She raised a gloved hand to her lips.

"Did it work?" he asked, somehow managing to get the words out despite the vice around his chest. "Did it feel like a kiss?"

CHAPTER FOURTEEN

Nova stared at Zhi, stunned amazement and aggravated irritation fighting for supremacy. How would she even know that?

She could still feel that alien pressure on her mouth. Even and firm, it had felt like a kiss, or at least what she imagined one felt like back when she still indulged in fantasy.

"Nova? Can you talk to me please?"

Her hands flailed in front of her face, gesturing for him to stop speaking. Conversation was beyond her.

"Nova, please answer me."

Why was it so hard to breathe? Blind, she reached out for the car's window control, fumbling with it a bit until it finally lowered with that discreet hum distinctive to expensive vehicles. The pristine forest air hit her skin like a wave of cool water.

She sucked it into her lungs like it was running out. Somewhere up above them the Spaceballs One Mega Maid was vacuuming off all the oxygen. What she was feeling was the breeze as it was siphoned off the surface of the planet.

To add insult to injury, Nova was drenched. She didn't usually sweat. Not like this. Her dress was sticking to her chest. Still blushing, she pulled the bodice away from her skin in a desperate bid to cool off, too uncomfortable to care that she wasn't alone.

Zhi's eyes were dilated, hot burning coals that were threatening to singe her clothing off. She could almost feel their heat across the space between the seats.

The predator camouflaged by a sharp suit tilted his head at her just before ghostly pressure skated across her cheek. Her mouth opened, gaping wide as it moved down to her neck.

Completely enervated, Nova let her head fall back on the seat. She was panting and hot everywhere.

"Does that feel good?"

The dark velvet whisper must have been in her head because her ears were thrumming. Actual sound wouldn't have gotten through. The pressure on her neck spread until it was as if an invisible hand was cupping her throat, the thumb stroking the sensitive skin above her collarbone, comforting even as it dominated.

"Oh my God." She couldn't catch her breath. Nova clutched the front of her dress, unsure what to do. And then the caress moved south until she could feel fingers skating over the tops of her breasts.

Her entire body throbbed in response. Lightning shot up her spine. A hunger sharper than any she'd ever felt had her in its grip, all claws and teeth.

Clenching her thighs together, she fought to regain control.

Trembling, she opened her eyes to see Zhi was breathing fast too, his attention hyper-focused on each tiny spasm that passed through her.

He looked like he was two seconds away from leaping on top of her.

"Please stop," she whispered, tears stinging her eyes.

Zhi jerked back as if she'd slapped him. The lust in his eyes cleared, and his facial muscles morphed into an expressionless mask.

"I..." he broke off, clearing his throat. "I apologize. I got carried away."

"It's okay." The words spilled out automatically.

"I know that's not true." His voice was harsh, and his chest was heaving up and down, although she couldn't hear the exhalations. All she could hear were her own.

"*Nova.*"

"*No.*" She straightened in her seat, needlessly tugging the hem of her dress down. But she still felt naked.

"We need to discuss this."

The laugh that escaped surprised her with its bitterness. "There is nothing to discuss. Except perhaps the fact that your fiancée arrives in less than two weeks."

Nova had been obsessing over that date on the calendar for the last month. It was her own personal doomsday clock ticking away. Unstoppable. Inevitable.

"I don't want her. I don't even know her. I want y—"

Her head snapped up. "Stop it."

The tears that had been gathering were well past the point of no return. One coursed down her cheek.

Zhi flinched.

Making an effort to regain her composure, she folded her hands in her lap. "It's not real. And I can offer you nothing."

All she could do was take. That was not enough for her. And no matter what he thought right now, it would never be enough for him.

It doesn't matter, she told herself as Zhi withdrew, the wall of ice rising again as he slid back into the window seat.

Zhi's fiancée would arrive in twelve days. The moment she did, he would forget whatever this was. Because he'd be able to touch Larissa... and be touched in return.

CHAPTER FIFTEEN

Nova stared down at the couple walking around the garden from the third-floor window.

She had mapped out this location with care. With the light hitting the house this way, shadowing this particular window, they wouldn't see her if they happened to look up.

Not that it would happen. Zhi and Larissa Zhou appeared engrossed in their conversation. Both were so attractive against the blooming backdrop of the garden that it could have been a scene out of her favorite romance film. The only thing missing was the period clothing.

This was good, she reminded herself as Zhi pointed out a particular species of plant to his lovely guest.

Larissa Zhou was everything a member of the Seven could want in a bride. Beautiful, poised, and cultured, she had flawless manners and enough magic to light up a room.

Nova just hoped Zhi found happiness in the match. Because while Larissa was impressive as hell, she didn't seem to have much natural warmth. Of course, it was still early days. There hadn't been enough time for Larissa to let her guard down.

Nova was so distracted by her thoughts she didn't hear the door opening.

Jing joined her at the window. She didn't speak for a long minute, but when she did it wasn't what Nova expected.

Jing kept her eyes on the couple strolling among the flowers. "Do you know how my twin brother Bai died?"

Startled, Nova twisted to look at her. No one ever spoke about the lost heir. "From cancer," she murmured. "Childhood leukemia."

"That's the story my father spread." The older woman's dark eyes fixed on her. "My father thought the truth would make us look weak. Bai was murdered."

Her shock must have been apparent because Jing nodded. "It happened while Bai and I were at boarding school. There was evidence pointing to a rival family. I was whisked home, and mother decreed no more of her children would be sent away. From then on we would be taught by private tutors. The house became an impenetrable fort. And, after a time, a prison."

Why was Jing telling her this? "I'm so sorry. I had no idea."

Jing brushed off her sympathy. "I was only seven but terrified because we were going to go to war with that other family. Then Zhi's gift flared to life."

"Oh, he was born a telepath," she continued when Nova frowned. "But until then we had no idea how strong he really was. Most telepaths can't get through a trained witch's mind. But there is no magic that can protect from Zhi's telepathy. He can cut through any mental shield or protection spell like a laser. Even shifters, who are impervious to telepathy, can't withstand him. Yes, their brains will be soup afterward, but despite what he claims about not being able to get through them they *can't* stop him. His ability can be a scalpel or a sledgehammer, and it has no limits. The only issue is whether the subject would live through it or not—and believe me when I say it's far easier for him to kill with his talent than he lets on."

Intellectually, Nova had known this, but hearing it from Jing made the reality of Zhi's world so much more stark and sad. The rigid level of control he had to exercise in his day-to-day life was inhuman.

She threaded her gloved fingers together. "How many shifters has he, um, liquefied?"

"Enough to be sure he can."

"Were they assassins?"

A nod. "Being one of the Seven is dangerous. But being the head of the family or heir to be the head is like dancing on a knife's edge all the time."

Jing tilted her head, looking over Nova's head straight into the past. "Most people think my father was being misogynistic when he passed me over as heir. But the truth was he loved me. He loved Zhi too, but at least Zhi's ability meant he could see any threat coming."

"Zhi was the one who realized the murder was a setup," she guessed.

"Yes. He was little more than a baby, but he told us who had done it and who had helped."

These events had happened years ago, but Nova's stomach tightened anyway. "It was someone close to you."

"Yes. My father's cousin. He thought pitting us against the Delavordos would lead to us dying so he could assume the throne."

She turned her gaze back out the window. "Father made Zhi take care of it himself, to avenge his brother and to show everyone that the new heir was as lethal as they come."

Oh God. Poor Zhi.

"I had no idea." She had believed the cancer cover story, had no reason to dig deeper. But she should have known. Zhi's intensity had been born of his brother's death. The fact he'd been able to let it go with her for a while had been a gift she hadn't appreciated.

Nova didn't know what the future held, what their relationship would be like. But she knew she couldn't ask for that brief ease to return. She couldn't do that to him. That would be Larissa's role from now on.

"Most people don't. But the right people do—the other heads of the Seven Families. And our family of course."

"May I ask how old Zhi was?"

"Seven."

Her eyes widened. "He was forced to do this at *seven?*"

"That's the thing. My father told him to do it, but Zhi was willing. He'd heard the killer reliving the death and his plans in his mind. It made him angry. He *needed* to avenge Bai. My baby brother still had baby fat on his cheeks. But Zhi turned into a killer because he realized he could protect us. So that's what he does. Sometimes it seems like that's all he does. Me and mother do travel a great deal, but we do it with a coterie of bodyguards. They check in with Zhi twice a day."

Nova nodded. She had noted this once the ladies arrived home. In addition to the guards, there was also a panic room and a small armory filled with weapons of every variety. The guards didn't patrol the grounds with guns, but it was because they didn't have to. They carried spell balls and were strong enough to cast curses. "With the exception of Han, I have noticed this zealousness to protect the family. It's probably why he bid on me."

And it wasn't because he thought she could help protect *his* family as intended. He hadn't known enough about her ability at the time of the auction to make that determination. No, it had been to protect her from the other families.

"That's not why I'm telling you this. You know why you're here. And we never have to worry about Han. He can take care of himself."

She heard that sentiment several times now, but no one was invulnerable. Moreover, she liked Han enough to be concerned. However, Nova knew better than to contradict any of the family.

"Why are you telling me all of this?"

Jing's head bobbed as if to indicate the couple no longer visible on the other side of the glass.

"My point is that you should be glad it's not you. I know I'm glad it's not me."

The words should have been a kick to the gut, but Nova's shields took the hit. "I wasn't up here lamenting my fate or your brother's upcoming nuptials."

"I'm not accusing you of anything," Jing said, surprising her. "I know nothing can happen between the two of you. From what I've observed, you've haven't put a foot wrong."

"Then..."

But Jing didn't explain why she had started this conversation. "Out of curiosity, what were you doing up here?"

Her smile was weak. "Contemplating the nature of human companionship."

Jing appeared to consider that. "Does it make you angry? That you won't experience it to the degree the rest of us can?"

Nova's eyes found the blue-black gleam that was Zhi's hair peeking over the top of the distant hedge maze walls as he walked behind his intended. The distance between him and Larissa had not grown smaller. On the contrary, it had expanded.

"Not today."

Jing raised a skeptical brow, making her look more like her brother than Nova thought possible. "It doesn't?"

She shook her head. "I don't get the highs, but I also don't get the lows."

"Hmm." Jing pursed her lips. "I guess I hadn't considered it from that perspective." She snorted suddenly. "Based on past experience dating among the Seven, you may end up being the more fortunate one."

"Well, I might not go that far," she muttered.

Jing smiled, giving her a predatory air. "What do you think of Larissa?"

Nova was too good a diplomat to answer that loaded question with complete honesty. "She's extremely poised. Confident. And her power is palpable."

And she looked amazing on Zhi's arm, even through a streaky third story window. "I'm hoping we can be friends," she added.

It was only now that Jing's expression became sympathetic, touched by pity.

"I hate to be the one to break this to you, Nova, but given the way my brother looks at you when he thinks no one is watching, that's not going to happen."

CHAPTER SIXTEEN

Zhi wondered, not for the first time, whether Larissa was kidding or if she was exaggerating because she was deliberately trying to shock him.

"I assume you weren't in the car when it went into the bay."

Larissa raised one perfect eyebrow. "Driving a car remotely is child's play. Don't tell me you've never done it?"

He looked at her sideways as they turned another corner of the maze. "Can't say I've ever had the occasion."

"It's a simple spell. I can teach it to you." Her expression was probably meant to be adorably smug, but Larissa was too coolly sophisticated to pull off the adorable part.

"Wasn't your cousin mad about his car?"

She shook her head, managing to toss her jet-black tresses back over her shoulder so it would catch a ray of sunlight just right. It was like the woman traveled with her own invisible lighting professional. "He recognized the error of his ways and wisely decided not to complain."

Zhi chuckled, wondering if he should applaud. With one anecdote, Larissa had framed herself as a grade-A ballbuster, one who put family loyalty above all else. "I'm sure he never made that mistake again."

Larissa's smile was both wicked and mischievous. He half-wondered if she practiced them in the mirror but then decided she didn't.

Larissa Zhou was everything she presented herself as. Intelligent, sharply incisive, and supremely confident. She couldn't have been more different from his first marriage prospect. Larissa would make a formidable partner. And she would never be afraid of him, because she didn't give a damn what anyone thought about her.

He hated to admit it, but his mother had chosen well. As little as three months ago, he would have been intrigued by her.

"You would be right." Larissa turned the next corner of the maze—the correct one—without looking. "I suppose your relatives don't test you that way. They don't want to risk being lobotomized."

"You would be right," he echoed, his tone a touch above deadpan.

Larissa tittered, the sound genuine. They kept talking. She told him about her travels, her education, subtly highlighting the connections she would bring to the table without being obvious or crass. She also managed to look and sound interested in everything he had to say.

But none of it rang true. It felt more like a performance. Both of them were players on a stage, and he was not as willing to play his part as she was.

By the time they were done with the maze, he was wishing himself exactly fifty-four miles away—at his private cabin, the one only Han knew about. Zhi had gone there after the incident in the limousine, taking a couple of days to clear his head. And to give Nova the space she so clearly wanted.

He still couldn't believe he'd done that to her. But the moment he realized his telepathy could trick her into feeling touch Zhi had lost his head, intent only on making her shiver in ecstasy. And she'd been with him for a brief intoxicating moment.

No, he had to stop lying to himself. He had crossed a line. And he still hadn't apologized for it.

He had tried, but Nova had shut down all conversation that wasn't about work or the Zhou family visit. The one time he pushed the flash of panic and pain in her eyes had been too much to bear.

Zhi couldn't keep hurting her. So, he'd given up.

Nova had joined his mother's efforts to let her take outside contract work. She'd gotten dozens of offers in his short absence. He'd told her he would think about it.

He'd been lying at the time until it dawned on him that living in his house wasn't part of their contract. She had chosen to live with them in order to serve his family at peak efficiency, but ultimately it was her choice. She could move out at any time.

The push to take contract work was an obvious ploy to get away from him.

Damn. He was going to have to let her do it, wasn't he? He hated the thought of having her out of his sight. And despite the fact he'd bought her, Zhi did not own her.

He tried to look on the bright side. If Nova took outside work, they'd find some sort of equilibrium. Their relationship wouldn't be the same, but they'd have a chance to forge it into something new. Something that wouldn't blow up in either of their faces.

As for Larissa, he didn't know if she was right for him, but too much work had been done, too many hours of sensitive negotiations for him not to give her a shot.

It wasn't as if Nova wanted to take him up on his offer. And why would she? *It's not real*, she had said. And she was right.

The only thing he could offer her was a lie.

CHAPTER SEVENTEEN

Han couldn't help but notice Nova's expression as she climbed into the limo after him. She wasn't smiling, but she seemed more upbeat than she'd been the last few weeks. There was a spring in her step, as if she felt lighter. He could relate.

"I'm relieved to be getting out of the house too," he confessed as she settled into the plush leather seat at the other end of the limo—Zhi's rule for traveling with Nova.

"I'm just happy to be resuming contract work," Nova said with a smile.

"And it has nothing to do with the fact we don't have to attend that tedious garden party Elizaveta organized to parade the happy couple in front of her cronies?"

Her expression wavered, but she recovered quickly. "More like I was afraid Elizaveta would slap a tray in my hand. She even conscripted Eduardo the backup driver to serve canapés today."

"As if Zhi would let her do such a thing," Han snorted. "He'd hogtie us if we put you within reach of the crowd coming today."

Despite how well Zhi's courtship with Larissa appeared to be going, he would pop a blood vessel if anyone came within six feet of Nova.

"That's very kind of him," she said noncommittally, tucking a stray lock of hair behind her ear.

"How do you think it's going?" he asked as the car finally started and they got underway.

"How do I think what's going?"

"The Zhous' visit. The courtship."

She folded her hands primly in her lap and appeared to give his question serious consideration. "From what I can tell, Ms. Zhou would make Zhi the ideal partner. Elizaveta certainly seems to approve. In fact, they're rather similar—down to their fashion choices."

Han raised a brow. "You noticed that too, huh. Do me a favor and don't mention that to Zhi. I doubt he'd enjoy the realization that he's about to marry his mother."

Nova wrinkled her nose impishly before her expression smoothed out. "I guess that tells me how you think the courtship is going."

He shrugged. "Larissa is smooth. I'll give her that. More importantly, she doesn't cower in fear around Zhi."

And his cousin wasn't asking for more than that. Although he should be.

He suppressed a sigh. Han would have felt better if this prospective wedding was something Zhi wanted to do instead of something he felt he *ought* to do.

"Of course, the real test happens after this weekend when Larissa's parents leave."

"They're leaving?" Nova fixed the full force of her cat green eyes on him.

"Yeah, early Sunday," he confirmed. "They want to give the happy couple a chance to be alone."

"Oh." Nova brushed invisible lint off her lap. "That's wise. Although I'm surprised. Larissa's parents seem rather protective."

That was the understatement of the year. Larissa's folks were classic helicopter parents.

"Well, the bodyguards aren't going with them."

"Hmm. That would explain their willingness to depart. Both of those men are rather...intense."

Han found her gentle euphemisms amusing. The bodyguards were just a hair shy of rabid. They left an impression of barely coiled violence, and this was *with* the parental units around.

"Pretty sure both are eunuchs," he snarked. "That's the only reason the Zhous are willing to leave their precious daughter alone with us, so pure and unsullied."

Her brow puckered. "Is virginity really a prerequisite for an arranged marriage these days?"

"No, of course not. But the ones who aspire to marry into the upper echelons of the Seven don't take chances with that sort of thing."

She hummed and opened the thick paper folio in her lap.

"Boning up on your assignment?" he asked.

She stroked the paper with her glove with undisguised pleasure. "Yes. This is for a private collector, a human one is my guess."

"Do you not know?"

"If the job comes through certain channels like Marchesi, then it's usually a given. All known magically adept clients are tagged in their dossiers. If the auction house is unsure, they leave that field blank. But the level of detail in the dossier is a giveaway."

She held up the pages to show him the crowded pages.

"Are they not typically this detailed?"

"For humans, they are the majority of the time, but most of the magic adept families prefer a cold read and so supply little-to-no information beforehand."

"Why? What purpose does that serve?"

She lifted a shoulder. "It's a test, of course. If I read an object without prior knowledge of what it is, then it's extra validation in their eyes. A cold reading also minimizes the possibility that I might be bribed in some fashion to do a false authentication."

He liked that she didn't bother to hide the annoyance in her tone. Of course, Nova would take exception to the implied insult of her honor. "It's a little irritating, but Llewelyn told me to think of it as the price of doing business with the Seven."

Han nodded before a chime on his tablet reminded him he also had work to do. He sent emails and texts, delegating and putting out the fires too small to bother Zhi with. By the time they arrived at the private antiquities gallery, he was done and free to observe Nova at work.

It was fascinating. After the pleasantries were over, he and Nova were led to a back room where the object was waiting, a delicately carved agate vase from the Byzantine Era.

"This is similar to a piece in the Walter's art gallery," she told the excited owner after making a show of a tasteful level of awe and appreciation. "See how the light passes through it. The delicacy of this one is superior, which should offset the fact it was likely carved approximately a century after the Walter's piece."

She then asked if the item was going to be sold and then suggested a price tag that staggered the owner.

"Now you could easily get twice that at auction," she informed him. "But that carries the risk of getting less money if the bidding doesn't go your way. Always remember the worth of an object is in the eye of the beholder."

Nova added more details that would flesh out the provenance, although the actual verification of the vase's path through history had already been done by the art broker who'd contracted her. She merely verified it.

"You wrapped that up fast," Han chided as they were leaving. "Too fast. If we head back now, we risk being forced to attend the tail end of that party."

"What do you mean 'we?'" Nova asked with a teasing grin. "I'm just the hired help. It's acceptable for me to hide in my room. Expected even."

He snickered. "Fine. Save me by accompanying me to a late lunch."

"I ate before we left." A slight pout told him she didn't want to go back any more than he did.

"I think you can squeeze in a few delicacies of the sliced fish variety," he said, naming his favorite sushi place in town, one with a private dining room so Zhi wouldn't give him grief later.

She took the bait. Nova couldn't resist haute cuisine. It was one of her few sensory pleasures. He took the opportunity to discuss his observations on her talent throughout the meal.

"I could feel the energy coming from your hands," he shared at one point, wondering if she was aware of the level of magic she pumped out during a reading.

Her lips parted. "You could? I have always been aware of it but had no idea it was detectable to others. Not at those levels."

"What level would that be?"

"Well, this was an easy job," she said, sipping the tiny cup of plum wine he'd coaxed her into ordering.

"How so?" he asked.

"Vases that ornate are not handled as much as say, a sword," she explained. "I have to expend far less magic digging through the layers to get to the answer the client wanted. That and the original impressions left by the sculptor were still quite strong. It's often that way with pieces made by highly skilled artisans."

"Does that mean you could have pinpointed the name of the artist?"

She nodded. "And the name of the emperor who commissioned it. It was uppermost in the artist's mind as he carved it. But a human owner doesn't need that level of specificity."

"I would have guessed the opposite would be true."

"I know it seems odd, but in most cases handing over that much detail would just make my assessment suspect. They don't know that it's magic giving me the real time and place it was carved."

"Or for whom," he said, acknowledging the wisdom of holding back with the humans.

They continued to chat about her past cases, eating delicate slices of fish served omakase style followed by a quick detour to a coffee shop. After a leisurely two hours, he judged it to be late enough to head back to the estate, deflecting more than one question about the exact nature of his talent.

A secret weapon was far more effective if no one knew about it.

Not that he didn't trust Nova. He did. But he was also just egotistical enough to relish the look on her face when he revealed his true self.

She was still trying to wheedle it out of him when they went inside. "I can't believe you won't tell me. I live here now," she laughed. "There's not much point keeping me in the dark about it."

But he didn't budge, teasing her until she gave up and left to change to go on a run before dinner.

Zhi found him in his office a short while later, catching up on paperwork. "How did it go?"

"Shouldn't I be asking you that?"

"Larissa performed admirably," Zhi said, passing a hand through his hair and dropping into the chair in front of his desk.

"A telling choice of words."

Zhi rolled his eyes. "The party went well."

"Does that mean you're officially hitched?"

His cousin scowled at him. "As if I'd decide on a life-long commitment over such a trivial reason. Now tell me how Nova's job went."

"It was fine. An easy couple of grand."

Nova had explained to him that most art appraisals paid by the hour. They billed at similar rates to lawyers, something that tickled him given his law degree. But Nova commanded several orders of magnitude more. Her word was as good as gold in the art and antiquities community, so she charged the big bucks—even in the human world. But the scale was relative.

Zhi raised one of his black brows. "Explain to me why we we're taking special trips to the city to make what is essentially chump change?"

"The price tag goes up for more dangerous objects. By a factor of ten or twenty." Han pointed his pen at him. "You know that."

He didn't bother to remind Zhi that he'd been the one to turn down other more lucrative requests because they required Nova travel out of state.

"She wants to keep her hand in the game. It's better if there aren't any overly large gaps in her appraisal record."

"It's not like her magic is going to atrophy for lack of use," Zhi sniped.

"Yeah, that didn't sound disgruntled." Han rose and poured them both drinks from the sideboard, handing his cousin the larger serving. "Not at all."

"Nova doesn't have to take these small jobs."

Han tried not to snap at Zhi in exasperation. "She wants to feel useful. And you're the one who nixed the big jobs unless they come here to her. Now stop stalling and tell me how you and Larissa are getting on."

Zhi shrugged and took a sip. "Both of us have a good understanding of the demands this marriage would impose. As for how we're getting along, well enough, I suppose."

What a ringing endorsement.

Han waggled his brows suggestively. "How well?" he asked, loading the question with as much innuendo as he could muster.

Zhi shot him a killing look. Han snorted, failing to wither away under his dangerous cousin's glare.

"What? Are you seriously considering shackling yourself to someone without knowing if you're compatible between the sheets?"

"Sleeping with Larissa would be tantamount to committing to the marriage, and I'm not prepared to do that. Not until we've spent more time together. Besides, you know how I feel about sex..."

"That you need to do it more?"

Zhi closed his eyes. "No, that one woman is pretty much the same as another."

Han shook his head. "It's sad that you really believe that. Maybe if you hadn't always gone for such mercenary women you'd have learned otherwise."

His cousin narrowed his eyes at him. "As if you've done any better. Or do you have some secret girlfriend I don't know about? Let me guess, she lives in Canada...right next door to Julie," he said, naming the fake girlfriend he'd made up in the sixth grade.

"You know I made up Julie strictly to make Amalia Quiñeros jealous."

"And it worked a treat," Zhi said smugly. Amalia had crushed Han like a bug under her dainty Mary Janes.

He flipped him off, polishing off his drink with his other hand.

Zhi rose from his seat. "I should let you get back to work. I just wanted to see how things went at the museum."

"You know there's a cool new way for you to figure out how Nova is doing." He set down his glass. "You can *ask* her."

CHAPTER EIGHTEEN

Nova limped through the mansion entrance with a curse.

Damn it. Her jog had been going great until the last few hundred yards. She'd completed a three-mile circuit in the woods surrounding the house to pump herself up. Larissa Zhou had finally taken her up on her offer of a guided tour of the family art galleries, and Nova was determined to knock it out of the park.

Her enthusiasm had been reflected in her run. She'd nimbly jumped over fallen logs and a little stream by hopping over the rocks someone had strategically placed for that purpose. And then the moment the house had come into view she'd slipped on some wet leaves.

Her legs had flown out from under her, leading her to hit the ground with bruising force. Worse, the tenderness in her ankle was bad enough to qualify as a sprain. Not great news in a house with no elevator and a million stairs.

It's not an omen, she told herself. Nova would make a friend of Larissa if it killed her. Sure, the woman had barely glanced in her direction the entire time she'd been here, but that was par for the course. Her parents and the rest of the entourage had been swarming all over her and Zhi. Now that they had departed, save for the bodyguards, she had a chance to connect with her.

Perhaps Elizaveta would reinstate the invitation to dine with the family this week. It had been temporarily rescinded with the Zhous in residence—not that Nova minded. Inserting herself at that stage of the getting-to-know-you dance would have been awkward. But when she lived with Llewelyn, she ate with him more often than not, only skipping out when he entertained his gentlemen callers or met with his closest friends who wanted to reminisce about the good old days.

Nova didn't want to dine with the family every night, but she did want the option.

I just want it to feel easy and natural. No awkwardness. The way it had those first few weeks when it was just her and the boys. Before things got tense with Zhi.

Trying not to picture how either Zhi or Han would react to being referred to as *boys,* she continued to limp through the grand foyer when a booming voice made her jump.

"What happened to you?" Her head snapped up to see Zhi rushing down the left-hand stairs as Larissa observed from the landing.

He stopped short as she waved him off.

"Just a little spill," she said, giving them both a bracing grin despite her watering eyes.

Glancing behind her to make sure she wasn't leaving a trail of muddy footprints, she explained about the wet leaves, trying to inject as much humor into her story.

"But don't worry," she told Larissa. "I have a poultice from the Gallardo family that will fix this right up. We won't have to delay our tour of the gallery."

"That is good news," Larissa said, inclining her head.

Limping past Zhi, Nova started her long and arduous journey up the stairs.

NOVA POINTED to a stunning emerald and diamond collar necklace nestled in its own custom-made special display case.

"And this was gifted to the family at the end of the nineteenth century by the Maharawat of Varanasi in appreciation for an unnamed favor by the first Bao Zheng. I believe Elizaveta wore this to the coronation ceremony of the king of England," she added enthusiastically to a distressingly indifferent Larissa.

The fact the woman had opted to go on this tour with one of her bodyguards trialing them didn't help. She waited for a reply, but Larissa maintained her silence.

Nova had already taken her through the major galleries. Larissa had shown little interest.

Despite Nova pulling out all the stops, the woman hadn't reacted to anything. Even the totem that had belonged to a notorious wizard who could summon arcane creatures only earned a polite nod coupled with a stifled yawn.

Which was why Nova had saved the family jewel vault for last. But her big gun was failing.

What woman didn't like jewelry? Even those disinterested in fashion would be impressed by this collection. The history of the pieces in this room could fill multiple volumes!

At the very least the setup should have gotten a reaction. The vault was a spacious steel-reinforced room warded to keep out intruders. Assorted jewelry pieces and the more valuable antiquities and magical artifacts were displayed on pedestals or special niches built into the wall. It had a thick steel and silver reinforced door that they didn't bother to lock while Zhi was in residence.

The threat of theft was negligible with a telepath of his strength around.

Nova could feel Larissa's attention flagging further—as if that were even possible. This was her last chance to crack the woman's icy facade, and she was failing miserably.

Stubborn to a fault, she was determined to persevere.

"With the exception of the handful of cursed pieces, the Zhengs make it a point to wear and live with their heirlooms." Nova waved to encompass the entire room filled with precious stones glittering under the brilliant track lights. "I think that's admirable—it keeps the pieces alive, rather than relegating them to museum status."

She leaned in conspiratorially. "If you feel like trying anything on, taking it for a test run as it were, that can be arranged."

Larissa's dark eyes flickered with amusement. *Finally*. But Nova's celebration was premature.

"I think I'll hold off until the appropriate occasion presents itself," Larissa said in a terse tone at odds with her high voice. "In fact, I'm not sure there will be a real run, to borrow your analogy."

"Oh." Nova tucked a non-existed stray hair behind her ear. Was Larissa looking for some kind of reassurance about the marriage negotiations? She didn't really know what to say, but she couldn't let that pass without comment, could she?

"I can't really speak from a place of authority because I haven't been with the family long, but from my perspective your visit appears to be going well."

No reaction.

"Of course, these things take time," she added, cracking slightly under Larissa's flat gaze.

Perhaps it was Larissa who found Zhi lacking, as unbelievable as that seemed. "To be sure," she added. "You'd want to be sure. It is a lifelong commitment."

Larissa began to walk around the room, her sky-high dark ruby heels strangely muted against the polished wood floor. "I understand your position is similar," she said—the longest sentence since the tour began.

Nova smiled and nodded, assuming Larissa was being amusing, trying to connect.

"In a way, yes, in that my contract is for life. But that means a lifetime of curse detection in addition to the other services I provide."

She proceeded to drop notable names from her network of shopping contacts, highlighting a few of the vendors who Elizaveta and Jing had discovered through her and the types of purchases they had made, mainly purses and shoes.

"Did Zhi give you leave to address him by his first name?"

Warning lights flashed in her brain, but Nova nodded gamely. "He prefers it. He doesn't wish to be formal in his own home. I understand his father, Bao, was the opposite, which is likely why Zhi insists on a more casual address."

"And you were the one who chose the aquamarine bracelet waiting in my room on my arrival."

"It's the piece Zhi selected from a range of provided choices," she said before lifting a gloved hand to her neck. "Aquamarine is typically tuned to the throat cleansing chakra. It's meant to promote clear communication when properly charged. I took the liberty of doing so before your arrival."

The charge on the stone wasn't strong, but as a member of a magic-adept family Larissa would have felt it regardless. At most it would have given her a small boost.

That was what Nova did for her clients. Her psychometry and curse detection were the marquee aspects of her magic, but her job was to smooth their way in a thousand other small ways. Little boosts, applied at every opportunity. It was what Llewelyn had trained her to do.

Nova suppressed a grimace as the bodyguard following Larissa stationed himself behind her. She didn't like to be between two people, but moving away would have meant brushing against one or the other.

"I suppose I should thank you for the bracelet," Larissa said, leaning forward to examine the emerald and diamond confection on display. "Charging it, that is."

Nova held her gloved hands in front of her. "Thanks are not necessary. It's my job."

Larissa pivoted to face her. "Yes, I suppose it is. But then your duties are rather broad, aren't they?"

Nova kept her growing frustration in check. Where was she going with this? "I've been trained to anticipate a client's every need, even those they aren't aware of yet."

The other woman's laugh was an odd combination of husky and brittle, like glass wrapped in velvet. Nova did not like the sound of it. Not at all.

Larissa wasted no time proving her misgivings right.

"Every need, how droll..." she said, pacing in a short semicircle in front of her. "But know this, I don't intend on marrying a man who keeps an in-house mistress. I know that sort of thing is quite common in the Seven, but it won't be an aspect of my marriage."

Nova laughed in outright relief.

"Oh. I'm sorry," Nova said as Larissa's face transformed into an offended sneer. She smoothed her hands over her midriff. "It's just that idea is quite impossible."

Nova took a small step to the side, but both Larissa and the guard trailed her.

She smiled uncomfortably. "I know this is the first time we've spoken, but either Han or Zhi must have mentioned that human touch is impossible for me. My psychometry is at the extreme end of the range." She held up her gloved hands. "I can't tolerate skin-to-skin contact."

Larissa crossed her arms. "I know that's what you would like everyone to believe. But after what I saw yesterday, I have formed another opinion."

Nova raised a brow. "I'm sorry. I don't understand. I wasn't working with Zhi yesterday. I only saw him with you very briefly after my run."

She'd been limping up the stairs for Pete's sake.

Larissa's expression went flat. "Yes, and I saw Zhi running to you. He would have picked you up and carried you up the stairs if I hadn't been there. But he stopped himself in time. Protecting your secret."

Did she really believe that? "I assure you I'm not faking my condition. I am not Zhi's mistress. I can't even touch him. I can't touch anyone."

"No psychometrist is that sensitive."

Straightening her shoulders, Nova shook her head. "Most aren't. I am an exception."

Her lips parted as she felt the bodyguard move behind her.

Nova held up her hands, about to warn them not to test Larissa's theory, but it was too late. The bodyguard's meaty hands closed over her upper arms at the gap between the end of her sleeves and the top of her gloves.

Pain tore through her, a raging river of red. It felt as if she was being twisted, fire and force tearing the very fibers of her muscles apart as her entire body began to jerk and twitch out of her control.

Her last act before blacking out was to let herself fall to the ground in the hopes the man behind her would drop her when forced to bear all her body weight.

But he didn't let go.

CHAPTER NINETEEN

Zhi was reaching for his coffee as he went over a contract update when the scream pierced the air.

The mug flew off the desk as his arm hit it, splashing over the hand-knotted silk rug. But Zhi didn't even look back. He was already rounding the desk, running for the door.

Han hit him on the shoulder as he barreled into the hallway, having been alerted to the disturbance with his own talent.

"What the hell?" he shouted as they bolted for the stairs.

"It's Nova." Zhi flew down the stairs, taking them three steps at the time. The sound of their pounding feet on the marble could be heard through the entire house—Han had magically amplified it in his panic.

What met his eyes was a nightmare. Nova was sprawled on the floor, blood all over her face. He took one look at Larissa's blank face and rounded on the bodyguard.

The mental scan was lightning fast and brutal. Blood began to pour out of the guard's nose and from his eyes, but Zhi wasn't satisfied with that.

The mental blow that followed sent the man flying back, blood streaming out of his eyes and nose. His muscled body slammed into the wall hard enough to crack the plaster coating the metal.

The bodyguard slumped like a side of beef slapping onto a butcher block counter, leaving a streak of red on the pristine white paint.

"It was an accident," Larissa protested, panic twisting her pretty features when he rounded on her. "She tripped, and he was catching her to keep from falling—it was instinct."

"*Liar*," he shouted, tapping his temple. "I know exactly what happened."

"But."

"No!" Zhi screamed, spittle flying from his mouth. He took one step toward her, only to be restrained by preternaturally strong arms.

"You can't kill her without starting a war."

"I don't care," he growled in his head, trying to break Han's hold.

"Nova needs a doctor."

It was the only thing Han could have said that would make him see reason again.

He took a sharp shuddering breath and pointed to the fallen man. "You have five minutes to pack your bags and leave this house, or you join him," he snapped at Larissa.

"Go," Han added coldly when Larissa opened her mouth to protest.

Not satisfied, Han let go of him, taking his former almost-fiancée by the arm and forcibly escorting her from the room. A moment later he was back and bending over Nova's prone body.

"She's breathing. How the hell do we help her if we can't touch her?"

Zhi waved at the doors. "I alerted the entire house staff. The maids are fetching every silk sheet in the linen closet. We'll use them to make a stretcher."

"Fuck," Han scrubbed a hand through his hair. "We should've bought gloves like hers for ourselves in case of emergencies."

Would've, could've, should've. It was an ugly refrain in his head. They hadn't prepared at all. Nova had been in danger from the moment he'd allowed Larissa Zhou into his house, and he hadn't done a damn thing to protect her.

"Hey." Han knocked into his side, able to read his expression. "This is not your fault."

"Of course it is! Larissa was convinced Nova was lying about being able to touch me. She thought we were secretly sleeping together behind her back because of the way I looked at Nova after she slipped jogging. Larissa had ranted about it to her guard. They *planned* this..."

How they thought he wouldn't figure it out when Nova had a seizure was beyond him.

Han swore in Mandarin as a group of servants led by Wen swept into the room. They brought the sheets and tied them together to make a litter and used silicone gloves meant to remove hot pans from the oven to pick Nova up.

After a brief discussion they ran for Nova's list of recommended concierge doctors, the one intended for *their* use, not hers.

A curandero from the Gallardo clan she favored for healing was flown in on a helicopter from his home on the coast. But despite the fact the healer had been vetted by Nova herself and was therefore the best, she remained unresponsive after hours of painstaking treatment.

She was clinging to life but slipped into a coma despite his efforts.

CHAPTER TWENTY

Nova squeezed her eyes shut against the bright light shining in her eyes.

"*Nova.*" Zhi was in her mind. "*Can you open your eyes?*"

There was an unfamiliar note in his voice, plaintive and persuasive. She'd never heard him sound like that.

"*I will if you turn that off,*" she muttered, turning her head to the side. It was heavier than normal, which was odd considering it felt as if someone had hollowed it out and filled it with cotton wool.

The light disappeared, accompanied by a harsh sandpaper sound that might have been a laugh.

With a great deal of effort, she opened her thousand-pound eyelids. She was in her room, but the bed was missing. In its place was a new hospital bed. The head had been raised so she was lying on an incline, presumably so the doctor in the white lab coat next to Zhi could examine her.

Blinking her dry eyes, she focused on her boss. He was sitting on the antique Louis XVI armchair next to her bed looking like something the cat had dragged in.

The sandpaper grated aloud again. "You're right. I do look terrible."

Though he was dressed stylishly in a white button down and gray slacks, his shirt was wrinkled and stained. His face was a touch paler as well, except for the skin under his eyes, which was dark gray.

"You're reading me," she said after a moment, slightly surprised. He'd stopped doing that before Larissa had arrived.

"I have been since you were injured—to monitor you. I've been trying to bring you out of the coma."

Nova sucked in a breath, regretting it instantly when the muscles of her diaphragm protested. *Ow.* Shallow breaths only. "I've been in a coma? For how long?"

"Thirteen days, six hours, and forty-three minutes."

Nova closed her eyes, senses reeling. The fact that he knew how long it had been to the minute...

"I don't remember what happened."

"Larissa's bodyguard grabbed your arms," he said, aggrieved. "He maintained skin-to-skin contact even after you started to seize."

A cold shiver passed over her, but it was less about what happened and how close to death she had come. If the coma had lasted longer than a week, it had to have been close. No, the shiver was about the expression on Zhi's face. It was as cold and dark as a cave in the arctic.

The man who had touched her was dead. She didn't even have to ask.

His features softened, and she remembered he was actively reading her. "My apologies. I'll stop now," he said aloud. "But it's become a habit since you were hurt."

"It's okay," she whispered, aware of what these days must have cost him. "I don't mind. But I still don't understand why the guard grabbed me like that. Weren't they warned against it?"

Zhi didn't answer. Instead, he looked at the two men in the room, dismissing them with a glance. When they were gone, he flexed his hands and grabbed the arms of the chair with a slow and deliberate movement.

"They *were* warned. But Larissa was angry. She thought we were having an affair."

Nova groaned. "But that's impossible."

"She convinced herself that your inability to bear touch was a lie or hoax of some kind." He sat back in the chair, passing a hand over his face. The level of exhaustion was both startling and disconcerting. No one had ever worried about her like this. Not even Llewelyn.

"That's absurd."

"I know that. But the way I look at you implied intimacy—at least in her mind. One that could not be achieved without sex."

Her laughter was weak. She had almost been killed over something she could *never* do. Subsiding, she fought to make her tone light. "I'm sorry if this puts a crimp in your marriage plans."

"Larissa is gone, along with the other guard. They were booted from the estate."

The other guard. Because the one who touched her was in the ground. Her throat swelled with emotion. She cleared it, but it still sounded as if she was being strangled. "You're not marrying her?"

Or would they revisit the idea once the furor of her attack died down? Because that was what it was, not an accident due to ignorance of her condition.

"I could never marry someone who doubted my word," he rasped, watching her with bloodshot eyes.

Nova stared, willing him to say more but also grateful that he didn't.

"Is your mother unhappy the wedding won't be happening?"

Elizaveta had chosen Larissa, researching all there was to know about her. She'd picked her from dozens of likely candidates and found her worthy of her son. All that effort...wasted.

"Mother was understandably upset over what happened, but most of that is anger that Larissa would endanger a nine-figure asset. Elizaveta warned Larissa and her guards about your inability to bear touch herself when the family arrived. As did I. As did Han. Even Jing thinks she mentioned it. They had ample warning. None can plead ignorance."

And still that woman had thought they were all lying to her, protecting the heir's secret side piece. "Thank you. It should have been enough."

"I'm sorry it wasn't."

He leaned forward, bracing his arms on his lap. "I understand if you'd like to terminate your contract. You have grounds."

Nova sat up despite the lingering pain, panic welling up in her chest. "What? No. I don't want to leave...unless you'd rather I did?"

There were certainly enough reasons for him to want her gone. This past week must have been terrible for him. The toll it had taken was right there, etched on his face. What if he decided she was more trouble than she was worth?

His brow drew down. "I don't think that. Don't ever say that."

Her lip quivered. "Technically, I didn't."

He snickered suddenly. "I promise I'll get out of your head now. I've just been worried."

"Don't apologize. I'm sure it helped." Telepaths were in demand in that small intersection of medicine and magic, helping comatose patients and those unable to speak due to injury or infirmity.

"That doesn't give me leave to continue." He gestured to his head. "My only excuse is that I'm a bit tired."

"More like drained. You need to get some rest."

"If you're awake, I'm awake."

She shook her head. "I'm going to have to insist."

"Nova—"

"You don't want to upset the woman who just got out of a coma, do you?" She reached out but stopped, belatedly noticing she wasn't wearing her gloves.

"We brought in a telekinetic, Nurse Rohan, to manipulate you without damaging you further."

"What?" Nova blinked in surprise. "Wow. I hadn't ever considered a telekinetic helping out that way."

"I got the idea from you."

She wrinkled her nose. "Me?"

"Yes. We were inspired by that time you hired a telekinetic who worked as a phone engineer, one accustomed to manipulating tiny electronic components to help restore an intricate solar clock."

That was years ago. "How did you hear about that?"

"Han." He shrugged. "It worked. As did Emmanuel Gallardo, the healer you recommended for family use in the list of recommendations you shared with him. We were able to fly the healer out on a moment's notice. He was here within the hour. You would have died without him or been permanently brain damaged. But it still took him working in tandem with other healers and myself to bring you all the way back."

"Oh." She closed her eyes, trying to absorb all of that.

Nova knew from experience that the damage done to her brain from skin contact was comparable to a stroke. Emmanuel Gallardo would have had to repair the tissue vessel by vessel. Most healers wouldn't have been able to do that. "Glad he worked out."

"The family is offering to put him on permanent retainer with the understanding he move to Seattle so he will always be within reach. He just broke up with a longtime partner, so he was amenable to the move. "

She felt relieved, not just for herself but for the whole family. "Oh. That's good. Not that I anticipate needing his services again. I'm going to take every precaution from now on."

Zhi's look was steady and grave. "We both know the fault was not yours." He looked at the door as if he could see behind it. "Han's coming. He wanted to come by as soon as you woke up."

"I'll be glad to visit with him," she said softly. "But you have to promise me you'll go to your room now and get some sleep."

He rolled his eyes and gave the door a dirty look. "Han agrees with you, but far less politely."

Rising, he slipped his hands into the pockets of his slacks. A knock announced his cousin. "Since he's here, I will go and take a quick nap. If you need anything, tell Han to come get me."

"I will," she lied. Nova had no intention of disturbing his rest, which he knew. But he was too tired to call her on it, letting Han take his place at her bedside.

CHAPTER TWENTY-ONE

Two Weeks Later

Zhi packed the new version of the contract Han had prepared for in his suitcase.

"Really?" Han snorted.

"What?" He peered at his cousin and checked his watch.

They were scheduled to meet with the board of Rilexa, ZZ8's newest acquisition, in an hour. It wasn't a meeting he had planned on attending himself. The deal to acquire the company had been finalized months ago. His presence was superfluous at this point, but he'd changed his mind about going to the closing when he'd learned Nova would be accompanying Han.

Rilexa began experiencing significant manufacturing problems after a supplier unexpectedly went belly up. Han had solved the problem by buying a faltering startup and repurposing its infrastructure to fabricate the parts the company required.

Nova had helped Han finalize the details, finding a company whose manufacturing arm could be converted to suit their needs with minimal effort. She always managed to get him what he needed. Her continued success in that was almost preternatural. Zhi was almost convinced it was part of her gift.

Han rolled his eyes. "The song you're humming."

"I'm humming?"

His cousin widened his eyes. "Yes...the same song that Nova was singing to herself downstairs just now."

"So?"

Han sighed. "Look, no one is happier than me that Nova has bounced back from her coma. She's thrown herself into work, and that's been good for me. Awesome really. She anticipates problems and makes my life ten times easier. She's also great company. I consider her a good friend."

Zhi straightened. "Then why the hell are you complaining?"

"I'm not. But we've all noticed how you've been since she woke up...so happy."

This man is family. You do not want to punch family in the face. "And this is a problem...why?"

Han's expression filled with sympathy. It annoyed the hell out of him. "Because you're back at square one—head over heels over a woman you can't touch."

Zhi sometimes wished he didn't love Han so much. It would have made it easier to punch him in the face sometimes. Especially when Han was right.

"I am happy," he admitted. "Do you think you can back off and let me enjoy it? Or do I not get to feel this way?"

Han raised his hands. "Of course you do."

"Then why the third degree?"

"Because I can *see* you tumbling down into this thing, and I'm not sure where you're going to land." Han threw up his hands. "Even your mother has noticed. Let me repeat that for the cheap seats. *Elizaveta*, the woman who had no idea Jing had a secret boyfriend for over a year despite meeting him half a dozen times and finding him in her room twice, knows you've fallen for your assistant."

Hell. Han wasn't exaggerating when he said Elizaveta was oblivious. It was a trait that had helped her navigate her fractious marriage to his father. "How did she figure it out?"

"What did you expect?" Han tapped his head. "You're obviously talking to her all the time. Or at least whenever she's awake."

"Nova doesn't mind," he said, annoyed at how defensive he sounded.

And while Elizaveta was unhappy that Zhi was falling for an employee, she was the one who had brought Larissa into their lives. She owed him, which explained this grace period where she kept from voicing her criticism.

"I know Nova doesn't mind," Han acknowledged. "And she is clearly pleased with the status quo. For now..."

He closed his eyes. "Then, as long as she is, leave it alone."

Han sighed but inclined his head, putting his hands in his pockets. "Alright. I've never known you to do something without overthinking it to death. So I'm going to trust that you know what you're doing."

Gathering his own paperwork, Han preceded him out of the office. Zhi followed a moment later, aware that in this case his cousin was wrong.

He wasn't thinking. Once Nova was well enough to leave bed, they'd slipped into their old pattern, talking all the time despite his intention to stop. But he couldn't. Not when Nova had welcomed his conversation, encouraged it.

The intimacy of being in her head had been a temptation too great to resist. Their rapport was precious to him. Enough that he was saying to hell with all the reasons why he shouldn't, as well as his family's concerns.

As long as Nova was happy, he didn't give a damn. Whistling, he went down to the car to meet her.

The meeting went well. Nova had found the perfect solution to the problem, something he didn't hesitate to tell her once they were alone in the car. Han had opted to follow in his own car so he could hit a club downtown afterward.

"You know that deal we just inked to be our own supplier will net ZZ8 around a hundred million in the first five or six years."

She shot him an amused look. "Is that your way of telling me I've just earned back my purchase price?"

"It is. But don't think that gets you out of your contract."

She grinned. "I would never. The point is to pay out my fee several times over."

"As long as we're in agreement," he said, affecting a superior air. "You're never going to leave me."

Her eyes widened as the atmosphere in the car thickened. "*Zhi*," she whispered.

He held up a hand. "No. Don't say it. Just...let's just enjoy being within one another's company."

Color flooded her cheeks. Thick lashes screened her eyes as she tugged on the ends of her gloves before jamming them back down. "I do enjoy being with you too."

"But?" He knew there was one.

"But nothing has changed. We don't have a future."

Zhi leaned back in his chair. "Can you do me a favor? Can we try not to discuss the future?"

She tilted her head. "No talk of the future. We live in the now?"

He nodded.

Those lush lips pressed together. "So, what do you have planned for tonight?"

A rush of warmth swept through him. "Dinner at a family-run Italian place in town. They have this tiny atrium built on the roof that can be rented out as a private dining room. The food arrives via dumb-waiter. We'll have total privacy."

Nova took a deep shuddering breath. "You know this is a terrible idea...I hope they serve *osso bucco*."

Pleased beyond reason, he gave Jaxson the go ahead. The driver changed course, taking the Aurora bridge. They were halfway across when he sensed the enemy.

They were in pursuit and coming in fast.

CHAPTER TWENTY-TWO

Nova was pleased when Zhi asked for her impression on the players from today's meeting.

Most of the staff had been inherited with the company's acquisition. Zhi and Han had previously assessed their expertise, but whether or not they were capable of continuing in their current roles as the company expanded was an open question. He wanted her to weigh in on their comfort level with all the big changes coming up.

She wasn't an empath, but she did spend a lot of time observing people, trying to get a bead on what a client might need. She had made copious mental notes.

Nova didn't care that Zhi was talking shop on the way to what was, for all intents and purposes, a first date. He could have asked her to recite stock numbers or read the phone book to him, and she would have been happy to do it.

But midway through her rundown on the engineer she considered pivotal to the success of the deal, Zhi's head jerked to look out of the rear windshield.

"Tighten your seatbelt," he ordered. All warmth had bled out of his voice.

"What's wrong?"

"We're being pursued by a team on motorcycles, at least seven strong. Maybe more."

"More?" she echoed stupidly.

He didn't take his eyes off the road. "They're shifters, and they're in motion. It complicates the read because I can't exclude all the shifters on the bridge—some might be innocent motorists."

"And you're sure the ones on the motorcycle's aren't innocent?" She craned her neck to look behind them. "Shifters like them. I know of at least two or three all-shifter motorcycle gangs."

Then she saw them, and the reason Zhi tagged these bikers as threats was obvious. Dressed head to toe in black leather with matching helmets with opaque visors, the bikers surrounded the limo like a black wave.

She stifled a squeak. "Okay. I take it back." These were hostiles out there.

Don't panic, she ordered herself. Nova had been in dangerous situations before. Llewelyn had been obsessive in his quest to collect magical artifacts. It had landed them in some tight spots. But this was next level. They were being swarmed by team of powerful Supernaturals who possessed superior speed and strength.

Zhi's hand thrust out in her direction, as if he wanted to grab her, protect her. It was his instinct. Always. "Hold on," he shouted.

Not wanting to distract him, she worked on slowing her breathing. Sweat trickled down her spine. Then they heard the sound of tires squealing, crunching metal, and breaking glass.

Screaming, Nova flung one hand up to protect her face, grabbing the door with the other as the limo slid sideways, slamming into the metal barriers of the bridge.

———

"Han we're under attack on the Aurora bridge. I need you here now!"

Zhi ignored the explosion of swear words in his head as his cousin changed course. *"I'm coming,"* Han yelled.

Zhi didn't reply, changing mental channels to contact his security team—the one he'd opted not to bring with him because he'd wanted to surprise Nova with dinner at his favorite restaurant. He hadn't wanted an audience, confident that between him and Jaxson they could keep her safe.

That was before half a dozen shifters tried to pin them down on one of the most dangerous bridges in the state.

Considering they were improvising, they had chosen their choke point well. Too well.

The Aurora bridge had three narrow lanes on each side and no median. Their assailants didn't believe Zhi would risk taking out their people, possibly causing a pileup with other vehicles, endangering himself or Nova.

As if he would hand her over to these people—that he would *ever* allow her to be out of his sight.

And there was no doubt she was the one they wanted. Shifters had trailed them the day of the auction all those months ago. He'd been out on his own since with not even a whisper of danger.

No, it was her they wanted. Why, he had no clue. Han had never been able to trace the group that had followed then. And not for lack of trying.

The *mudaks* were flanking them. The limousine was too big with no maneuverability. Not in these narrow lanes.

The bikes whizzed past the window, trying to get in front of Jaxson to force them to a stop.

That was not happening.

Two quick non-lethal mental strikes, and the two lead motorcycles in front of them lost control.

"Keep going," he ordered Jaxson. *"I don't care if you have to drive through them."*

But the shifters were stronger than he'd anticipated. The one on the left had shaken off the mental blow, maneuvering his bike in front of their vehicle as he leapt off.

The bike hit the front of the limo with a crash. Steel tore like paper, their momentum carrying the limo over sharp debris. The front right tire blew despite being armored.

They were run-flat radials, but the mass of metal trapped under the axle was too much.

"Brace!" Jaxson shouted as the limo began to careen, the back swinging like a pendulum. It careened too far.

The end of the car crossed the center divider and right into the path of oncoming traffic—right into the path of a large pickup truck.

NOVA'S SHOUT was drowned out by the noise of breaking glass and crushing metal. She and Zhi were slammed violently from side to side as something heavy plowed into the tail end of the limo. Her head thumped into the window in a glancing blow, but it didn't break.

When the world stopped moving, she was bruised, and her head hurt, but she didn't think anything was broken.

A groan snapped her to attention. "Zhi!" His head was hanging down, a drop of blood on his crisp white shirt.

Unclipping her belt, she reached out for him. Her gloves slid over his sleeve, but it was enough to rouse him. Dazed eyes cleared as he blinked at her. "Are you okay?" he asked.

"Yes, but you're *bleeding*." She pointed to his forehead.

Zhi raised a hand to his hairline. It came away stained with red. "It's nothing."

He glanced out the window. The driver of the truck had hit his break, not enough to avoid impact, but it could have been far worse. The truck had slammed into the side of the limo, blocking his door. "We're lucky it didn't crush us. We have to—"

A crash splintered the air, and glass flew over them as a fist punched through the black windscreen. Nova screamed and leaned away from the grasping hand. It disappeared, only to be replaced by a boot.

A man wearing head-to-toe leather and a motorcycle helmet kicked at the broken windshield, roaring when the shattered shards held together, keeping the assailant out. He crouched to yank at the laminated glass.

"Don't touch her!" Zhi yelled.

The giant's hands flew to his helmet before he slumped down. But the door on her side flew open, and another man in black appeared in the opening. They reached for her with gloved hands, but she reared back, falling to the floor, screaming and kicking out.

Her ineffectual strikes wouldn't damage them, but they did what they needed to do—buy time for Zhi.

He struck out on the mental plane. The second man clutched his head and staggered away. A third assailant appeared at the opening in the back windshield, and she knew they had to move. "Zhi, we have to get out!"

Clambering up, she began to climb, stepping over the arm of a fallen man. Zhi's mental blow had been strong enough to knock him out—possibly killing him. All she knew was he wasn't moving.

"Ignore him." Zhi was right behind her. But no sooner had her heels hit the asphalt than the door of the car was ripped off its hinges. A massive man in jeans and a helmet reached for her barehanded.

A strangled squeak escaped her as she dodged—right over the side of the bridge.

NOVA WAS RUNNING from the largest wolf shifter Zhi had ever seen when she slipped. She fell through the gap in the metal rail *and* the suicide fence behind it, a hole created by his car slamming into the dual barriers.

She flailed at the edge for one endless moment, one hundred and sixty-seven feet over the water.

But his smart girl threw herself to the side, reaching out to grip the bars of broken fencing with one hand. Her legs swung out, but she maintained her hold, clinging to the metal on the wrong side of the fence.

"Hold on," he shouted, striking out at the two assailants barreling toward them. They fell over each other as he battered their brains, their hands flying to their ears—which did nothing to protect them from him.

He swung back to see Nova's foot slip on the metal support she was trying to climb. One of her black heels fell off, dropping the more than fifty meters to the water below.

"Zhi, I'm here," Han said. His cousin was still in his car at the end of the bridge, unable to get closer because of the stopped cars, most abandoned by their panicked drivers blocking the road.

"Change and give us cover."

A familiar roar filled the air as Nova whimpered, sliding down. Her left foot braced against the intact bottom rail, but the right one was in the air, feeling blindly for a toehold.

No longer caring if there were innocent shifters on the bridge, Zhi sent a crippling mental blow to every werewolf in the area.

Grabbing the edge of the ripped-open fence, he braced his legs at the edge of the broken asphalt. "Give me your hand," he rasped, reinforcing his words with a mental command in a gentle but firm voice. *"Do it now."*

Between the bars, Nova's pale face turned ashen, but she obeyed, reaching out to him with a straining hand.

That was when Zhi learned how slippery silk was.

"No!" He lunged forward when Nova began to slide out of his grasp. Reaching out, he caught her by the dress collar, cursing himself for not wearing gloves himself. But that tenuous handhold was not enough.

"*Zhi.*" Her face was bone white against, her dark-red lipstick in stark contrast to her ashen complexion. She looked down and sobbed, a jagged, terrified sound.

That was what broke him, forcing him to do the unthinkable.

Time slowed. He saw himself reach out to grasp her upper arms, the bit covered by the short sleeves of her double-breasted wrap dress. Then he was hauling her up, muscles screaming as he lifted her up and out of danger.

She crashed against him, the entire front of her body smacking into his chest. They stood there, their rapid breaths ragged and overlapping, back on the solid deck of the bridge.

She hadn't gone over. Nova was safe in his arms.

Holy shit! Nova was in his arms.

"Zhi?" A male voice intruded into their frozen tableau. "Zhi!"

It took him a full minute to realize his cousin was standing next to them, yelling at him. But Zhi didn't turn his head to look at Han. He didn't dare move a muscle.

Because he was touching Nova. She was pressed against him. One hand was wrapped around her upper arm *below* the cuffed sleeve of her dress. And the other—*fuck*. The other was wrapped around the back of Nova's neck, because he was *holding her to him*.

And she wasn't having a stroke. She was staring at him wide-eyed, breathing rapidly, stunned. But she wasn't seizing.

CHAPTER TWENTY-THREE

Nova didn't dare move. She even stopped breathing in fear that this strange stalemate with the universe would end.

Every iota of her awareness concentrated on the foreign warmth on her arm and neck. Heavy. Zhi's hands were heavy and hot, the skin of his fingers rougher than hers. Their heat was intense and *mobile*, as if his hands covered more than the actual surface area they occupied.

Why wasn't she hemorrhaging? According to everything she knew about herself, she should be mid-seizure right around now. But there were no spasms at all. Not even a twitch.

"What is happening?" The voice sounded as if it was coming from a great distance.

She turned her head, jerking in surprise because it wasn't Zhi speaking. Han was standing next to them. Nova blinked slowly, but when the bizarre vision didn't change she blinked again.

Han. "Where are your clothes?"

Han raised his brows. "That's what you're choosing to focus on right now? Really?"

She opened her mouth, but then Zhi's big, rough hands cupped her face and neck.

Holy shit. Nova staggered, the unfamiliar sensation of being touched nearly cutting her legs out from under her.

"*Nova.*" Zhi's dark eyes burned like coals into hers. And then his impossibly handsome face got closer, and there was pressure on her lips, sweet and painful.

The world blurred, and her knees dissolved, losing the fight to support her.

"NOVA, NOVA!" Zhi shook her shoulder as she collapsed against him.

Her eyes were open but glazed over. He shook her again, but though her lips parted she didn't reply.

He swore under his breath. What had he done?

"That's not a seizure, dude." Han snorted, interrupting what promised to be a mental spiral into hell.

Panicked, he jerked his gaze up to his cousin's amused face. "What?"

Han crossed his arms, covering the bottom of the intricately detailed script tattooed to his chest. It was the reason he was so blasé about being naked in public in broad daylight at the site of an attempted kidnapping.

"She's not seizing, man. That's a good old-fashioned swoon."

Zhi stared down at Nova, shamelessly delving into her mind. But his scan showed nothing wrong. She wasn't in pain or experiencing any sort of trauma. Her mind was just quiet, almost sluggish, as if she was just waking up from a deep sleep.

"A swoon?" he asked in disbelief. "This is just a fainting spell?"

Han snorted. "You just grabbed a woman unable to bear being touched. Well, anyone else's touch. And then like a gigantic butthead you doubled down and kissed her." He threw up his hands. "It's too much sensation, butthead. She can't process it. Back off."

Of course, Han was right. He might not be hurting her, but Nova had gone her whole life without touch. Her body had never learned to process the sensory input.

Zhi reluctantly moved his hands, shifting them so that the cloth of her dress was between them. As long as she wasn't seizing, he wasn't letting go. She'd fall to the asphalt. No way was he letting that happen.

His intentions were good. They really were. But just then Nova roused, her thick lashes fluttering as her eyes opened. She looked confused.

Slowly she reached to bring her fingertips to her mouth, biting at the tip of her glove until she tugged it off with her teeth. Then her trembling fingers touched his cheek.

Her touch burned in the best way possible. Zhi covered her hand with his, pressing her fingers deeper into his skin.

Nova burst into tears. But she didn't snatch her fingers away.

Zhi's arms tightened, clutching her to him with an inarticulate sound that sounded suspiciously like a sob. But it came from him this time. Whatever was happening to let her bear his touch was not going away.

But they didn't have time to marvel at this miracle. The shifters were stirring. Unless he wanted to kill them once and for all, then they had to move.

He swung Nova up into his arms and carried her down the bridge as the first sounds of distant sirens pierced the air. "Jaxson is fine, but the limo is stuck. I need you to deal with that and the cops. Where the hell is your car?"

Han jogged beside him. "Are you seriously leaving me here?" He raised his hand to gesture at his nakedness.

"Don't you have a gym bag in your trunk?" They had a state-of-the-art gymnasium at the house, but his cousin favored shifter-run boxing gyms. They were the only opponents he didn't have to hold back with.

Han's face twisted. "Yeah," he said unenthusiastically. "But I forgot to take it out after my last workout. Shit's not washed."

"Sorry you're going to stink, but I have to get her the hell out of here."

Zhi hitched Nova closer. Her face was buried in his shirt, one hand fisting the cloth, but she was out now. Too much touch and her body had shut down into a peaceful sleep.

That was going to be a problem, one he was determined to solve.

They reached the end of the bridge, and he spotted Han's

gunmetal-gray Aston Martin DBS. Running ahead, Han popped the trunk and grabbed his gym bag. He pulled on the pants and sneakers, but Zhi stopped him before he threw the smelly tank top over his head.

"Wait," he said, shifting Nova to a fireman's carry. He slammed his free hand over the script tattooed over Han's chest.

His cousin stood still while he activated the obfuscation spell they had worked out in high school. Han winced as Zhi grunted, shoving more magic at him.

"You know this might be easier if you actually let go of her," Han said, then raising his hands in surrender when Zhi glared at him. "Yeah, yeah. I get it. That's not going to happen anytime soon."

"Good. Glad you understand."

He jerked at the car, waiting until Han opened to deposit Nova inside. He ran around to the driver's side, taking the key fob still on the dash, because anything on Han's person disintegrated when he changed.

Han hesitated, bending to look past him to where Nova sat unmoving in the passenger seat. "Zhi, I don't know what the hell is going on, why you can suddenly touch her, but try to go easy on her."

He nodded, reaching over to fasten Nova's seatbelt. On impulse he took her hand and tugged at the bottom of his shirt. When he'd exposed some skin, he settled it on his abs, skin to skin.

Han smacked himself in the face. "What did I just say?"

"I don't want it to go away."

"Fine." Han sighed, waving him on. "But you better get the hell out of here now."

The sirens were much closer now. Zhi swore. "Find the *mudaks* who ran us down before I do."

His cousin snorted. "Like you're going to be doing anything but Nova for the next week. See you after the sexathon."

Zhi would have blistered Han's ears, but he wasn't a hypocrite. And Han had told no lies.

The sirens were almost on top of them. Closing the door, he turned the engine and peeled out of there before his fragile miracle evaporated, blowing away like smoke.

CHAPTER TWENTY-FOUR

The scent of expensive car leather permeated her mind first. Then the motion of the car. Finally, she registered the heat under her hand. It was nestled under Zhi's shirt, resting on the hard surface of his ridged abdomen.

Nova shivered. She was touching Zhi and was still alive.

He shifted gears on the manual transmission. Hazily, she watched him drive, weaving in and out of traffic with the ease of race car driver, finally understanding the meaning of the term "competence porn."

Briefly he lifted one hand, covering hers before returning it to the wheel. "*It's okay*," he said in her mind. "*You can sleep. Just keep hold of me.*"

She wondered what it said about her that she wasn't even tempted to disobey. It should have bothered her, but Nova wasn't doing great with complicated thoughts at the moment. The only thing she could focus on was the rock-hard abdomen under her palm.

Was her touch as distracting for him as it was for her? How did the contact not consume his every thought like it did hers?

It must not feel as intense, she decided. Else, how could he focus on driving?

"Trust me, I feel it as fiercely as you do. Your skin on mine...it's like being hit with a sledgehammer," he said in a voice like sandpaper as he suddenly put the car in reverse. He backed it up and brought the car to a stop, removing a space-age key from the dash.

"Where are we?" All she could see was the narrow track they'd driven down and a sea of pine trees crowding around them.

Zhi stepped out of the car coming around to the passenger side door.

He reached over and unclipped her seat belt before putting his hands on her skirt-covered thighs, tugging them gently until she was facing out. But he didn't step back to help her out. Instead, he knelt on the ground, staring at her.

"Zhi?" Her voice was steadier than it had any right to be.

He put his hands out, hovering them over her legs. A head-to-toe buzz of sensation went through all of her. She chalked it up to anticipation. Nova was waiting for his touch. Craving it. But then it hit her. The frisson was *him*. Zhi was scanning her, making sure she was fine with what happened next.

Those big hot hands lowered, those big, surprisingly rough hands touching her through the sheer hose covering her legs. They both sucked in a breath. Nova sat dumbly, utterly transfixed as he slowly ran his fingers up her thigh. He stopped when he hit the elastic border of her stockings.

Zhi closed his eyes as if he was in pain. "You're wearing stockings with garters."

"I like them better than pantyhose," she whispered.

His grin was both feral and a little sheepish. "I like them better too."

She snickered just as his fingers moved up to caress the naked skin above the tops of her stockings.

"Oh my God," she breathed, shivering as her head drooped forward. He leaned forward as if he was pulled by a magnet until their foreheads were pressed together.

They stayed like that for a long moment. Ever so slowly, he angled his head closer until his lips pressed against hers, soft but determined.

Do something. Wracking her head, she tried to recall kisses she had seen in the movies. *Damn it, I shouldn't have fast-forwarded through all of them!*

Zhi's head drew back, the expression on his face amused. "You fast-forward through the kisses?"

Blushing, she bit her lip. "I don't watch romance movies," she admitted. "Not even romcoms. And the movies that have a couple falling in love as a subplot, I skip through all the physical stuff."

Why rub your nose in what you could never have? It was the reason she liked action and gritty crime thrillers best.

"I understand," Zhi said softly. "But since this unexpected opportunity has presented itself, I would really like to change your mind about kisses. Starting with the fact that they're not just for other people."

"Okay. If you want…"

Good lord, she'd turned into a blithering idiot. But Zhi didn't seem to care. He almost hopped forward, and then there was that delicious pressure again.

It should have been less shocking this third time, less debilitating. But it was as powerful as before. And who could blame her. Nothing had prepared her for the visceral reality of kissing Zhi Zheng. Nothing could.

I can do this. Nova told herself she was doing well, holding her own —until the moment his lips parted, and his tongue stroked the seam of her lips.

Her blood rushed out of her head.

"Nova, *Nova.*"

Blinking, she came to in his arms. They were sitting on a long, plush couch inside a luxe wooden cabin.

"Hey." Zhi's face was a mixture of concern and possessiveness. Both emotions were clearcut and strong enough to be a little concerning.

One hand shifted, stroking the skin of her cheek, down to her ear. Her vision began to tunnel, and she grabbed his hand. "Don't do that unless you want me to pass out again."

"I'm sorry," he whispered, regret and desire warring for supremacy on his face. "Han was right. I have to go slower. Now that we're here, we have time."

His words sent a thrill through her. Nova Navarro was no coward. She would see this thing through, no matter what. But there were things she needed to know. Starting with where they were.

She cleared her throat, looking around at the unfamiliar walls around them. "Where is here?"

"It's my cabin."

His what? Nova sat up straighter, taking a better look around.

The single room was shaped like an L with an exterior door in the middle of the base. It opened onto a small area with coat hooks and a table with a bowl for keys and other sundries. There was a kitchen with a breakfast nook with a small dinette set off to the left. The couch they were sitting on was on the long part of the L, facing some overstuffed bookshelves.

There was a king-sized bed at the far end. A second door stood open to the right, with a bathroom beyond.

She furrowed her brow at their minimalist surroundings. "This is yours?"

His chuckle vibrated through her. It was startling. "Why so skeptical?'

"I don't know," she said, her sluggish mind working it out. "I guess this place doesn't fit my mental image of a Zheng-family property."

Not that it wasn't nice. The modern lines combined with a rustic exterior and handmade furniture made for a peaceful and attractive space. But it didn't have the opulence she'd come to expect from a Zheng.

A corner of Zhi's mouth pulled up. "That's because it doesn't belong to the family. It's mine and mine alone. No one comes here but me."

She swung her skeptical gaze to him. "Not even Han?"

He lifted a shoulder, but his hands were busy stroking her legs. Apparently he could do that now without her losing consciousness.

"He knows where it is, but he's only been here once or twice. Han bought the land and organized the construction through a shell company. We're safe here."

She clapped a hand over her mouth to stifle a swear. "I had almost forgotten we were ambushed."

The aftermath had been more shocking than the crime that led up to it. And she was still sitting on his lap! No wonder her synapses were fried.

"Yeah, I figured. I was tempted not to remind you," he confessed, "but I don't want you to worry. Han is on it. He has our people poring over all the traffic camera footage. He's going to find them. I'm not going to let them take you."

"*Me?*" Nova's lips parted. "They were after me?"

He frowned. "You didn't realize that?"

"No. I thought they were after us because of some business related to the Seven." She shook her head. "Going after me doesn't make sense."

His hand stopped stroking her knee. "How can you say that? You're a multi-million-dollar asset."

"I am," she acknowledged, "but I'm also one that can be bought."

He made a disgruntled, growly noise, and she poked him with her ungloved hand, part of her still in disbelief that she could. "You know what I mean. My services can be contracted. You have been taking bids, right?"

"Not all bids," he muttered.

Her brow puckered. "You turned down these shifters? Is that why they're resorting to trying to kidnap me?"

He shook his head. "No shifters have tried to contract your services. Han would have flagged them. No, these assholes have plans for you, and they didn't like losing the auction. At least two were part of the group that followed us after it ended."

She tilted her head. "How do you know? I thought you couldn't read shifters."

"Oh, I can. I just tend to kill them in the process," he said. At her wide-eyed look, he shrugged. "Like some of the stronger witches, they have rock-solid mental shields. But I can still get through them. It just involves a lot of smashing and inevitable brain damage."

"Shifters have off-the-charts regenerative abilities. Don't they heal?"

"Not from everything," he muttered. "And a quick mental imprint can be done at the surface. They're unique. Like a fingerprint."

She had never heard of a telepath having that ability. "Do they know you can do that?"

Zhi squeezed her knee. "Trade secret. Shifters are better off not knowing I have the ability to identify them in this fashion."

"Yes, of course."

Shifters were notoriously secretive and volatile. If they learned someone could ID them so easily...that would be problematic. "Regardless, kidnapping seems a bridge too far for them. Why wouldn't they just hire another psychometrist?"

He considered that. "What if it's curse detection they want?"

"Then they contract a witch. I know plenty for hire. Some of them must have ways of detecting magic, even the subtler curses."

"We won't know why they want you until we track one down. Unfortunately, they took their wounded with them."

Nova had been so out it she hadn't realized there had been any shifters hurt severely enough to be considered wounded. "Did you have to kill any of them?"

"I don't think I did any fatal damage. I was trying to leave one alive for questioning, but as I said they all managed to escape. It's possible one succumbed after that. I hit a few of them pretty hard."

"Okay," she said, sounding a little lost.

His head tilted forward, those coal black eyes intent on her face. "Know this, I will end anyone who tries to take you from me."

Good lord. He really meant that.

Dazed, she scrambled off his lap. She had a split second to register and regret the distress on his face before it was transformed into stunned awe as she began to unbutton her dress.

"What are you doing?" he said, sounding hoarse.

"I don't want to waste whatever time we have," she explained as she shimmied, pushing the dress down when it caught at her hips.

Nova was out of breath by the time it hit the floor, but it was nerves, not exertion.

Her body was flashing hot and cold like a strobe light as she stood before him in her bra, panties, and gartered stockings. "I want to take this as far as we can go."

Zhi's hungry gaze skimmed over her limbs. Was she experiencing his lust as touch again? Or was it her imagination? A ghostly finger ran over the top of her breasts, and she knew it was him, but it didn't bother her. Not this time. She could touch him back now. And the fact of the matter was that with Zhi there were no lines.

Judging from his expression the ghost touch wasn't something he could control around her. She liked that.

"Look at you," he breathed, rubbing his slack mouth with his hand as if it had gone numb and he was trying to wake it up. He slapped his own face, making her jerk, startled.

"You know someone up there really screwed up," he said, pointing at the sky, his eyes eating her up. "It shouldn't be you who hurts when someone touches you. It's everyone else who should seize up and convulse. That is the appropriate punishment for having the balls, the sheer effrontery, to touch the divine..."

He shook his head in disbelief and reached out, his fingers stopping just short of the bare skin of her midriff. "You're a goddess, Nova. Anyone who dares lay hands on you should fucking burn."

Wow. This man. He was going to ruin her, wasn't he? Yes, yes, he was. But even knowing that Nova had to fight the urge to run at him full-tilt and leap on him, slamming their bodies together.

Instead, she took one small step forward, pressing herself against his hand. "Are you afraid of fire?"

He hissed, *actually* hissed as his big hand covered her taut belly, shifting to take hold of her hip in a tight, possessive grip. His eyes were molten and full of things that made her heart keep skipping beats.

"It's criminal to take this bra and panty set off you," he said, both hands stroking the satin and lace. "You should never wear anything else. Seriously, someone should paint you in this right now—"

His hand spasmed on her hip. "Not that I'd ever let anyone else see you like this."

Her face flamed. Despite her show of bravery, Nova had never been this exposed in front of anyone before. But the look on Zhi's face was worth the embarrassment. It was worth everything.

Zhi dropped his forehead on her stomach with a groan. "I want to strip you bare more than I want to breathe. But I promised to take it slow. However..." he began when he registered her disappointment. "...slow doesn't mean stop."

Zhi tugged her hand hard, and she fell forward, landing in his lap.

His hands were everywhere, all over her, adjusting her until she was straddling his legs. The heat of him was intoxicating. An instant addict, it only made her want more.

"Skin," she panted, tugging on the buttons of his shirt. "I want to feel skin."

But the experience of being in his arms without barriers was too much. She could barely process the bombardment of sensory input to function. She couldn't make her hands work with the dexterity necessary to get the buttons out of the holes.

Zhi was smelling her hair, taking a huge lungful of it when he noticed her problem. Taking over, she yanked the rest of the shirt open. Buttons flew all over. One smacked her right breast, sliding into her bra.

A nervous giggle escaped when her attempt to retrieve it only succeeded in pushing it further down.

"Let me."

Transfixed, she watched Zhi raise a hand, reaching into her bra with two fingers. She held her breath as he lingered, letting his fingers go farther than was strictly necessary. Nova squirmed as he grazed her nipple.

He tossed the button aside and pulled her flush against his chest. *"Don't test me, baby."* The voice was a growl in her mind, presumably because he was breathing too fast to speak.

His hot breath fanned down her neck as he buried his face into her hair. Then he opened his mouth against it, and she whimpered, clutching the back of his head, urging him to maintain contact.

The sound seemed to inflame him. He moved like lightning, throwing her down onto the couch and stretching over her.

She couldn't help the cry that escaped. His heat, all that skin touching hers, threatened to send her into sensory overload, but she hung onto consciousness, fighting tooth and nail to stay with him.

"This is either the best or the worst thing I've ever done," the guilt-tinged voice reverberated in her head.

"Best," she gasped, undulating under him. "Definitely best."

His strangled laugh cut off when she raised her head, pressing her lips to him. Her tongue tangled with his as he pressed her into the cushions, grinding his cloth-covered cock between her legs.

Zhi had the wrongheaded notion that he shouldn't remove her undergarments, but that didn't mean he couldn't shift them, shoving the cups up to expose her breasts.

He stilled, staying motionless for a long moment. Then he was on her, hands and mouth kissing and licking. He consumed her breasts with abandon, all the while pumping and grinding. Her body reacted, opening and softening for him.

His fingers thrust into her panties. He squeezed and caressed her clit, rubbing in a circle with firm pressure. And then lips closed over her nipple, sucking hard.

Nova's hips bucked as her body fragmented. Sobbing, she tumbled down in a dark wave of ecstasy.

CHAPTER TWENTY-FIVE

She had never woken up in a man's arms before. Why did it feel so natural?

Zhi's throaty chuckle warmed her. "Because it's me," he said, running a finger down her cheek.

"Arrogant," she chided. But that didn't stop her from cuddling closer to him, marveling at the feel of him. She would be happy staying here forever.

"You love it." He tapped her nose. "And I'm not sure about there being no precedent now that I've had some time to think about it. We've been laying the groundwork for this for months."

"We have?" she asked skeptically.

"With my telepathy. I've never used it as liberally as I have with you. Not outside my family. Not in it either."

"Not even with Han?"

"Cumulatively maybe. But no one has ever welcomed me into their mind the way you did." His face sobered. "And then there was the amount of time I spent digging through your mind when you were comatose, trying to bring you back to consciousness."

His hand closed over her hair, which she belatedly realized was now loose, hanging down to her shoulders. "I still feel responsible for landing you in the hospital to begin with, but it may have had an unexpected benefit."

Her lips parted. "You think your ability has somehow carved an exception for itself—my ability no longer sees you as other."

He nodded. "It makes sense. You always felt my telepathy as a form of touch. I don't know if we could have done this before your coma, but I bet we were heading in that direction. The time spent attempting to rouse you might have put us over the finish line. At the very least it appears to have desensitized you to my touch."

"Then this might not be a fluke?"

"I don't think so. As long as we keep talking mind to mind, we should be safe to keep touching. Han agrees."

Nova bit her lip, disconcerted. "He does? When did you speak?"

"We were bouncing a few ideas back and forth while you were sleeping."

They had? She sighed. "How long was I out?"

He scratched the back of his neck, reddening a touch. "An hour or so. Long enough to get an update from Han and, um, shower."

Nova reached out to touch his hair, belatedly realizing it was wet.

"Oh." Nova was mortified. She was sitting in his lap in a sweaty, unwashed ball, and he had *showered*. He'd even changed into loose pants of some stupidly soft fabric, and she hadn't even noticed.

Nova curled her limbs, trying to get up.

But he wouldn't let her go. "Don't feel bad you haven't had a chance to wash up yet. I'd still be naked too if I hadn't had to...uh, take care of business."

Her brow puckered. "Was there a ZZ8 emergency?"

"No." Zhi waved over his groin, a flush creeping up his neck. " I didn't want you to feel awkward if you found me sporting a raging erection when you woke up. I thought it best to hit the shower to take the edge off."

Nova could feel her cheeks turn as red as her hair. She snickered, peeking at him from under her lashes. "Oh."

"I'm sorry. I'm not trying to embarrass you. I think the constant mental contact is erasing too many boundaries, way too fast." He gave her an adorable, self-deprecating smile. "My only excuse is I like being close to you."

She threw her arms around him, burying her face in his neck. "I like it too. And it was very thoughtful of you to take care of your arousal before I woke up. Sorry I wasn't there to help."

Zhi burst into laughter, loud guffaws that shook her whole body. "Oh, you'll get your chance, but for now you have to stop looking at me like that. Being playful makes me want to pillage you."

"I wouldn't mind being pillaged."

He groaned, dropping his head against hers. "You're going to be the death of me."

Nova decided to take pity on him and change the subject. "How could you not tell me that Han is a shifter?"

"Because he's not one."

What? "Then why was he running around buck naked on the bridge?"

He put a finger to her lips. "Clothes don't make it through the transformation. But he's not a shifter, not in the traditional sense of the word."

Employee Nova wouldn't have pushed. Even a long-term retainer couldn't expect to be taken into the family's confidence. Sometimes secrets were necessary. But the Nova who'd orgasmed in her boss's lap less than a few hours ago decided she had a little leeway. It wasn't as if this was a secret they'd be able to keep. Not with Han streaking in public.

"Come on. You know you want to tell me."

But Zhi held firm. "I can't. Han made me swear on my father's grave he could be the one to show you his second form. He likes to surprise people."

"You just said second form. That means he's a shifter."

He shook his head, smug and secretive. "Worlds away."

"I can't believe you're not going to tell me!"

"Patience is a virtue. Trust me, the wait will be worth it. " He leaned over to nuzzle her hair, starting the slow melting of her nether regions. "There's a reason Han is our head of security. His magic is unique and formidable. He's the only person I trust with your safety—other than me, that is."

"You realize half the drivers on the bridge saw this mythical other form."

"But they won't remember it. There's a contingency in place for that."

Her brow puckered before clearing. "Han's tattoo. You did something to it before we got into the car. It's a spell, isn't it?"

"Yes." Another nuzzle.

"Obfuscation?" Nova's brow picketed. "I've never heard of one that had worked in tattoo form."

"It was the best solution. It's a complicated spell designed to work not just on people but also technology—Han's second form can't be captured on camera."

"How is that possible?"

"He appears as a big bright or dark spot, depending on the amount of ambient light. As for the witnesses, the average human will register what they're looking at only while they continue to have eyes on him. As soon as they turn away, they forget what they saw. Their brain autocorrects, filling in his image with someone else more likely—a big dog, a lion. Someone even reported a runaway riderless motorcycle once."

Stunning. "That is some seriously impressive magic."

"It is complicated," he acknowledged. "We can't do it on the fly. But we figured out how to lay the groundwork in high school, condensing it into a tattoo. There are a few missing ingredients that have to be fresh, but we figured out ways to incorporate them into Han's toiletries without losing its efficacy."

Her mouth dropped open. "Is that why he always smells like mint?"

"That's the Chinese basil extract you're picking up. We put it in his pomade. It gels up nicely, and all he had to do is pass a hand over his head and rub it on the tattoo before I activate it." He shrugged. "He doesn't mind. The ladies like the scent."

"The tattoo is a conduit for some sort of enhanced telepathic push? Do you have to be there to activate it?"

"Han can activate the spell on his own, but it is more effective when I do it because I can channel more power. When it comes to the mind manipulation, I am a natural catalyst. The tech obfuscation works regardless of which one of us turns it on."

"Wow. I would have expected the opposite." Modern technology didn't play well with witchcraft. Attempts to circumvent or manipulate magic through tech often failed in a spectacular fashion. But for Han and Zhi it was the stable, most infallible part of their spell.

"I'm starting to feel kind of inadequate here. Outside of my psychometry, which is innate, my spell craft is rudimentary by comparison."

Zhi scoffed. "No, you're only an expert on everything else under the sun. Do me a favor and leave the spell craft to me and Han, or else you'll leave me nothing to do."

"Says the man who saved me." Nova cupped his cheek. "Thank you for watching out for me. But now that I know those shifters are after me, I need to do something to be able to take care of myself."

Most witches learned some form of defensive spell work as children, but the Seven took this to another level. And who could blame them? Theirs was a world full of predators.

"If that's what you need for peace of mind, I will help you with that, but until the threat passes I'm your shadow. Closer than that now that I can touch you. With your permission of course."

"You have it." Nova stroked his muscular chest, almost purring. "How long will we be staying here?"

Zhi cupped his hand over the back of her neck, a possessive gesture that made her want to melt into the couch cushions. "The answer I want to give is that we'll stay here till we get our fill of each other. But the realistic one is a few days, however long it takes for Han to track down those shifters."

Or his family ran them to ground. She would happily put off that next meeting with Elizaveta for as long as he wanted...

Wait, was she more afraid of his mother than the shifters who wanted to kidnap her? Nova had the sneaking suspicion the answer was yes. But that was a challenge for another day. Today there was another hurdle she had to acknowledge.

"I should warn you that I've never even slept in the same room as anyone else. For all I know, I may snore. I have no idea."

His lips quirked. "You don't."

"How do you know?"

"The plane. You were out for a few hours. But you're out of luck. I snore like a freight train. Brace yourself."

"Oh no!" she giggled.

He pressed a kiss to her forehead. "I'm kidding. I do snore, but only when I have a cold or have had too much to drink, which hasn't happened for years."

"Good to know," she said. "But the snoring was just an example. What I really want to say is that I don't know how to be around anyone in an intimate way."

He held her closer. "I understand. And even though I have a little more experience than you, I'm not sure how to behave either. You're the first woman I've ever been with who didn't fear my telepathy."

She studied him. "But you've had girlfriends."

"A few in high school," he acknowledged. "But those relationships did not end well."

"What happened?"

"Different things, but the core problem was the same in all cases." He gave her a mirthless grin. "Eavesdroppers should know not to expect to hear something good about themselves."

She nodded sagely. "You scanned them. Did they know?"

"One did, the other didn't. Ironically that was the uglier breakup. Mainly because she thought I was spying on her when I accused her of hooking up with a football player." He sighed, the sound coming from deep in his chest. "I stopped trying to have deep and meaningful relationships after that."

But he hadn't been celibate. She didn't even need to ask. A man as attractive as Zhi, with his aura of power, would have been tripping over women. "You stuck to short and shallow liaisons. Understandable."

Zhi closed his eyes and sighed, appearing to choose his words carefully. "The ability to stay separate tends to fall away during intimacy, so keeping it to one night with no expectations of more was easier. Well, as easy as that sort of thing gets. But enough of my semi-sordid past."

He rose, swinging her up into his arms so fast she squealed. "For now, I'm going to introduce you to my favorite amenity in this cabin—the hot tub on the deck."

CHAPTER TWENTY-SIX

Feeling relaxed and decadent, Nova lounged in the saltwater hot tub while Zhi fixed them a platter of food to share.

It went against the grain to allow Zhi to serve her. But though this was his space, he was concerned she'd pick up an echo from one of the men who'd installed the cabin or one of the manufacturers.

Truthfully, she didn't fight him too hard. Nestled in between the two branches of the L in the cabin, the tub rested on a redwood deck overlooking a valley full of pine trees and a small lake somewhere near Snoqualmie Pass. It was a breathtaking view, the pristine snow-dusted mountain caps and sea of evergreens almost painfully perfect.

As a bonus, the temperature on the deck was spelled to be a comfortable and balmy seventy-eight degrees. She could streak across the deck in perfect warmth. Not that she would do that. Nova had used up her bravery when she'd stripped down to her lingerie. Now it was wet, and she didn't have a change of clothes.

No going backward. Even if she had to run around the cabin naked, she'd do it.

"As much as I would love that, there's no rush."

She turned in the water to find Zhi at the sliding door. His grin was infectious. "That, and if you got naked right now I'd need another cold shower.

He approached holding a towel as big as a blanket. Setting the tray down, he leaned against the hot tub wall, dipping his fingers in the water. "I'm glad you like that tub, but I've learned from experience that soggy canapes are not that appetizing. Why don't we eat this inside?"

In a near-blissed-out state, she was more than agreeable. "Sure."

Taking his hand, she let him wrap her in the towel where they ate in front of the fireplace before he found her a flannel shirt to sleep in.

Despite spending most of the evening in his lap, Nova couldn't help but look at the bed with trepidation. Zhi, who'd been digging through his drawers for sleepwear for himself, turned back and swore.

"Damn it, I forgot about the sheets," he said, misinterpreting the reason for her expression.

Oh, yeah. She'd forgotten too. Normally she carried a set of silk sheets with her, but their original outing had been a short business meeting. Now the only thing between her and the vast expanse of Egyptian cotton was Zhi's flannel shirt.

"I've been reacting well to the cabin and its contents," she reasoned aloud. She hadn't been brave enough to walk around barefoot yet, but it might be possible here. Although maybe she wouldn't. The sight of her walking around in her heels seemed to please him.

He made a rough sound in his throat. "I do like it, but I also want you to be comfortable and safe."

She twisted to look at him, reminding herself this was *his* place. "I will be."

Turning back, she bent at the waist to place her bare hands on the bedding at the same time Zhi reached out and said "Wait."

But she was faster. Nova stroked the down comforter over the king-sized bed, pulling it back to reveal the thousand thread-count sheets.

Relieved, she giggled and dived between the sheets enthusiastically. "I think it's okay." She rolled, somehow managing to keep the towel around her.

Nova undulated over the mattress, rubbing her cheek on the sheets. "Ooh. Silk is supposed to be the most luxurious fabric, but these feel so good. Different but good."

The texture was rougher than her normal silk but still soft. Nova enjoyed the contrast.

Zhi didn't say anything for a long moment. He cleared his throat. "So you're fine?"

She rolled onto her back, feeling slightly drunk. "Uh-huh. I think it helps that you never bring anyone else here. Your magic is so potent that it has coated everything you touch." A thick, protective layer of it sheathed everything here. And that magic didn't hurt her. She didn't have to worry about wearing her gloves or brushing up against something here.

Euphoric at the realizations, she giggled again and rolled in the sheets.

"Your psychic scent is all over these," she said, burying her face in the sheets, trying to touch them everywhere. "Your actual scent is strong too."

Zhi didn't wear cologne. This delicious smell was a product of his body wash and him, combining in an alchemy that made her mouth water. Combined with the crisp scent of the laundered sheets, she had no chance. The effect was drugging to the point where her lids were growing heavy. "Mmm," she hummed, bringing the pillow to her face, drawing the smell deep into her lungs.

A hoarse, rasping sound made her flip over on her back. "Sorry. I got carried away," she apologized, flushing bashfully under the heat of his gaze. "It's just that this is so..."

"Freeing."

She sat up and nodded enthusiastically. "Yes, exactly! Since this place is new, and with your magic as a buffer over everything, there is no question—this is the safest place I've ever been in."

Her amusement died a quick death. The way he reacted to her words, the look in his eyes... It made her heart rocket around in her chest like a trapped bird.

Good lord, he must *never* look at her like that in public. They'd get arrested.

"Beg to differ," he growled, tearing off the flannel pajama top he had thrown over matching pants after getting out of the hot tub. "This is a very dangerous place for you."

Nova yelped when he took hold of her legs and slid her down the mattress. Zhi climbed on the bed, rising over her to unbutton her shirt. He spread the flannel open, exposing her bare breasts and neatly trimmed mound.

It was as if a switch had been flipped. His hunger bordered on feral. Blushing, she resisted the urge to cover herself. "*Zhi.*" His eyes were glowing. "I think your magic is leaking."

Zhi adjusted himself through the flannel. *"That's not the only thing leaking."*

Nova burst out laughing, grateful for the moment of levity. The pants rode so low it was obvious he wasn't wearing anything underneath. Unable to resist, she sat up and traced the sharp divot made by the V of his abs.

Zhi groaned, collapsing on the bed next to her. They reached for each other at the same time. Time stuttered, but not because she lost consciousness. Not this time.

His hands covered her breasts, cupping and caressing, making her insides liquefy. "I'm sorry this isn't what I intended. We were just going to sleep—up until the moment you started rolling around like that."

She giggled and flipped to one side, intending to roll away. But he pinned her down, pressing his palms to her nipples. Panting, she watched transfixed as he lowered his head and licked one before sucking it.

The feel of his lips and tongue on that sensitive area made her whimper. She buried her hands in his hair, tugging gently to press his mouth tighter against her flesh.

His hands moved all over her skin with possessive, greedy strokes.

It was as if her self-control never existed. Each protective barrier she put up between her and the world melted as Zhi's body settled between her legs. Then Zhi began to move, his rhythm punctuated by his harsh breathing.

His heat and weight were the most delicious pressure she'd ever felt. But it was a little too intense. Her head began to swim. He murmured under his breath and backed away. "I'm getting ahead of myself."

The richness of his voice didn't cut through her sensual haze. Instead, it wrapped around her, pulling her back into the here and now. "I don't want to stop," she confessed.

"Then we won't." His fingers moved to her cleft, tracing the moisture gathered there, eyes fixed on her face to keep a careful watch over her reactions.

"*Fuck*," he said in her mind as she clamped around him. "*I have to taste this pussy now.*"

Nova squeaked as Zhi pressed her legs wide, making room for his broad shoulders. But the squeak turned into a moan as his lips closed over her clit. His tongue teased her as his fingers began to penetrate her.

Every part of her body trembled as he licked and sucked, his fingers working in counterpoint to his tongue, teasing and thrusting until her sheath began to flutter.

That was when she learned one of the fringe benefits of having a telepath for a lover.

"*Like ambrosia,*" he said in her mind while he continued to eat her out. His teeth grazed her clit, his tongue working it over like a piece of candy. "*This pussy is the food of the gods.*"

She would have laughed if she wasn't out of breath. "*Please, please,*" she begged as inarticulate cries escaped her mouth. "*I need you inside me.*"

Her hips squirmed. She tried to grab the waistband on his pants, but he held her down, pinning both her wrists with one hand.

"*Not yet, love. I need you to come in my mouth first. Cause when I bury my cock in this sweet cunt, you need to be able to stay with me. I can't have you passing out on me while I fuck you. You need to be aware enough to scream my name as you come around my cock. And you will. Consider that a promise.*"

Nova shuddered, too out of breath to protest. Which was a good thing because she was prepared to say anything to make him take her now. But her orgasm was barreling down on her, leaving her incapable of speech.

Zhi groaned as the rhythm of her hips stuttered and her sheath clamped down on his fingers. Nova wailed, her vision blinking in and out as spasms wracked her body.

"Your climax is the most gorgeous sight I've ever seen..." The last thing she heard was Zhi continuing to praise her as he petted her still-throbbing pussy.

CHAPTER TWENTY-SEVEN

Zhi wasn't upset when Nova lost consciousness as she came. Given where they'd started just a few hours ago, it was remarkable she'd held on as long as she had. And he had enough of a male ego to be proud of himself. Nova had passed out with a smile on her face. It matched the one on his.

Satisfaction welled. Nova was building endurance for touch in leaps and bounds. One or two more sessions like tonight's would make her ready for him. Damn, he couldn't wait. He had a long list of fantasies to indulge in.

Images of what he wanted to do to the criminally sexy woman in his arms filtered through his mind before he crushed that door closed. That campaign would resume tomorrow once Nova had a chance to rest and recover.

Ignoring the fact he was hard as a rock, he shifted her, arranging her lax limbs until she was curled up into the perfect spooning position. Then he pulled the down comforter over them, mentally reciting Mariners' batting stats until his erection finally relaxed enough for him to sleep.

"*It would help if you didn't sound so smug,*" Han telepathed the next morning.

It was almost nine, the sun high and shining bright through the windows because he'd forgotten to close the blinds last night.

Zhi never slept this late, but Nova in his bed was an experience that needed to be savored, something his cousin was having far too much fun teasing him about.

"*I think I'm entitled to a little smugness, all things considered.*" He rolled over to admire the view. With her gold-kissed curves and deep-red hair, Nova was a fantasy come to life. "*I wonder if Nova can knock now too.*"

Few non-telepaths could give him that mental nudge requesting the initiation of mental contact. However, the mental connection with Nova was so effortless he was betting she'd be more than capable.

Han agreed. "*I'd be surprised if she couldn't. But to test the theory you'd have to close the mental channel between the two of you.*"

He pursed his lips. "*How did you know I keep it open?*"

"*Because you and Nova have no boundaries. Hey, I didn't say that was a bad thing,*" Han added when he sensed Zhi's displeasure over the line. "*I'd love to have no boundaries with a smoking hot sweetheart like Nova. Although you should work a little harder to keep those walls up with me, because I'm getting mental snapshots from your perspective. Before you freak out, she's covered with the blanket.*"

A snicker in his head. "*If you're going to send me pics, at least show some skin.*"

Shit. Zhi used to be too disciplined to leak like that. But his rigid mental control had taken a beating the moment Nova walked into his life. "*Hell no. And if I ever do send one on accident, please know I'll have to lobotomize you. I'll be sorry after, but I'll do it anyway.*"

Han continued laughing, taking the threat in stride. "*Here I am running interference with Elizaveta for you out of the goodness of my heart, but do I get a thank you? No, you ungrateful swine.*"

"*I texted her and Jinx,*" he protested.

"*And said nothing about nothing. All you told them was that you'd be in touch after the situation was resolved. The key word in that phrase being 'after.'*"

Zhi wrinkled his nose. They didn't keep score, but he might owe

Han naming rights to his firstborn if he'd been keeping his mother at bay.

"What did you tell them about Nova?"

"As little as I could, but they know enough, like the fact that you can touch her now. Otherwise, your absence wouldn't be explainable. No place is safer than the mansion. Going elsewhere didn't make sense unless there were other reasons. Sexy-time reasons. Not that they asked for details, thank God."

His face curdled, picturing the conversation that had taken place when Han arrived home without them. *"Uh, thanks, I guess."*

"At least you and Nova won't have to spring your situationship on them when you get back. I'm laying the groundwork here, reminding your darling mother just how valuable Nova is so she won't be tempted to hex her when you get back."

"I would never let that happen." But Han had a point. Zhi liked to tell himself his father had been the real hardass, but Elizaveta was just as rigid in her own way. And she had invested a lot in her search for his bride...

No, Elizaveta would not be happy when he announced he intended to marry an employee. One with no connections and an unknown pedigree.

"That's a problem for later. I really hope you have an update about these shifters."

Han's rumbling growl sounded remarkably like a bear's. *"Tracking them through traffic cameras failed. They split up. Some drove into the city. They either changed vehicles or dumped their gear so they could blend in with the crowds. A few others disappeared into the woods. Our people found two abandoned bikes. They torched their clothes, shifted, and ran out of there on foot."*

"And you couldn't catch them?" The wolves might be fast, but Han was built for endurance. Over long distances he could run a werewolf down.

"They had too big a head start. Even the tracking spells failed. I decided to cut out the middleman."

Zhi raised a brow. *"You contacted Douglas Maitland."*

The Canus Primus of the Americas was a powerful chieftain. He was the alpha of the largest werewolf pack in the country and overseer to the rest. By and large he let the smaller packs run as autonomous units, interfering only when a situation exceeded the local alpha's ability to deal with.

Zhi had never met Douglas, but they'd had some business dealings. These had been conducted through intermediaries, as befit their respective stations. The deals had been big enough for them to be active, if silent, partners in the negotiations. Douglas was tough but fair. And he chose the people who represented him with care.

That made it really surprising that wolf shifters were antagonizing them. He couldn't picture Maitland signing off on somethings as reckless as this attempted kidnapping.

But the North American coalition was a loose confederation. Each pack was answerable to their own alpha. They were supposed to report any issues too big for them to handle to Maitland, but it also didn't surprise him that they hadn't. Wolves were an arrogant lot. One of them might have decided Nova was the solution to a problem they needed to solve, and they'd been stupid enough to go it alone, keeping the Maitlands in the dark.

There was a small chance that these wolves were foreigners, but Zhi doubted it. There had been too many of them—the attack too coordinated to be done by anything but pros or members of a pack, many of whom served in the armed forces. Even after they left the service, many pack members trained together, trading off duties to secure their territories.

If a team of mercenaries had entered the country, it would have been flagged by the Maitland clan. A big group of foreign shifters wouldn't have been allowed to fuck around without finding out what it was like to be crushed under a hiking boot, Maitland's footwear of choice. And if that had happened, he wouldn't be dealing with this mess right now.

"Yeah. He's looking into the issue," Han confirmed.

"Good."

Zhi didn't need to ask that Han had also issued a warning. The wolves were risking a war with his family if this didn't get fixed. And despite the fact the American branch of the Zhengs was outnumbered, his family in China was vast and vindictive. They would retaliate. That and there were several other witch clans that would be happy to join forces against "the animals."

As a group, the Seven and the upper echelon of aspirants to their thrones weren't known for their open and enlightened attitudes. He didn't share their opinion, but if the wolves kept threatening his family he would use whatever means at his disposal to crush them.

"Keep me updated."

"Will do. I'm on my way back into town by the way. Maitland's agreement to investigate didn't come quick enough for my taste, so I'm going to turn a few stones of my own."

This was his cousin's area of expertise. Han had a labyrinthine network of contacts and connections, but he still had to ask. *"Will anyone useful talk to you?"*

He could almost hear his cousin's shrug. *"Shifters are notoriously insular, but they still need to eat. They know we pay well for actionable intelligence. Plus, this fits in with their whole survival of the fittest mindset—messing with our clan is terminally stupid, and they know that. Anyone who crosses us deserves what's coming."*

Zhi couldn't agree more. They talked a little longer, discussing security protocols. He also relayed a few instructions to the staff at the house. Things would be different when they returned. Nova would no longer be staff. It was best to make that clear sooner rather than later.

Nova's brow wrinkled in her sleep as if she'd heard him plotting.

"Got to go, Han," he said when she began to stir.

His cousin's tone was suspiciously even. *"Do me a favor and make sure you close this mental channel. You're like a brother to me, but there are some things I'd rather not see."*

CHAPTER TWENTY-EIGHT

Nova went from sleep to consciousness in a blink. She sat up abruptly, her heart going a mile a minute as she clutched at Zhi, scrabbling like a wild woman.

Her immunity to his touch *hadn't* gone away like she'd dreamed. There had been no reset brought about by sleep. Nova tried to breathe but choked on the lungful of air. Overwrought, she burst into tears.

Hard arms closed over her. Zhi's lips skated over her face. "It's okay, love. We're okay. It wasn't temporary."

Nodding, she tried again, hiccuping and wiping her eyes with one hand. Zhi waited patiently, holding her until the small storm passed.

Nova wiped her eyes with the heel of her palm. She'd just woken and already felt like a wrung-out kitchen towel. "I can't believe I cried. I never cry. I'm sorry I'm so emotional."

Zhi rubbed his cheek against her hair. "You have every right to be. This has been a monumental change in your life. And full disclosure you did this twice last night—not the crying part," he clarified when her face crumpled. "You woke up convinced things had gone back to normal. But once I assured you they hadn't you fell back asleep."

He stroked her hair soothingly. "I know it seems strange and hard to believe, but I know in my gut—*this* is our new normal."

Sucking in a shaky breath, she nodded, trying to believe him. But her resolve was shaky.

Zhi rolled over. Nova landed on her back with over six feet of muscular male stretching out on top of her. "Do you think fate would give us this gift only to snatch it away?"

Nova wasn't immune to his heat. He was bracing most of his delicious weight with his arms, but what was left was wrecking her, yet she wasn't ready to relax. "In my experience, fate is a cruel mistress."

"Not anymore. Not if I have anything to say about it."

It was such an arrogant statement. But of course Zhi Zheng would think he could take on fate and win. A family head was groomed and trained to do just that.

He let her bear a touch more of his weight with a look both hungry and calculating. However, that intent expression melted away when her stomach growled. Judging from the light streaming into the cabin, it was long past her normal breakfast hour.

"Sorry," she giggled when he took her hand to tug her out of bed. "I think I need to eat."

"The apology is mine." He shook his head as if berating himself. "Your needs are my priority, but I forgot in the face of my own hunger. I was being selfish."

"You were being a mind reader," she said. He looked confused. She raised her brows, waggling them suggestively.

Catching on Zhi reddened and laughed, melting her heart into a useless pile of goo. She didn't think she'd ever seen him blush before.

His lips kissed along her hairline. "Hold that thought for after we eat. Fortunately, I keep this place fully stocked with non-perishables and frozen food. Each meal was specially designed by Chef Sam to be prepared fast and delicious."

He proceeded to demonstrate by putting an assortment of frozen pastries in the oven. They baked while he thawed out strawberries and sliced peaches mixed with a sweet dairy-infused crumble as well as little bottles of orange juice.

Not well versed in the kitchen, Nova helped by brewing the coffee before excusing herself to take a shower. She washed up, snagging an extra toothbrush from the medicine cabinet and claiming it as her own.

If only the clothing issue could be solved as easily, because as much as she wanted to be intimate with Zhi, she wasn't comfortable running around stark naked. Turning her nose up at yesterday's dress and used underclothes, she bit the bullet and raided Zhi's closet, choosing a tailored blue shirt and a pair of white boxers before arranging her hair into a messy bun.

Zhi paused in the act of setting two coffee mugs on the table. He gave her a long, lingering appraisal that made her temperature soar. "I really like you in my clothes."

"That's good," she said, trying to appear nonchalant. "Because I didn't exactly get a chance to pack a bag."

He grinned before scowling as something occurred to him. "*Govno.* Neither did I."

She twisted to do a questioning sweep over their surroundings. "What are we missing?"

The cabin was better stocked than a survivalist bunker, one with way more fashionable clothes. The shirt she had borrowed was Fendi.

Zhi offered her a coffee mug with a pensive expression. "I don't suppose you are on birth control?"

Nova nearly spit out the sip she had just taken. "*No.* I never thought I would need it."

"Of course you didn't." Zhi gave her a hapless shrug. "I also don't have any protection here either, for obvious reasons. Although now that I think about it, condoms are probably not something we should use anyway. You might react to it."

He was probably right. Nova wanted to sink through the floor, a mix of mortification and self-recrimination flooding her. *Damn it.* She hadn't considered this aspect at all. Playing with Bob was one thing. Condoms were something else.

Zhi's expression darkened. "Who the hell is Bob?"

"Oh, err..." Face flaming, Nova cleared her throat. "That is what I call my, um, my electronic aide."

His scowl dissipated. "Your what?"

She put her hands on her cheeks, but that didn't change the fact it felt as if they were on fire. "Bob is short for battery-operated boyfriend."

The light dawned. "I see," he said in a carefully neutral voice.

His cheek twitched, but at least he didn't laugh. "Can I ask...how did that work?"

Nova snorted, and he shook his head. "I mean, obviously I know *how* it worked. But I thought your aversion to certain objects meant you avoided those kinds of..." He raised his hands, spreading his fingers out in surrender. "You know what—never mind."

Nova buried her face in her hands but forced them back down. She had nothing to be embarrassed about. And she and Zhi had no secrets. He may as well know it all.

"I had to carry that vibrator around for over a year before I felt safe handling it in the manner it was intended." That was how long it had taken for her to feel like the brand-new device belonged to her.

He tilted his head, the gesture incongruously boyish. "Sorry, I was jealous." His brow creased, his reply tongue in cheek. "Or should I be intimidated? Having not met Bob, who knows how I'll measure up?"

Nova crumpled a napkin and threw it at him. "Bob is discrete."

She had carefully considered her plan and had decided she'd need to keep the device in her purse, so she'd gone for something on the smaller end of the spectrum. Enough that Zhi was rather intimidating by comparison.

He beamed at her. "Thank you."

She snorted and covered her face. "I begin to see the drawback of being involved with a telepath."

It was a lighthearted jibe, but Zhi sucked in a breath as if she'd sucker punched him. "Shit," he said. "I'm sorry. Maybe Han is right. We might need to establish some boundaries."

"No." Nova rose and threw her arms around his neck, her heart picking up speed. "I was kidding. I don't want boundaries."

Zhi's arms wrapped around her waist. "You say this now, but having an open channel will get old for you sooner rather than later."

Burrowing closer, she made a protesting noise. "I doubt that."

Nova didn't want to return to that time when Larissa had been around and Zhi had stopped speaking to her mind to mind. It hadn't lasted very long, but after experiencing that singular intimacy of his voice in her head she didn't want to live without it.

He hugged her closer, reading the confused jumble of her thoughts as if they were his own. "All tight. We won't go backward—for now. But we're in the honeymoon period. You've never had the chance to be close to anyone, and I've never had a partner so accepting of my ability. Your utter openness has made me selfish and more than a little greedy. In time this level of constant contact may wear thin. I don't want to smother you."

"I don't feel smothered. Not at all. I want you with me all the time." She sat down in the chair with a scowl. "Even in my head. And believe me I don't want to know what that says about me."

Zhi knelt in front of her, taking her hands in his. "Then we have matching neurosis. Because I want to stay in your head all the time too. Hands down it's the best place I've ever been. Just touching your mind. But I predict that we'll soon settle into a natural rhythm, similar to what Han and I maintain."

He broke off to stroke her cheek. "Well, maybe a bit more frequent than that. Regardless, I think we can safely scale back our telepathic conversations, especially when we're together. Your immunity isn't going to go away."

His confidence bolstered hers. She smiled up at him. "I guess you're right. I'm borrowing trouble worrying about the future. Let's just live in the now."

He raised an eyebrow, waggling it up and down. "So back to Bob."

"No," she giggled. "I don't need him anymore."

"I'm actually grateful to Bob," said Zhi, taking her chin in his hand. "It means I don't have to go easy on you."

Nova gasped, her chest swelling as a very graphic scene unfolded in her head. "You can send me your fantasies?"

Zhi's only answer to that breathless question was a salacious grin. "Let's eat breakfast and then we have some preparations to make. I think I have a solution to our dilemma."

THERE WAS no problem magic couldn't solve. At least that was what Elizaveta had always told him.

Growing up, Zhi had really believed it. He knew better now, of course, but the fact he and Nova couldn't rely on traditional means of contraception wasn't going to be an issue.

After breakfast, he surprised her by opening the floor safe concealed under some false floorboards.

"I can't believe this thing was hiding under there," she said as he opened a small trunk with many compartments concealed inside.

"Every one of my family's properties contains one of these," he said, patting the emergency spell kit. "It contains a book of defensive curses and charms and all the raw materials needed to prepare them."

Nova bent to read the tiny print affixed to each of the compartments. "Mugwort, Yarrow, Belladonna...all the basics. But how will a defensive spell help us have safe sex?"

Zhi could tell from the color in her cheeks that she was still embarrassed by the frank words, but after the Bob discussion Nova appeared determined to let go of her shyness.

"They won't. For that I'll have to check the family's online grimoire."

Her mouth parted. "You keep all of your family's secret spells *online?*"

"Just the non-lethal ones," he explained, taking his phone and logging into the encrypted server. "The dangerous family spells are stored the old-fashioned way, as dusty tomes. There's a hidden vault just off the library. I would have shown them to you, but they aren't used very often. I've consulted them less than a half-dozen times at most since reaching the age of majority."

He hadn't needed them because he'd memorized most of their contents. So had Jinx and Han. Regardless of their innate talents, all three of them had been taught the basics of spell craft from the cradle, adding to that knowledge year after year as part of their formal education. Most of the Seven families did the same thing with their children.

Thanks to that training, Zhi could come up with complicated spells on the fly. But he never had occasion to mix a contraceptive potion.

Maybe Jinx had, he thought with a shudder. But Hell would freeze over before he asked his sister for help with his.

"Well, you and Han hardly need spells given your innate abilities," Nova said with a grin, having caught most of his internal reflection.

Zhi didn't consciously lower his walls for her. When it came to her, they didn't exist.

He nodded, scrolling until he found the folder he wanted. "We've been taught not to rely on our inborn gifts too much. That obfuscation spell was one of the rare occasions we needed to refer to the grimoires. We altered an existing spell, updating it for the modern age to incorporate a block on cameras."

He held up his phone to show her the recipe for a basic contraceptive potion. "As for this, it seems relatively simple. We have most of the ingredients in this box."

She examined the list and tsked. "Not all of them."

There were two ingredients that had to be fresh, including recently running river water. Fortunately, there was a rather romantic spot he wanted to show Nova that would fulfill their needs.

The only impediment was her lack of outdoor gear. But he was willing to make some sacrifices to remedy that. More willing than Nova. "Those look new!" she cried when he took a pair of scissors to his insulated North Face pants.

"We'll order you proper hiking gear when we get back," he promised, cutting the leg length down so it wouldn't drag on the ground. He glanced up at her, picturing her in a cute ski bunny outfit. "I would have had some delivered, but that would defeat the purpose of being in hiding."

"UPS or drone?" she teased, lifting her arms so he could tie one of his belts around the waist of the mangled pants.

Rising, he tapped her on the nose. "Jokes on you because *ZZ8 does* have drone subsidiary. We're months away from a drone delivery launch. It's going to work well for rural areas like this."

Laughing, she took the scissors, finishing the job of cutting the pants to a usable length. They paired them with one of Zhi's thick parkas. There was no footwear option, forcing Nova to do the hike in her vintage heels. Fortunately, their destination was close by, along an easy path.

Nova loved the waterfalls. The small but picturesque natural wonder was a scant quarter mile from the cabin.

Her pleasure was his own. "The first time I saw these was in the dead of winter. I needed a break after a particularly hectic holiday season," he explained. "This was shortly after my father fell ill and decided he was retiring, handing me the reigns. I wasn't yet accustomed to my new responsibilities, and half our relatives from China had descended on us to pay respects to the new family head. It coincided with a particularly fraught negotiation at ZZ8. Come January, I was fried and needed to get as far away from people as I could. I drove out here with no plan, no gear, nothing."

He wrapped his arms around her, wishing it was summer so he could feel her without the impediment of so many layers. "I hiked aimlessly for hours before stumbling on these falls, frozen over."

"That must have been spectacular." While there was a light dusting of snow on the ground now, it wasn't cold enough for the water to freeze.

"It was. The ice glittered like diamonds in the sun. I have about a thousand pictures of it," he said, taking out his phone to show her.

"And you decided to build the cabin then?" she asked after marveling over the images. "It explains why everything is so new."

He nodded "I contracted one of those prefab housing developers, modifying one of their basic designs and had them deliver it to us at a rest stop on the highway. Han and I drove the pieces here, bringing the equipment needed to move and install them after. It took several trips and a crash course in crane operation because Han didn't want anyone else to have the location of my bolt hole."

She threw him a teasing grin. "Is he going to break out the thumbscrews to ensure I don't tell anyone where we are?"

"You were unconscious most of the ride," he pointed out. "You have no idea where we are."

She chuckled. "True enough."

Zhi kissed her brow. "But no. It's a non-issue. I trust you. And so does Han. And before you ask—yes, our magic tells us that you're good. But I would know that regardless of whether I could read your mind. Because I know you now. I feel your goodness in my heart, not my head."

Nova snuggled into him. "No one who looks at you would ever suspect you're a closet romantic...or so incredibly cheesy."

She squealed as he swung her up, putting her over his shoulder. He smacked her on the ass. "I'll show you some cheese."

"Stop. I can't take this much romantic prose!"

His laughter vibrated through her. He swung her back down, stopping for a hot, all-consuming kiss before collecting the water and a bit of lichen on the way back to the cabin.

CHAPTER TWENTY-NINE

The cold spoiled the romance of their brief outing. Nova's feet, shod only in her low heels, were little blocks of ice by the time they returned.

Nova squeaked as Zhi stripped her and helped her into the bath he insisted she take once they were safely indoors. Pins and needles shot through her feet as the warm water did its work.

Her entire body sighed in relief as she submerged up to the neck. She lifted her chin to meet Zhi's gaze. The fire in them was banked now, but only temporarily.

"I'm good now," she assured him, lying back to rest her head against the angled end of the tub. "And I would have liked to see more of the woods. It really is beautiful around here."

"I'm glad you like it," he murmured, his voice dropping to an intimate pitch. "But we won't be taking any more walks outside. Not until we outfit you with proper gear."

"I was warm otherwise." All of those layers had done their work, even if she'd been swimming in his clothes. His shoulders were just too broad.

Speaking of...Nova tilted her head to the side. "You know I think I'm starting to get used to being naked around you."

It was freeing, being without so many layers between her and the world. But she could only be this way with Zhi.

He knelt, his fingers dipping into the water. "I will reciprocate once I'm done mixing up our contraceptive potion. It requires heating some volatile ingredients on the stove, so splattering may be an issue. And I don't want to damage anything sensitive."

She smirked, but it turned into a gasp when he ran a finger over her nipple under the water. "I have big plans for tonight," he shared.

That touch combined with the hunger he didn't bother to hide was enough to send her body temperature soaring. The cold was a distant memory. "Then by all means let's get cooking."

"I'll take care of it." He leaned over to kiss her forehead. "You stay here and make sure frostbite doesn't set it. I'll be back in time to wash your back."

But Nova didn't need to soak to get warm. Not with the reality of what would happen with Zhi tonight. Getting out of the tub, she dried off quickly and put on one of his shirts.

He was pouring a steaming, cloudy brown liquid into a mug when she entered the kitchen. He put the pot back on the stove without looking, keeping those intense dark-brown eyes fixed on her.

"I like the sight of you in my shirts so much I may have to give them all to you."

She began to walk toward him when he held up a hand. "Hold that thought," he said, raising the mug to his lips and blowing on it before taking a sip. His nose wrinkled. "Now I know why most witches use human contraceptive methods."

He blew on it a little more before proceeding to drink the rest of the mug.

Nova's lips parted. "Wait. I thought that was for me."

Zhi gave her a chiding glance. "It works for either sex. And I would never give you a potion I wouldn't take myself."

He finished the contents of the mug with a wince. "Lucky for me having some wine after this won't interfere with its effectiveness. Pour me a big one—it'll take a whole glass to get this taste out of my mouth."

Touched by the proof of his caring, Nova opened the Zinfandel he'd chosen to pair with a pasta dish he'd thrown in the oven. They ate in the kitchen and retired to the couch with their wineglasses. A few kisses later, Nova ended up in his lap, her bare bottom against the rougher material of his pants.

His hand and mouth caressed her, stoking the fire higher and higher. He kissed and licked her neck until Nova pulled away.

"Do you remember when I said no to you that time in the car," she asked in a low voice.

Eyes wary, he nodded. "When I offered to trick your mind into feeling sexual pleasure."

She pressed her hand to his cheek. "I didn't think of it as a trick. I knew you were offering me a gift. I refused because I couldn't return your affection. I could only take it. "

He began to interrupt, but she squeezed his shoulders. "I know what you're going to say, but you know it wasn't fair. And that would have eaten away at me."

He wrapped her arms around, stroking her back. "*Nova.*"

But she wasn't done. "I don't know what the future holds for us. I'm trying not to think about it. All I know is that here and now I'm ready to take whatever you're willing to give."

Big hands cupped her bottom with a rough, pleasurable noise. "Your future is with me, at my side."

"But—"

He pulled her tush so that her sex abraded his covered crotch. "Love, you're sitting in my lap, going commando under that shirt. I know we have a lot to discuss, but I'm not a saint."

His lips covered hers, his tongue stroking into her mouth with barely leashed hunger.

Giving in with a feminine whimper, she let herself go lax, melting against him in a way he seemed to love.

He didn't stop kissing her as he undid the buttons, pulling open the fine cotton to cover her breasts with his hands. He squeezed them with a groan, plumping them up with his hands so he could take the rosy nipples into his mouth.

Her last shreds of restraint broke. She tugged at the hem of his shirt. "Really glad you're not a saint or I'd have to go to confession for this."

"I have it," he panted, laughing as he helped her pull off the sweater and thermal shirt underneath.

Zhi stopped her when she began to attack his zipper, picking her up and off the couch. He tugged off the open shirt.

She landed on the bed, totally bared to him.

Leaning back on her elbows, she watched him kick off his shoes and pants. His eyes met hers as he pulled off the boxer briefs underneath. She had a quick impression of a large, rigid cock before he crawled over the bed, and then she was feeling it hard and silky against her slick folds.

Dark suffused her vision, but it wasn't loss of consciousness threatening. Her brain had stopped processing what she was seeing in favor of cataloguing what she was feeling. And it was *so much*.

Hands parted her folds, caressing and opening her slick petals as his mouth suckled at her breasts.

Each pull on her nipple sent a shooting thrill straight to her pussy. When Zhi penetrated her sheath, she was halfway to orgasm, the muscles fluttering and clamping on his fingers.

Swearing, he didn't fight her when she pulled him on top of her. The hot, stiff length teased her, running up and down her folds to hit her clit. Each strike made the swollen bud throb.

"Watch me fuck you, love."

Sucking in a harsh breath Nova obeyed, looking down as Zhi took his length in hand, pushing the flared head against the tight ring of muscles at her entrance. Her head fell back as he filled her, pressure and pain-edged delight overwhelming her as he claimed her in the most primal and elemental way.

Zhi didn't wait, he kept pushing until he was pressed flush against her. He swore in Mandarin and then again in Russian for good measure. Pressing his forehead against her hair, he slipped into her mind.

He pumped experimentally but kept the movement shallow, letting her savor the feel of him. *"You're so tight around me. Am I hurting you?"*

"No." Nova clutched at his arms. Her inner muscles fluttered

around his thickness, so much fuller and hotter than her skinny little vibrator.

His laugh was sensual against her ear. "I guess I do measure up to Bob," he said aloud. "However, size isn't everything. You'll have to excuse me for this, but I still have something to prove."

Zhi pulled back, withdrawing until just the tip of him remained inside her. "I can't buzz, and I don't vibrate, but I can do this."

With that he thrust back in, driving home with a slick, steady motion. Nova shivered, wrapping her arms and legs around him. "That feel good, baby?"

"Yes, so much," she panted, hips rising to try and get closer. "Do it again."

He was only too happy to oblige. He began to pump in and out, a slick, hot glide accompanied by a filthy wet smacking sound. Nova took it, using her muscles to try and hold him deeper.

"*You love it, don't you?*" he whispered in her mind as her hands raked against his back. "*You love me stretching out this sweet little pussy.*"

"*I do. God help me, I do.*" She clung to him, grabbing the taught muscles of his ass as he pistoned into her flesh.

All decorum flew out the window. Her every sense was dedicated to the sweat-sheened body drilling her into the mattress. His taste in her mouth, the cedar and apples she could almost lick off his skin paired with the rough silk of his skin abrading hers was too much.

Her inarticulate cries rose in pitch as her sheath began to spasm.

"That's it, little love. Squeeze my cock." His mental voice was deeper, tinged with sensual command. "I want you to take my come, every drop."

He broke off, grinding against her hard with a rumbling sound of victory. "That's it. Clasp that cunt around me, drain me dry..."

He stroked through the spasms as the waves of ecstasy crested. They were too strong to be hers alone, and for a split second she could see herself through Zhi's eyes, swollen lips and half-masted eyes worshipping him as her breasts shook with the force of his thrusts.

The tight twisting pleasure wasn't all hers either. Part belonged to him. She was experiencing his emotions, the possessive satisfaction too sharp and primal to be her own.

Oh, dear lord. If this was how he felt about her, she was in trouble.

But she had no time to think about that. Another wave of his pleasure hit her. It magnified hers and bounced to him, only to surge back, as inevitable as the tide.

His length jerked, hot jets of fluid flooding her. That coiled spring of tension broke. Nova cried out, shaking as electricity shot through every nerve ending, shorting them out. When sense returned, she was a panting, seething mess fighting to catch her breath.

Zhi stroked into her a few more times, his head thrown back, neck cording as he savored the last precious seconds of his own climax. With a last wrenching thrust, his cock jerked one last time. He groaned and collapsed, pressing her into the mattress.

Nova wrapped her arms around him, holding him close as his labored breathing fanned her neck. When he recovered, he looked down at her, concern mixed with a proprietary gleam in his eyes.

She put her hands on his face and whispered in his mind. *"More."*

He grinned down at her. "My thoughts exactly."

CHAPTER THIRTY

Eyes half-lowered, Nova moaned as Zhi's tongue stroked up her folds. "Zhi, please take me."

Raising his head for a moment, he grinned at her for a second before lowering his head to suck on her clit. *"But you like this more."*

"Untrue." Nova loved it, but she loved being penetrated more. Having him inside her, being joined so intimately that they were one... There was nothing like it. Taking his cock, so silky smooth and hard, was the most decadent pleasure she had ever felt.

It had been almost a week of near-constant sex. Nova and Zhi had done it on the bed, floor, and the couch in all sorts of positions. And she was still greedy for more.

Zhi was just as hungry—for everything. Especially her pussy.

"Your barriers drop when you come," he'd confessed after the first time he'd gone down on her. "I don't just feel your pleasure. Your thoughts, the passion you feel for me, it's all there."

"But that happens during regular sex too."

"It does, but I'm a little distracted when I'm inside you." The abashed expression on his face had melted her, wrapping yet another tendril of love and affection around her heart.

Which was why she never argued whenever he unbuttoned the

dress shirt she'd borrowed before lifting her onto the kitchen table. Then he'd spread her legs and just stare for a long minute.

"You're my favorite work of art," he said in a rough whisper, making her heart swoop to her feet before soaring high.

Eventually his hunger would get the better of him, and he'd toss one of her legs over his shoulder, letting the other dangle over the edge of the table as he buried his head between her thighs. Then he'd lick, suck, and fuck her with his fingers until she screamed.

Which she was about to do now. The kitchen blurred as his lips closed over her clit and sucked hard. "*Zhi.*"

Nova's legs shook, her back arching as she writhed, the orgasm making her sheath clench on nothing. Enervated, she reached blindly for him when the sound of the zipper warned her he was about to give her what she wanted most.

Zhi hissed when her hand closed over his hot, hard length. "Can I lick you too?" she asked.

"*After,*" he promised, his thoughts borderline feral. "*I can't wait.*"

She was disappointed but understood. Their connection was at its strongest when he was buried deep inside her.

Pushing up on her elbows, she watched the thick flared head of his cock trace the rim of her entrance.

"Ready for me, baby?"

She nodded so hard she made herself dizzy. Then he began to slide in, and all of her awareness narrowed down on their joining.

The mix of Russian and Chinese genes had gifted Zhi with his height and broad shoulders. The rest of him was built in proportion— nothing she couldn't handle. But this would never be a casual act. His size made his possession almost primitive. She felt possessed... claimed...every time.

Zhi groaned. His hard length forged inside a little slowly. A few inches in, he groaned and withdrew, pumping back in a little farther on the return stroke.

"*Yes, more,*" she pleaded, wrapping her legs and arms around him when he finally pressed all the way home.

Zhi gathered her up, easily bearing her weight. "Anything. Anything you want."

She thought he'd pin her to wall—he loved doing that—but Zhi didn't move. Instead, he stood his ground, using those muscular arms to lift her then letting gravity impale her on his cock. He did this over and over, the feat of strength that left her helpless, the rhythm defined and controlled by him.

Helpless in his arms, she held on for the ride. All too soon the ripples of a second orgasm began. Crying out, she clutched his shoulders, one hand rising to tighten on his hair.

"Tell me you love me."

"I do," she gasped, bouncing up and down, trying to clamp down so she could possess him too. "I love you."

"Good. Now come."

A flood of images rushed into her brain. Zhi naked, coming down on top of her on the bed. His cock teasing her pussy from behind when she was on her knees on the couch, and her breasts and pussy from his point of view from the oral sex on the table just now.

Convulsing, she screamed as he pushed her down on his cock, grinding hard. The taut coil of pleasure broke hard as hell, making her vision blink in and out.

Spent and utterly boneless, she felt Zhi move. He landed on the couch with her draped over him.

He wrapped his arms around her back, thrusting his hips up, endless hard drives. A minute or two later, he pressed his mouth to her ear. "Come again. Come with me."

"I can't."

"You can." His hands took hold of her hips, twisted her ever so slightly to increase the friction. His cock swelled and jerked as he exploded. Another impossible orgasm broken as his hot seed flooded her.

"That's it," he urged in a taught tone as she sobbed, her pussy milking him reflexively. His hand reached between them, swiping at the cream that had escaped. Zhi lifted a wet finger to her lips. "Take all my cum. I want it in your pussy and your mouth."

Obeying, she licked, sucking the cream off the tip until it was clean. He closed his eyes and thrust up a few more times, his face suffused with pleasure. Removing his fingers, he cupped the back of her head, tongue invading. His other hand held her in place, tightly joined to him.

Zhi raised his head after a few sipping kisses. Dark eyes gleamed with amusement that ever-present hunger he stopped hiding from her. "That was breakfast. What should we do for lunch?"

Groaning, Nova collapsed against him.

NOVA BLINKED, looking around in confusion. "How did we get back to the estate?"

She was sitting in one of the plush armchairs in the library. Muted sunlight was shining through the windows.

Raising a hand to rub her eyes, she frowned down at her glove. Alarm shot through her, and then a crushing wave of pain brought tears to her eye.

The coma. Her ability to touch Zhi had been a coma dream.

"Please stop. Such histrionics are unseemly."

Startled, Nova looked up to see Elizaveta sweeping into the room in one of her trademark embroidered dresses.

Zhi's mother sat down in the chair opposite her. "I do apologize for interrupting your private time with my son in such peremptory fashion, but it appears you two are intent on avoiding the family for the foreseeable future, so I had to take matters into my own hands."

Nova gripped the armrests, staring dumbly at the other woman. The realization sank in slowly. "I'm not really here."

Elizaveta examined her nails. "No, of course not."

Confused, Nova looked around her. The library was exactly as it was in her memory. "Then where am I really?"

"Still with my son in his little hidey-hole."

Her lips parted. "I'm asleep." The hairs on the back of her neck rose—which was so weird. How could these panic responses be happening in a dream?

Amusement flickered over Elizaveta's face. "Very good. Most people never catch on. Then again, I'm not usually this visible in a dream. I prefer to observe. You learn much more that way."

"You're a dream-walker." It was a rare witch who could dream walk. Nova had never met one before—not that anyone would admit to being one. That would negate their advantage.

Nova waved at the library. "Was I dreaming of this place, or can you control the setting of my dream?"

Elizaveta waved a languid hand. "This is my choice of venue."

"Oh." Wide-eyed, Nova fought to control her breathing. Elizaveta was scary as hell on a normal day. Finding out she could flitter in and out of her dreams and control key elements was downright terrifying.

"I suppose it makes sense that dream-walking is related to telepathy."

"It does indeed."

Nova blinked as a fully laden tea set—a Russian samovar—appeared next to Elizaveta's seat. The older woman reached over to lift a fine porcelain cup. "Tea?"

Clearing her imaginary throat, Nova rose to accept the cup. She sat back down and sipped the clear brown brew. *Holy cow.* She could *taste* it.

This dream was far too detailed for her peace of mind. Fervently hoping the old wives' tale about dying in a dream was only that, she sipped again before setting the cup in her lap.

You are no coward, she reminded herself. She was tangling with the world's most feared telepath. She could deal with his mother. "Is this the part where you warn me off your son?"

Elizaveta was amused. "As if Zhi would allow you to leave him." She set her own teacup down, her expression wry. "My son is more like his father than he cares to admit—possessive to a fault."

"Then why am I here?"

She crossed her legs in a graceful motion, leaning back in her chair. "Please forgive me for being blunt, but in you my son has a potential bride who is guaranteed never to betray him with another, one so starved for affection that she is not just willing to allow him into her mind but actually invites it. Add to that a significant magic reservoir, and it may just negate your other deficiencies as a bride."

"Oh." The description stung a little, but she couldn't fault it for being untrue. She'd been trying very hard not to think of what kind of reception she'd get from this woman. "I should point out that Zhi hasn't asked me to marry him."

Yes, he'd spoken of a future together, but Nova didn't take anything for granted.

Elizaveta dismissed this with a delicate snort. "It's only a matter of time. And I feel it's better to set expectations up front. I don't have to tell you that marriage into the Seven is a demanding proposition, one you haven't prepared for."

The understatement of the year. "That's true," she said, thinking on her feet. "But I have mixed with a great many of the Seven. And while I may not have the same defensive training as some others, I have made a study of all the major families and can offer my insights on their motivations and interests. My chief concern is you. I would have thought you'd object to a bride without a pedigree or connections."

The older woman waved an airy hand. "To be blunt, the price we paid for your service is more than the dowry we expected from the Zhous. As for your general suitability, I've decided to be grateful that Zhi appears to have attached himself to a witch of considerable talent, warped thought it may be. Which brings me to the chief topic I wanted to discuss. Your future children."

Nova was starting to wish the tea had been poisoned. Or at least drugged. "I never planned on having children, for obvious reasons."

It wasn't just the sheer impossibility of pregnancy before Zhi. The very idea of passing on her magic was anathema.

"Before you start to spiral, I suggest you hear me out." She stared until Nova nodded.

Elizaveta crossed her legs. "Good. You possess magic in surfeit, enough that it has held you prisoner. But thanks to my son, you've already begun to break out of your metaphorical shackles."

She folded her hands together and leaned forward. "It is my firm belief that your touch aversion can be further ameliorated. Zhi jump-started the process, and even though you've had to lean heavily on him, that success likely means you can go further. With more training, I think you'll be able to bear touch from others in a few years."

Nova was starting to get dizzy. "Wouldn't that negate my advantages as a bride to Zhi?" She would never betray Zhi with another, but in its current form her magic meant built-in fidelity.

"You'll be married by the time this becomes an issue."

Nova swallowed more tea in self-defense. "And your theory is that between me and Zhi we'll be able to shape the magic in our child if they're unlucky enough to inherit my psychometry?"

Elizaveta lifted a shoulder. "My point is that you shouldn't fear passing on a burden. Magic is much more malleable in children. I still think my nephew Andrei could have developed proper shields had he been given the training as a child, instead of being tossed into that god-forsaken *mukhosransk*."

"I see." Nova didn't know what to say. Her mind was racing. "I should discuss this with Zhi." She assumed he wanted children, but was that because he wanted them or because his family expected them? "You've given me a great deal to consider."

Elizaveta gave her a regal nod. "Good." She rose to her feet. "And tell my son to get home if he wants any say on the choice of wedding venue."

Hundreds of miles away, Nova jerked awake in Zhi's arms. Aware she was breathing too fast, she fought to calm her racing heart. The last thing she wanted was for Zhi to wake up right now.

But her jumbled thoughts must have been very loud, because he stirred almost immediately.

"What's wrong?" he muttered groggily, followed by a string of Russian swear words.

He sat bolt upright on the bed, dislodging his cock from inside her —his preferred way to sleep.

"My mother did *what*?"

CHAPTER THIRTY-ONE

Nova was being far too diplomatic, sitting quietly on the bed as he ranted and raved to his mother.

Pacing, he swore when Elizaveta, predictably, dismissed all his arguments about ethics and respecting boundaries in favor of pursuing her own agenda. Which included getting him and Nova married as quickly as possible, followed by a quick hop onto the baby train.

He disconnected more frustrated than he was at the start of the conversation. Tossing a pillow aside, he growled, pouring all his frustration into the bear-like sound.

"This is your future mother-in-law," he said, scrubbing his face. "Please don't leave me."

Nova's tense expression softened. "I'm not going anywhere. I'm aware Elizaveta is a force of nature. I would never hold you responsible for her actions."

He snorted. "Well, that puts you heads and shoulders above most of the people I know. Not that many people know the true nature of her magic. Most people think she's a moderately strong telepath."

"It is an interesting talent." Nova looked a little green, but she felt calm in his head. Or was that resignation?

"It's not considered a particularly dangerous ability," Zhi shared. He wanted to be as transparent with her as possible. "But that's only because very few people can do it skillfully. And my mother is the best. She can jump into dreams and manipulate them, controlling the environment and other people in them. The dreamer has no idea the other characters are just spitting out her words. She can appear as anyone, leading the subject down whichever path she wants."

Nova sank back into the cushions. "Wow. I guess I never realized what a dream walker could do. With enough effort they can influence and manipulate power brokers at almost any level, from politicians to CEOs. All she has to do is reinforce a decision they made by showing them dreams of success or give them unsettling nightmares undermining their choices."

Her complexion was considerably greener now. "Applied consistently, she could influence global markets and governments."

Zhi leaned over to tap her on the nose. "Except Elizaveta is far too self-involved to invest that kind of time. She did it more when my father was alive, at his request, to further whatever agenda he was pursuing at the time. But as far as I know she hasn't bothered to pursue any economic or political schemes since he died and I took over the family business."

She raised her brows. "That you know of."

He sat down next to her. "You don't have to worry. I have a lot of experience with her talent. She taught all of us how to stop dream walkers so I could protect myself. Once you know what you're looking for, she won't be able to slip into your dreams undetected."

Her relief was palpable. Nova threw her arms around his neck. "Oh, thank God."

Groaning, he pulled her into his side. "I'm sorry. I should have warned you what she was capable of. But I wasn't thinking about her at all."

Her hand ran up his bare chest. "That's alright. I can't exactly blame you for being distracted."

Zhi squeezed her tighter. "And don't let her talk about marriage and kids scare you. Well, the kids part anyway. I'm really hoping you're good with the marriage part."

Her big green eyes fixed on him. "Are you sure you want to marry me?"

"Of course I'm sure. I want to spend the rest of this life with you."

There was a glimmer in her eye, as if she didn't quite believe him. "I'm nowhere near as accomplished as your other marriage prospects."

He snorted. "No, you're more accomplished. Not that I give a damn about that. I just want to be with you. I'll take you however I can get you. But for full disclosure, my mother's insistence on marriage isn't just her being old-fashioned." He didn't want to dwell on the downsides to a union with him, but he had to be transparent about the dangers. "You know what kind of waters we swim in. The status and trappings of marriage will protect you to a degree."

There were certain parties among the Seven who would target a girlfriend without compunction. But those same people would hesitate to look sideways at a wife. Especially his wife.

"I don't doubt that." The words were even, but her smile was weak. "It's just all happening a little fast."

"Do you want to get married? Not to me, but generally? How do you feel about the institution?"

She held up her hands. "Honestly, I don't know. Marriage was always something meant for other people. I do know I want to be with you."

He pounced. "Enough to accept Elizaveta as a mother-in-law?"

Nova laughed. Her fingers drummed her cheek. "Hmm. Let me think about it."

Zhi put a hand over his heart, miming being stabbed.

Climbing over him, Nova pressed him back into the mattress. "I love you. As long as you're willing to wait a few months before offering me a ring, I can deal with whatever comes next."

A few months was more than he'd planned. "You need that long to get used to the idea?"

"Wouldn't you?" she laughed before the mirth suddenly died away.

"What's wrong?" Zhi asked.

"Something..." Nova bit her lip, chewing on it as she sorted through her thoughts, trying to remember what it was that was bothering her. And then she remembered. "Oh."

Zhi was starting to look alarmed. "What?"

"Elizaveta... She hesitated when I pointed out that she was being a little too accepting of a future daughter in law with no connections, no knowledge of her people."

Fuck.

"Yeah," she whispered.

The look on her face was tearing him up. Because it wasn't betrayal. It was just hurt.

"I knew of course." She pulled away, sitting on the bed with her hands wrapped around her knees. The little bit of distance she put between them was tiny but was already killing him.

"There is no way a member of the Seven would allow someone in their home without doing a full background check. A detailed family history."

She looked at the art on the wall, but clearly didn't see it.

"Before you ask, I don't know all the details. All I know is what Han told me.."

Nova jerked. "Which is?"

Zhi shook his head. "He confirmed what you told us about Greenfield and your time there—how Montclair took you. But Han did go further after my interest in you became clear."

He held up a hand when she began to interrupt. "It's a matter of safety. If you and I marry, we need to know that there are not going to be any surprise family members popping out of the woodwork. We're not at war with anyone, but we have enemies. Knowing your history is important. We need to get ahead of any problems our union might cause."

"Do you really think anyone is going to come forward now? After all this time? I'm a grown woman."

He sighed. "Blood is forever. For all we know you could have been the illegitimate child of one of those other families at the auction. If that came to light after the fact, things could become complicated, diplomatically speaking."

Nova snorted. "So I need provenance like the other artwork and artifacts from the auction?"

He winced. "You're not one of theirs, by the way," he said softly.

"Han confirmed you have no ties that will compromise you somewhere down the line."

Her exhale was harsh. Tears glittered in her eyes. "In other words, my family is dead, or they didn't want me."

Zhi wished he could lie. It would be so much easier. "They're not dead."

Her face crumpled. "So they just didn't want me..."

He rushed to her, wrapping his arms around her before the first tear fell. "Whether they gave you up out of a sense of desperation or weakness doesn't matter. They don't matter. Because you're not that girl anymore. You built an amazing life for yourself. You know everything about everything and developed an enviable professional reputation. People can and should pay for the privilege of speaking to you. And have a wardrobe any woman would kill for."

She snickered, but it was edged with pain and resignation.

Nova rested her head on his shoulders, putting her hand over her heart. "And I have you. In here."

"Always."

There was more talk. More promises made in soft voices then sighs and soft cries.

Never had Zhi been as grateful for his training and the consequent mental discipline that resulted in as he was that night. It allowed him to send a painfully hard blast on the mental plane, a very firm warning to stay put, even as he held Nova protected and unaware in his arms.

He waited till she was in a deep sleep before climbing out of bed to get dressed. Pissed off beyond measure, he slipped out the door and walked up the trail to face the pack of shifters waiting less than a mile down the road.

CHAPTER THIRTY-TWO

Zhi was in a murderous mood when he finally reached the clearing where the werewolves were waiting.

There were a half dozen of them, three tall men and three women. Two of the males had bodies so muscular they looked almost comical to him. The females were shorter and sleeker, two of them downright petite in build. But Zhi didn't make the mistake of thinking they were any less dangerous than their male counterparts. The smallest was no taller than Jinx, who had taught him firsthand how deadly a woman could be.

He directed his scowl at the wolf in the middle. This one was a touch leaner than the others, his muscles corded steel cables to the others' bulky cement blocks. But Zhi knew he was the most dangerous. Power pulsed off him, that wild shifter energy flaring across his senses like someone blasting a flamethrower a few yards away. The pack alpha.

Zhi came to a stop, his legs braced wide. He crossed his arms. "Is this a formal declaration of war?"

The big male on the left snorted, rolling his eyes.

Zhi didn't hesitate. He threw a mental blow that sent the fucker staggering back. The fact he kept his feet was a testament to his physical strength, but then Zhi hadn't struck a killing blow.

"I don't have to read your mind to crush it beneath my boot," he said, aware that his voice was more intimidating this way—flat and emotionless. "I'm going to repeat that slower for you, so you'll understand. *Is this a declaration of war?*"

"*No.*" The man in the middle held up his hands in surrender. "That's not why we're here. Also, you should know were not part of the pack who've been harassing you."

"Then why the hell are you here?" Zhi spat. "This is private property."

He owned the ten square miles around the cabin and was willing to buy more if it meant asshats like this stopped traipsing through his land. Not that this was some random visit. That much was obvious.

The leader raised his head. "Private doesn't mean untraceable. The pack possesses some skilled hackers, the ones who can get past purchases made by shell companies." He took a step forward. "My name is Rafe Hawkins."

Zhi had heard the name, but the mental image he had didn't fit the man standing in front of him. "Seriously?"

His opponent threw up his hands. "What, a black man can't be a werewolf?"

Idiot. "They can. They're just not usually named *Rafe.*"

"It's short for—"

"*I don't care what it's short for.*"

The group took a collective step back. Zhi hadn't yelled. He'd broadcasted the words as loudly as possible.

Predictably as the strongest, Hawkins was the first to recover. Giving Zhi a narrow-eyed glance, he shook it off, the move reminiscent of a wet dog drying itself.

"I thought you couldn't read shifter minds," he accused.

Zhi's imitation of an iceberg would have done Bao proud. "I don't have to read your minds to be heard. Or to liquify them into soup."

"*Fine.*" Hawkins's voice had distinctly more growl in it now. "Douglas Maitland sent me."

That didn't wash. "Han is our contact with the Maitland clan. He's our contact with everyone. You have no business in these woods." He put his hands on his hips. "Want to know how I know that—because *Han isn't fucking here.*"

The wolf's neck drew back. Zhi had rung his bell with that last blast. "Except you're the one we need to convince, the one gatekeeping access to the psychometrist."

Vindicated and angry, Zhi pointed an accusing finger at the alpha. "I *knew* this was about Nova. Well, forget it. There's no way you bastards are getting anywhere near her."

Hawkins closed his eyes for a long moment, flexing his long fingers. But they didn't sprout claws, a testimony to his control. "I get it. I really do. The other pack did everything wrong. Their alpha was just killed—that's not an excuse, but it is an explanation...or the start of one," he said, frustration bleeding into his voice. "But the problem they needed Nova Navarro's help with has gotten worse, spilling over into other packs—namely mine. That's why I got in touch with Douglas Maitland in the first place. To report it. He didn't know what was going on until your cousin contacted him and they put two and two together."

He looked behind him, signaling one of the women. She handed him a backpack. "We understand Ms. Navarro has signed an exclusive contract with your family. We'd like to subcontract her. Though the matter is critical to us, she would be in no danger. I guarantee it."

Unbelievable. "What part of no don't you understand?"

Hawkins took another step forward. Zhi hit him with a warning tap. "That's far enough."

The werewolf slapped a hand to his forehead. "Ow, damn it," he snarled. "Was that necessary?"

"That was a warning shot," Zhi warned. "And before you get ideas, no, you can't rush me all at once to take me out. I don't care how fast you think you are."

The hulk-sized shifter muttered loud enough for him to hear. "He's bluffing."

Zhi straightened, lobbing a mental strike that would have resulted in a stroke in a normal human. Each shifter clutched his head, all but

Hawkins. The pack alpha clenched his jaw, the tendons in his neck standing out in stark relief. But he stood his ground.

"Alright, you've made your point," Hawkins snarled, eyes going wolf-bright yellow before he pivoted and snarled something subvocal at the future Darwin Award winner. "If you're done proving you can hit us with your magic, we need to get down to business. We're prepared to negotiate a sum worth your while."

"House Zheng doesn't need money."

The wolf's lips tightened. "Yeah, but it's still nice to have, isn't it? And your pet psychometrist takes contract work outside your family. We know cause our people tried to hire her the normal way." He put his hands on his hips, widening his stance. "If you'd said yes the first time, none of this would have been necessary."

"What the hell do I look like?" Zhi scoffed. "That's the first thing I checked. No shifters have attempted to hire Nova since the auction."

It looked as if Hawkins was about to argue when he closed his mouth. He turned to the woman on his left. "Tell me he was upfront about shit," he growled.

The woman walked closer to whisper something in his ear. Rafe rage-reddened so much he looked like he was about to wolf-out. But that wasn't going to happen. Zhi knew what few outside the wolf shifter community did, Hawkins's secret.

The man was an alpha wolf who couldn't shift, which meant the eye thing was probably as far as the alpha's transformation could go. They called that kind of thing a partial shift, and his was barely one at that.

"There are other psychometrists," he said, wishing these wolves had their shit together. "Nova knows them all by reputation. She can recommend one."

"Maitland said Nova Navarro was the best. That's who we need." Hawkins signaled to the woman on the end. "And before you say no again, show her this and ask her if she wants to turn this job down."

He took something wrapped in several layers of plastic from the woman and tossed it to him. Zhi caught it, glowering at the opaque plastic bag.

"I know what you're thinking," Hawkins warned. "But if I were you, I wouldn't toss that. She won't thank you for keeping her in the dark. Trust me."

With a rumble that would have done any of the shifters proud, Zhi undid the ties and opened the bag.

There was Ziplock inside. He pulled it out and swore at the small plush bunny rabbit visible beneath the clear plastic. It had a pacifier attached to its mouth.

CHAPTER THIRTY-THREE

Nova stared down at the Ziplock bag on the cabin table, horror in her eyes. She reached out but hesitated, her hand hovering over it.

When she lifted her head, her green eyes were crystalline with unshed tears.

"Babies are hard," she whispered hoarsely. "They're so new and innocent and don't leave strong impressions on their belongings until they're a little older. Not unless the object in question was in their hands when they were ki—"

She caught herself before spelling out the worst-case scenario aloud, swallowing hard.

"But no. That's not what's happening here. I would feel the child's death through the plastic without touching it." She took a deep shuddering breath. "Something that violent would bleed through."

Zhi had to fight to stay where he was, to sweep her up and away from the table and the child's toy lying on it. He could have kicked Hawkins in the head for putting Nova in this position. *Repeatedly.*

Unfortunately, that ass of an alpha had been right. There was no way he could have kept this from her.

It went against his every instinct, but Zhi was going to have to let

Nova help the shifters. Whether she could was still in question. Failure would break her heart.

Zhi tensed when he saw Nova wringing her hands red. He covered them with his own, pulling her out of the kitchen chair and settling her between his legs and down on his lap.

A tear coursed down the porcelain skin of her cheek. His first impulse was to wipe it away, but he didn't. Instead, he pressed the side of his face to hers, so the tear was trapped between them.

She leaned into him, taking comfort in the firm, almost rough contact. "Unless the kidnapper touched it, I probably won't get anything from this."

He tightened his hold on her, bracing her for the impact to come. "If that's the case, you'll have other opportunities."

She twisted in his lap, consternation slackening her features. "What?"

Zhi inhaled deep before letting it go. "There are other missing children. Some teenagers and a couple of adults too. The first group of shifters—the ones who attacked us on the bridge have lost eight of their people. Five of those were kids under fourteen. The youngest of that group was four. The pack leader was killed trying to protect them."

Nova's hands flew to her mouth.

He pressed his forehead to her hair. "For some truly incomprehensible reason, the pack's lieutenants decided to keep the whole affair quiet. They didn't report the kidnappings to the Maitland."

Nova was responding to his voice, so he kept talking, giving her Han's synopsis on the wolf packs and their confederation.

"They were trying to kidnap me so I could help them?"

"Somehow they got it into their heads that you were the only one who could."

Werewolves were arguably the best trackers in the world. If they couldn't find their missing children, then they needed something more. Someone exceptional. They needed Nova, the most gifted psychometrist in the world.

"The Maitlands hadn't heard anything about this until Han reached out. Then they started digging around. When a second pack was attacked, the children targeted, their pack alpha went straight to their leadership. That's who came here. Rafe Hawkins, leader of the second pack, came to plead their case."

Nova nodded slowly. "There will be other items if this one fails."

"Yes. But they brought the baby's because they wanted to make the strongest case for help."

"I understand. And I feel terrible for being relieved there will be more—"

Zhi gave her a squeeze. "You don't have to explain. Not to me."

Twisting her head, she pressed a kiss to his lips before reaching for the plastic bag.

Zhi put his hand over hers. "Let me. I can drop it in your hand. If it overwhelms you, let it fall on the table."

"Okay." Readying herself, she extended both hands, palms up. Zhi opened the bag and shook the contents out.

Nova flinched as the baby plush and pacifier hit her skin. Zhi began to move as if to take it from her, but she shifted her hands away from him, her fingers curling over the toy.

Pursing her lips, she ran her bare hands over the furry surface. "I feel love—maternal love. And a bit of the infant feeling safe and secure. If this was on the child when they were taken, it fell before he or she was under duress and without touching any of the kidnappers."

She opened her hands, letting the plush hit the table.

Zhi rubbed her back. "It's okay. This was a long shot. I'll get something else." He pulled out his phone.

She shook her head. "If the items they brought were all like this, it won't work. We need to go."

He paused in the act of dialing Hawkins. "Where?"

"To the shifter's hometown."

Zhi began to argue, but she stopped him with a hand to his mouth. Her eyes pleaded with him. "We can't take the chance the next object they bring us will fail."

He scowled. "You want to go to the scene of the kidnapping? For all we know it's a dirt road or a common street. Is your plan to pick up vibrations from asphalt?"

Nova sucked in a shaky breath. Her eyes filled with tears.

Zhi winced. "I'm sorry. Of course you'll be able to pick something up from the scene."

"It's not that." Nova hung her head and sighed. She rose from his lap and squatted in front of him, taking his hands in hers. "There's something I haven't told you yet. There's an aspect of my magic Llewelyn warned me to keep secret—including the people who might employ me in the future."

"He did?" His head drew back, brows drawing down.

As far as Zhi was concerned Llewelyn Montclair had been a shit guardian. He'd taken a vulnerable child and had molded her into the ideal *employee*. While he provided Nova with a home and education, he'd also exploited her talent and taught her that the most she could expect were crumbs of affection and occasionally being told "good job."

If that mercenary piece of shit warned her to keep some facet of her magic secret, it was a big deal.

"What aspect is that?"

She began in halting words then stopped. "This is harder than I thought."

"You don't have to tell me."

"No. You need to know this. You most of all." Nova swallowed and tucked her hair behind her ears. "I don't need an object related to the kidnapping to find the victims."

She began to explain in fits and starts. Zhi closed his eyes, his pulse kicking up as the importance of her words began to sink in.

"*No.*" His gut tightened in instant denial. "You are absolutely *not* doing that."

CHAPTER THIRTY-FOUR

Han's shocked face would have been comical in other circumstances. "She can do what?" he hissed in disbelief. "And you're going to let her?"

Zhi rubbed his aching temples before unclipping his seatbelt. They had to be at cruising altitude by now.

It would be a short flight to Hawkins's pack territory. But it was long enough for Nova to shower and catch a quick nap in the small bedroom in the back of the plane—at his insistence.

She was tired and would need every ounce of her energy for the ordeal ahead.

The bedroom wasn't as isolated an environment as his cabin, but Han had brought Nova's silk sheets, as well as a suitcase full of clothes and another bag with a bunch of shoes. They had been packed by his staff using thick silicone gloves, for her protection. According to Han, they had done this without asking. He wondered how they would react when he asked them to move her things into his bedroom.

Probably better than his mother. Or not, given that she was already pushing Nova for grandkids.

"I didn't have much of a choice," he confessed, wishing he could pour himself a drink to take the edge off. But he had to be at his sharpest when they landed in Alaska. "Nova would never get over turning her back on children. Not with her history."

Han was skeptical. "The good thing about dealing with wolves is that they clean up their own messes, which is why I'm having a hard time accepting that they're seeking outside help."

Zhi released a tired sigh. "It's the youngest and most vulnerable of them being preyed upon—the cubs. We both know Nova is incapable of walking away from that."

"You're her lover," Han said, elongating "lover" like a thirteen year old discussing a middle school crush. "Couldn't you talk her into, gee, I don't know, *not* painting a huge target on her back?"

Zhi collapsed back into the chair. "Don't think I wasn't tempted. But the need to help others is weaved into the fabric of her soul. Denying her the chance to help would severely damage her."

"So will finding all those shifter cubs dead or dissected somewhere," Han pointed out, the thought too terrible to voice aloud.

"Let's hope that's not going to be the case. But it's going to be a clusterfuck either way. Knowledge of Nova's other ability must be out there or they wouldn't have been so insistent on getting her. The best we can do is limit knowledge on the true scope of her ability by controlling the conditions. I told Hawkins these measures are to protect her after the fact, and if he didn't agree to the concessions she was out."

He handed Han his phone, letting him read through the texts he and the alpha had been exchanging.

"It's better than nothing." Han returned the phone with a scowl. "But this is still weird. Of all the types of shifters, wolves are the most insular, the most independent. They take pride in not needing help and are feared the world over for their hunting abilities. If they can't find their own people, it can only mean one thing."

They both thought the words at the same time. "*Witches.*"

It wasn't the only explanation by any means, but it made the most sense. However, they would be on alert for other possibilities. They had to be ready for anything.

"I really don't like that one of these damn wolves knows about this aspect of her talent," Han muttered.

"That's why I want you to find a connection between Llewelyn Montclair and the wolf shifters or any of their known associates."

"You think he told someone?" Han frowned. "But he's the one who warned Nova to keep this part of her magic secret, drilled it into her."

Zhi grunted. "He did. But he was also a selfish, pleasure-seeking dilettante. Somewhere along the line he shared her deepest darkest secret."

"A case of do as I say, not as I do?"

"Exactly."

"The number one suspect for this is the ass currently in charge of that first pack."

"Or someone close to him or her."

"I'll get on that," Han said, taking out his phone to text instructions to his investigative team. "Although it may be too late. Cat's out of the bag."

Zhi inclined his head, tamping down the pulse of anger threatening his composure. Nova needed him in control. She also needed his ruthlessness, a detail he planned to gloss over for the greater good, until she was in so deep she'd never think of leaving him. He was the head of a house after all.

"That doesn't mean I can't threaten to drown the cat if someone else learns this secret."

Han nodded philosophically before turning with a grin. "This mission of mercy has a side benefit. You get to avoid Elizaveta a little longer. God only knows how she'll react when you bring Nova back home, not as an employee."

"The only reason I was letting her spearhead the search for a bride was because I thought I had no options. Well, I have one now, and she's my match in every way. Not that I'd let Elizaveta's disapproval stop me. I'm a grown man. In any case, I believe Nova and mother have begun to come to terms."

His cousin snickered. "Really?"

"Do you doubt Nova's ability to deal with my mother?"

Han thought about it. "You know what? I don't, which makes you the luckiest S.O.B. ever. You know that, right?"

"I do." And not just because his future bride was brilliant and beautiful or that she had the strength and fortitude to deal with his mother. Zhi's relationship with Nova was fated, a fit so perfect he believed it had been written in the stars.

And he'd do anything to protect her.

Han had confirmation from Douglas Maitland that Hawkins was a trustworthy alpha, but Zhi was not prepared to extend the benefit of the doubt to Rafe's people. And he damn well didn't extend it to the members of the first pack who'd attacked them.

Hawkins had guaranteed none of those wolves would be present. Anything they needed from that group would be handled by intermediaries.

If they didn't, if they tried to fool him or endanger Nova in any way, Zhi was prepared to go nuclear.

NOVA WAS BUNDLED in cashmere from head to toe—a cashmere sweater dress over cashmere pants paired with a cashmere coat and leather boots. It was the warmest clothing she owned and utterly inadequate for the frigid cold that blasted them when they disembarked at the little no-name landing strip in southern Alaska.

Scowling he peeled off his thicker wool coat and draped it over Nova at the top of the stairs. Han snorted, poking him in the back. "Don't expect me to give you *my* coat."

Nova pushed his hands away, trying to give back the coat. "I'm fine. You have to keep this." But her chattering teeth belied her words.

"I'll get another one from my case before we head out," he promised, ushering her to the car.

A specially outfitted Range Rover had been driven up by a ZZ8 subcontractor for their use. Given the distance it had traveled, the driver had broken the speed limit to get it here, but Zhi was adamant about the safeguards required for their transport.

Hawkins had snorted over the phone when he'd told him they wouldn't be accepting transportation from the pack, but Zhi didn't care. He wasn't going to be dependent on anyone else's goodwill. And without one of their regular combat-ready drivers available, they were better off with Han behind the wheel.

The trip took over an hour on bad roads. When they got to the small highway turnoff where the kidnapping had taken place, he saw the pack had blocked off the road, marking off a wide patch with traffic cones and police tape. Just past this on the left was a clear patch on land where the wolves had set up electric lights powered by a portable generator as well as a large weatherproof tent big enough for the entire group.

But the wolves weren't inside the tent. They were milling outside it, over a dozen of them in jeans and flannels or sweatshirts, showing off their cold tolerance in that smug wolf way.

"You sure about this?" Han asked, scanning the group from the passenger seat with a jaundiced eye. He would never speak aloud so close to the wolves. Never mind that they were still inside the car and the shifters were outside. The wolves would hear them if they spoke aloud.

Zhi nodded, including Nova in his reply. *"According to Hawkins, most of these are close relatives of the victims. The rest are soldiers at the top of the hierarchy, sent by Douglas Maitland himself and in his own pack. They're here to act on the information Nova gives them. They're the team that will be sent out to rescue the children."*

Han eyeballed the soldiers, their build and bearing giving away their status. They walked with a predatory grace, even compared to others of their own kind. Those standing relatively still had a coiled readiness to them, as if they were ready to spring at you at all times. *"How many can you take out all at once?"* he asked.

"In one blow?" Zhi considered. *"All of them. But I'd have to kill them."*

"There's the rub." Han sniffed. *"Since we don't want to start a war, you better not do that. If they rush us, I'll take care of them."* He snapped the collar of his coat up and grinned, the ultimate badass.

Zhi turned to Nova. *"I think you should wait here. Let us get the lay of the land before you come out. I'll leave our channel open so you can hear everything.*

She nodded, her anxiety bleeding into her posture. She was sitting so straight and tense she might snap in two, her eyes fixed on the tent.

Not wanting to prolong a second of her anxiety, he slipped on a ski cap and his spare coat before climbing out of the SUV.

CHAPTER THIRTY-FIVE

Zhi stopped where the police tape marked off the scene of a vehicular collision. Broken glass and skid marks covered the asphalt. He sent Nova a mental snapshot. *"More physical evidence than I thought."*

"Has it snowed since the kidnapping?" he asked the wolf who stood on the opposite side of the tape.

Unsurprised he was dispensing with the pleasantries, Hawkins put his hands on his hips, shooting a look at the car behind them. "No. Which is good. I wouldn't want Nova to have to dig through the snow to reach the road."

Han smiled at the alpha, his teeth pearly white in the combination of artificial lamps and moonlight. "You will address her as Ms. Navarro."

Hawkins looked Han over in a long, appraising sweep. "Is this your very interesting cousin? The one I've heard so much about?"

Zhi's smile was genuinely amused. "That description would apply to several of my relatives."

"Of course it does." Hawkins sounded both annoyed and resigned. He straightened, wrapping his arm around a red-eyed woman who broke away from the crowd behind him to join him. She had obviously been weeping. "My people are eager to begin."

"Did they bring the things Nova asked for?" Zhi asked, nodding to scattered glass. "Because this might not be enough."

"We tried. Given the requirements, we had to guess if they were right or not."

"Don't worry. She'll be able to tell if you chose poorly. If you did, we'll accompany you to the children's homes and try again."

Hawkins made a rumbling sound. But he nodded. "Are you ever going to let her out of the car or just keep quoting Indiana Jones?"

Zhi faced him, bracing his legs apart. "Before I get her, I will remind you again that if you harm her in any way I can and will—"

"Turn our brains into soup," Hawkins finished in a flat voice. "We got it. Let's begin."

"So glad you understand." He gestured to the SUV. *"Come join us."*

Nova climbed out of the car, her svelte form appearing bulky in the two coats. That didn't stop her from looking drop-dead gorgeous. Her alabaster skin glowed against the backdrop of his charcoal coat. Paired with her striking green eyes and rich auburn hair done up in a fancy knot, she was an unexpected bit of beauty and grace on this barren stretch of road.

He wasn't the only one who noticed. Despite his obvious concern for his people, Hawkins stared at Nova with undisguised interest. Zhi could almost feel the alpha vibrate when Nova came next to him, introducing herself in that throaty, butterscotch voice.

If Hawkins could shift to a wolf, he would have been licking his chops.

"Thank you for coming," the alpha said, the pitch of his voice suddenly as smooth as silk. "I hope you can help."

Nova's voice was breathy, but Zhi knew she wasn't flirting. She was nervous. "I hope so too."

Zhi hadn't taken his eyes off the shifters, so he saw their reaction. It was as if a ripple passed over them, their tension easing a notch as they registered her sincerity. The pulse of strong magic that accompanied her wherever she went didn't hurt either.

He made a mental note to teach her how to shield a little better. In the future it would be better if other members of the Seven weren't able to gauge her strength. But here and now it helped. The wolves' keen senses felt her magic, and it comforted them.

Nova pivoted to face the taped-off section, crouching to examine it from behind the line of cones.

Zhi suppressed a grunt when Hawkins knelt on the other side of the tape, directly in Nova's line of sight as he gave her a rundown of everything they knew about the kidnapping in that same smooth voice he appeared to reserve exclusively for her.

Zhi caught Han's eyes. *"Could he be more obvious?"*

Hawkins's normal speech sounded like he was chewing rocks. These silky bedroom tones were a complete affectation.

Han snickered in his head. *"Better get used to it. Nova is a beautiful woman. As your partner, she's going to get a lot more male attention than she did as a faceless employee."*

"Nova was never that." His first glimpse of her had been when she'd opened the door at Montclair's estate, directing them to the ballroom. He'd been stressed about the outcome of the auction, but he hadn't immediately dismissed her from his mind the way he should have.

He should have known then who Nova was meant be to him.

"I suppose not. But you've got a built-in 'keep out' sign, don't you?" Han added. *"Must be nice knowing that no one else can touch her given your innate possessiveness—even as kids you never did like sharing your toys."*

Nevertheless, Han narrowed his eyes at the alpha when Hawkins shadowed Nova as she moved from one spot to crouch over another. *"Although if he keeps eye-banging her like that I may have to find out how much he's worth out of principal."*

Zhi was in full agreement. *"Be my guest."*

After a minute or two, Nova rose from her squat, her lower lip caught between her teeth. "You can't trace the other vehicles?"

Hawkins shook his head. "From the scene we know there were two. But this is an isolated stretch of road. There are no traffic cameras out this far. We have a few possibilities based on the tire impressions and skid marks, but there's not enough scent markers for us to follow."

"Cameras wouldn't have done you any good," Nova said with a wince. "They were disguised. I can sense the magic of a concealment spell, a big one. I don't think they masked just their own personal scents. It's possible that they used magic to alter the vehicle's appearance. Once they were back on the main road, they removed the spell."

She snapped her fingers. "In a blink the car was a new make and model."

"Isn't that overkill?" Han asked.

"They didn't want to take any chances," Zhi guessed, jerking his head at the wolves. "They knew who they were dealing with."

"Concealment spells are frequently paired with curses," Nova explained for the shifters' benefit. "I've learned how to discern their signature up from the residual resonance. Masking the car is the only explanation for a disturbance of this size. But there's nothing of the kidnappers at first glance. I need to do a more detailed examination."

Giving them a grim smile, she began to remove her gloves.

Zhi hovered protectively, cupping the back of her neck with one hand. *"Remember there's a good chance you'll get nothing from the actual scene. The real trigger objects are in the tent."*

She nodded, the corners of her mouth turning up a fraction. *"Thank you for threatening to turn everybody into soup."*

His back to the shifters, he risked a small private smile. *"You're welcome."*

Zhi kissed her quickly and stepped away, pulling the police tape up to let her duck underneath.

When he looked up, Hawkins was watching them with a suspicious glare. "I thought she couldn't be touched."

Zhi drew himself up to his full height, voice cold enough to frost the air. "I am the exception to the rule—the only one. Try and do the same, and you will hurt her. Even accidental contact can send her into a seizure. Know if that happens, I won't just kill you. Everyone else you love dies too. I will wipe your entire pack from the face of the earth."

"Zhi," Nova chided, reaching out to him. "No one here intends to hurt me."

Hawkins grimaced, ducking under the police tape on the other side of the road.

He was two yards from Nova when he stopped short, lifted off his feet by Han, who'd appeared next to the alpha between one blink and the next.

"What part of no touching did you not understand?" Han growled, his voice reverberating with an inhuman frequency that in no way resembled the shifters' growls.

Startled, Nova sidled to the side, closer to him. *Zhi, what is Han?*

It's complicated, he replied, keeping the other wolves in his direct eye line, warning them off immediate retribution with his forbidding expression.

"I wasn't going to touch her, you ass." Hawkins pulled out of his cousin's grip, landing on his feet and jerking the hem of his shirt back into place. His eyes were wolf-yellow. He leaned toward Zhi and took an audible sniff. "You could have just said," he growled.

"Said what?" Nova asked.

Hawkins turned to her, visibly softening. "That you were a mated pair." He waved a hand to encompass her. "His scent is all over you, deep enough that it's imprinted on your skin."

"It is?" Nova glanced at Zhi, her pleasure sparkling down their mental channel, a shaft of sunlight illuminating a shadowed path.

"Yes. And for future reference, you wouldn't have to be intolerant of touch for us to avoid any unnecessary contact—not when your mate is a predator as lethal as a wolf."

He grinned at her, brushing imaginary lint off his shoulder. "Well, as most wolves anyway."

Ignoring the posturing, Nova gave him a polite smile, softening the fact she was making a shooing motion toward the police tape. "That's good to know, but accidents happen. And Zhi isn't exaggerating. I can't tolerate touch from any but him. So, if you don't mind waiting behind the line I'd be much obliged."

"No need to explain," Hawkins continued in that infuriating bedroom voice as he retreated behind the police tape. "Magic bends itself in a pretzel for mates."

Nova rewarded him with a smile. "I hope so."

The alpha nodded, a hint of wistfulness in his expression. That was when Zhi knew that despite the many obligations and bonds of pack, Rafe Hawkins was a lonely man.

He turned to Nova, forcing himself not to intervene when she reached for a piece of broken glass. She dropped it a moment later. "I'm getting images of a man cleaning the window," she said. "Also, a more faded snapshot of the factory where the glass was manufactured."

"Isn't the man who cleaned it relevant?" Hawkins asked. "It might be his vehicle."

"I don't think so. He's wearing a shirt with those oval name tags." Nova indicated placement with a gesture. "It could be from a car washing place or a rental agency. It's too generic to tell."

She didn't look up before placing her palms flat on the ground. This time she flinched, snapping her hands back. "The barest hint of violence, but nothing specific. Whatever happened was too fast to leave a lasting impression. This will fade soon."

Zhi was there before she stood back up. He took her hands, chafing them to keep them warm in the cold. "We knew the scene was a long shot," he said aloud, for the shifters benefit.

She nodded, shrugging off her dejection. "Yes, you're right."

He held out a hand. She took it, letting him guide her to the tent. With a murmur, Hawkins ordered the soldiers to wait outside.

The interior was larger than he expected, a long, fat rectangle with openings in the thick plastic on the longest sides. There was no furniture save for half a dozen tables lined up in a row.

Each had a lone object on it. Most were wrapped in big plastic Ziploc bags like the bunny pacifier. The two that weren't were resting on something that looked like hastily opened Saran Wrap.

Artificial heat had been pumped inside for their comfort. It blasted from portable space heaters with a rush of hot air that made Nova blink. Too hot, she wiggled out of both her coats, handing them to Han.

"Drop them if there's trouble," Zhi told him. His cousin would need his hands free.

Han inclined his head a fraction, his eyes measuring the distance between Nova and the others as she moved to the tables.

Three displayed toys, a bedraggled stuffed wolf with a pirate patch over one eye, a small handheld gaming device, and a long-haired doll that looked like an antique with eyelids that opened and closed. Next to it was a purple cellphone. Down from that was a plaid shirt. The last item was a geode amethyst the size of his fist.

Nova stopped in front of the cell phone. She rested her index and middle fingers on the cracked surface, almost as if she was taking its pulse.

She removed them almost immediately. With a frown, she did the same to the gaming device.

"I'm sorry," she said, turning to the wolves in the room. "These two devices won't work."

One of the women stirred. "But my daughter loves that phone. It's always with her. The only reason we have it was because she dropped it when they took her."

Han shifted his weight. *"I thought Hawkins said they left the scene undisturbed. That would have been better for her reading."*

"He probably didn't think bagging the phone counted," Zhi guessed. The alpha's impulse must have been to protect it from the elements or to fingerprint it. They wouldn't have known to ask Nova for help at that time. Not until well after the kidnapping when Hawkins had called Maitland.

"I realize it's special to her," Nova told the woman gently. "But just because it was valued doesn't mean it wasn't replaceable. What your daughter loves most about her phone is in the cloud. If she lost the device itself, she'd get another and download the data to it. For me to do what I need to do, the object in question must be truly loved—a thing that is irreplaceable to the person I'm seeking."

"So, it's like a witch's tracking spell?" the woman whispered, hope lighting in her eyes despite the failure with the phone.

"In a way. Except I don't have to cast a spell." Slipping on her glove, Nova picked up the phone and handed it to the woman, who took it without touching her.

"Just because this doesn't work, it doesn't mean those others won't. And based on the M.O. and timing of the kidnapping it's likely the children and other hostages are all being kept together in the same place," she said, repeating what Han had told her on the ride over.

His cousin's explanation had been intended to prepare Nova for the worst, but she used the knowledge to comfort others now. It was her way.

Han's K&R crash course had been short but detailed. Kidnapping a single person was a difficult proposition in and of itself. You needed a place to hold them, an isolated location, or failing that one that was heavily soundproofed and had an entrance that wasn't monitored.

The issues increased exponentially when multiple victims were involved, a mixed group that included adults, babies, and children. Not to mention the fact that these were wolves. Even the teenagers could be dangerous.

The woman nodded, visibly soothed by Nova's words. She stepped back and clutched the phone to her chest, going to Hawkins when he opened his arms. She wiped her cheeks as she curled into him, literally leaning on her alpha's strength.

Nova approached the doll next, hands hovering over it like it was a live cobra she snatched it up, sucking in a breath as if it stung. But she gritted her teeth and held it for several seconds before setting it back down.

"This is valued by someone but not the child you seek."

Someone sobbed. Zhi pivoted at the unexpectedly harsh sound. It had been made by one of the men. "Her grandmother left my baby girl the doll in your will. She did play with it a lot," the male said.

"Yes, I can feel it has a long history." Nova put her hands down, rubbing her fingers together. Her face was noticeably paler than it had been a moment ago. "But the connection we need has to be deeper, more personal than that. I'm sorry that this can't be used to find her."

Zhi's jaw clenched, resisting the urge to go to Nova and take her out of here. He could see the toll it was taking on her, the strain in those delicate features. And she'd barely touched two of the objects!

Her voice was like music in his head. "*Stop. I'm okay.*"

"*Please don't lie to me.*" But he didn't interfere, gritting his teeth when she went to the plaid shirt. She picked it up and held it for a long time. When she turned around, there were tears in her eyes.

"I'm sorry. This connection is broken."

Shit. Zhi strode forward, taking the shirt from her unresisting hands. He hauled her against him.

A man spoke up. "If that shirt doesn't work, then this woman is a fraud who can't help us at all," he growled, pointing an accusing finger at Nova. "That is Carrie's favorite shirt. It was her dad's. She wears it all the time. It fits all your requirements."

"That's not what she means," Zhi said, trying to gentle his tone. "The shirt *is* important enough. But the connection is broken because the owner is dead."

CHAPTER THIRTY-SIX

Nova didn't fight when Zhi pressed her trembling body against him, hiding her tear-stained face from the suddenly hostile crowd. But while she appreciated his attempt to comfort her, she couldn't hide from this. With effort, she lifted her head, facing the grief caused by her declaration.

Hawkins held up a hand, silencing the arguing wolves. "Nova, are you sure?"

She sighed and nodded. "I'm afraid so. The shirt was loved, prized just as you said." Her hand hovered over her heart. "But the tie has been severed."

Carrie. The woman's name had been Carrie. Nova could see her in her mind's eye, slipping on the shirt as she readied herself for her day. A woman, a mother, full of purpose and life.

Now she was untethered, cold in an unmarked grave. But Nova didn't know where that grave was. All she knew for certain was that Carrie was gone. She couldn't follow the thread to her. Nor could she identify her killers. There was no murder weapon to read, nothing that could tell her where that strong and capable woman had made her last stand.

Zhi squeezed her harder, putting her behind him. That was when Nova noticed Hawkins was holding back the man who grieved.

"C'mon." Han gestured to the exit. "They need a minute."

Deciding he was right, she let Zhi usher her out. Outside, he took the coats from Han and put both over her shoulders, holding her to him instead of buttoning them because she kept rubbing her chest with her fist.

"What are you feeling?" Han asked.

Nova stopped. "The connection wasn't made, so technically nothing."

"That's not nothing," Zhi scowled, putting his hand over hers.

She closed her eyes, raising her head to the moon. "It's a difficult sensation to describe. When this works as it should, it's like there's a physical tie from me to the other person. Their loved object is the rope linking us. When the person is dead, the rope is untethered. It flies loose over the void. It's a very unsettling feeling."

She rubbed her chest again. "But it will go away in a minute," she added.

The grief of the wolves inside would last much longer.

Nova hung her head. It didn't do any good telling herself this was not her failure. There was nothing she could have done to save Carrie. Getting here sooner wouldn't have helped. Well, it might have, but there was no way of knowing for sure. In all likelihood Carrie had died in the vehicle minutes or hours after the kidnapping. She had been a fighter. Nova had seen enough of her life to know that for a fact.

Carrie would have fought to free herself and the kids she was carpooling that day.

"Her kids were grown," she said aloud, extricating herself from the memories of a life not hers. "The children she was driving that day weren't hers. She was just being a good neighbor, a good packmate."

That was what shifters were known for. A healthy pack was a vital community with bonds than ran deeper than similar human enclaves. They were stronger and more varied than most witch clans too, with few exceptions. Like house Zheng.

Zhi's warm hand cupped the back of her neck. The heat and comfort of it was everything. *"You don't have to do this alone."*

"I know." Nova lifted her heavy lashes. After doing multiple readings back-to-back, it felt as if they had weights attached to them. "Thank you."

Zhi nudged her chin up. "If this is what a bunch of missed connections does to you, what is a real bond going to do?"

"It won't feel like this." That lost, desolate feeling was like someone walking over her grave.

"But it will still be hard on you," Han pointed out.

"I'll be tired, but I should be fine."

Zhi scowled. "Should be?"

Nova's impulse was to vacillate and soften the truth, but what was the point? Zhi was in her mind and in her heart. He would know the truth. "I've only ever done this on purpose once. The other times before were happenstance with objects I came across on accident or through my work."

And she had broken those accidental ties to the living as soon as they were made. It wasn't as if those people she'd made a connection to had wanted to be found. Quite the contrary in most cases.

Zhi cupped the back of her neck, massaging the tight muscles with small circles. "The intentional effort, you did it for Llewelyn."

She inclined her head. "It was a favor for his friend. The woman's son Felix had begun experimenting with drugs in college. He had gone to the Caribbean on spring break with some classmates and got separated. His friends searched for days, but they couldn't find him. The time to return to school came and went. He missed his flight. He was still lost weeks later and wasn't using his credit cards or spending money in a way that could be tracked."

"Let me guess. Rich kid flashing lots of cash—even if he wasn't wasted half the time, that's a stupidly easy mark. He was practically begging to get kidnapped."

She nodded. "To make matters worse, he'd wandered off without his ID. The kidnappers somehow misidentified him, making ransom demands to the wrong family. He was so stoned in the beginning and later gagged that he couldn't tell them they had made a mistake. The other family knew their child had come home, so they dismissed the ransom demands as a prank. No one informed the school. By the time everyone realized what happened, Felix had been held for over a week. The kidnappers were on the verge of killing him."

Han crossed his arms. "So Montclair had you do your thing."

"He brought me Felix's father's watch. It had been passed down to him, and he'd taken it off to swim, leaving it behind at the hotel. Llewelyn's friend, Felix's mother, didn't know the details of what I'd done. She just thought I was able to see his location because of my psychometry, and Llewelyn didn't disabuse her of that notion. He's the only one who knew about the heart-bond." She smoothed her skirt with her gloves. "That's what I call the connection. Because it has to start with love or great attachment and only works while the other person's heart still beats."

Zhi scowled. "But someone else must have learned about it or we wouldn't be here now. Did Llewelyn confide in anyone at the time or in the aftermath?"

"If he did, he didn't say so."

Han lifted his head, attention trained on the tent entrance. A moment later, Hawkins parted the plastic folds. "We're ready to continue if you are."

Nova straightened away from Zhi's embrace. "Yes." She turned to Zhi. *"I can do this. I promise."*

He looked over her shoulder to give the wolf alpha a warning glance. "I know you can. That's not what I'm worried about."

CHAPTER THIRTY-SEVEN

Nova knew the pirate plush wolf was a beloved object before she touched it. It was the ear. Ragged and noticeably more worn, it had been stitched back on, presumably because little cub teeth were constantly gripping it so they could carry it around.

You can do this. It wasn't Zhi's voice in her head but her own. But it may as well have been his. To use the wolves' terminology, she had a mate. She was only now beginning to understand what that meant.

Whatever complications arose in the future, whatever sacrifices she would be asked to make as the wife of one of the Seven, they would be worth it. Because she'd never have to face a battle like this alone. Not anymore.

Bracing herself, Nova picked up the stuffed wolf. The connection flashed in her mind's eyes from the toy, a golden lasso that stretched out into the aether.

"I have him," she whispered. Nova knew the wolves were reacting to her news, but she couldn't hear what they were saying over the rush of blood in her ears. But she heard Zhi's voice loud and clear.

"Where is the child?"

Blinking to clear her blurry vision, she turned. "Han, may I have the tablet?"

Han produced a thin white box from his bag, one of a dozen they had brought with them.

Zhi crossed his arms, glowering. He had argued against this but kept silent now as Han tore open the packaging. It took him a few minutes to ready the device, opening the map application and holding it out.

Technically, Nova had never done this part. When she had helped track down Felix, the kidnapped college student, she'd been a child. This technology had been in its infancy at the time. Instead, she'd spelled a paper map of the island, revealing the boy's location with an X, like a treasure map. She'd been worried that the X wouldn't adjust if they transferred the boy to another location but that hadn't been an issue because his kidnappers hadn't moved him.

It hadn't occurred to her to use a map application until Han suggested it.

Here goes nothing. Reaching out with her ability, she touched the golden threads only she could see, peeling them off the stuffed wolf one by one. They stuck to her fingers, crawling over her hands and arms, arrowing toward her chest. They would wind around her, strangling her if she let them.

"What's wrong?" Zhi's tone wasn't alarmed. More like concerned.

"I forgot how involved this was." Carefully untangling the strand from around the bear, she mentally wrapped it around herself, letting it wind around her thoughts and her heart.

Someone growled. In her mind.

Nova jerked a shoulder. She'd forgotten that she was in a room filled with predators, and her man was the most dangerous one.

Except Zhi wasn't a threat to her. He was her lover, her protector. That protective drive was what she had to contend with. He'd stop her if he thought she was harming herself.

"I'm arranging the strands," she told him, giving the ones trying to crawl around her heart a hard yank. Working more quickly, she tugged them toward the tablet Han was holding out to her.

Closing her eyes, she focused on weaving the newly separated strands together. The result was a thin glimmering rope of sparkling gold. It stretched from her into the aether. Nova guided it to the screen, touching the end of it to the glass surface. It was as if she was threading a needle. The strands spread on contact, forming a net of glowing gossamer fibers around the tablet. It was like a weight on a fishing line with her and the bear on the other end.

The map view whirled, spinning as if she'd swiped across the app. When it stopped, a pin dropped on a small island off the coast. She took the tablet from Han, displaying the screen to the wolves.

"Holy shit," the alpha muttered, his eyes nearly bugging out of his head. He reached for the tablet then snatched his hand back as if afraid it would break the connection.

He, Zhi, and Han crowded around the screen. Rafe scowled. "It's one of the Aleutians."

"There are inhabitants on little islands in this chain," Han said, his eyes narrowing on the dot. "But there's nothing on this one according to the map. No towns, no houses."

Zhi touched the screen, zooming in on the dropped pin. "Somebody must have built a structure here, one that's not on the map."

The wolf alpha pointed to the tablet. "Will the pin disappear if I take this?"

"No. The connection can't be broken unless I cut it." Or if she died, but she wasn't about to say that aloud.

Rafe accepted the tablet as if it was made of spun glass. "Take this," he ordered one of the soldiers. He turned back. "I'm sorry to ask, but we need to continue and do the other objects."

Zhi swore, gesturing to the soldier holding the tablet. "Why? Do you think they'll have two such strongholds? Matching his and her prison islands?"

The alpha growled. "I'm sorry, but we need to be certain. Maybe the children *are* being isolated from the adults. Maybe all the—"

He stopped before shouting that all the adult wolves might be dead.

"He's right," she told Zhi when he began to argue. "It would be easier to care for the children if they kept the group together. But the one thing I know about wolves is that they are feral about protecting their cubs. The children don't have to be their own for that drive to kick in. If that gets in the way with the kidnappers plans one too many times, they'll separate them."

"Unless they already took them out of the equation," she told Zhi, aware Han was also on the channel. *"It sounds as if they only want the children."*

Speculating on why would only give her nightmares.

Nova turned to the remaining objects. "I should be able to settle this issue in a minute."

There was a tense moment when it appeared as if Zhi would bar her from continuing. But after giving her a silent glance, he stood aside, and she continued, adding threads for twelve-year-old Matthew's geode. The rock meant the world to him because he'd found it when on a hike with Rafe. His alpha had praised him for his find. Then there was a baseball, signed with the name of a famous baseball player. Eight-year-old Sarah had caught the home run ball at a game she had gone to see with her father. An avid athlete, she considered it one of her most precious possessions.

It became more difficult to manage the threads with each success. *One more*, she thought as she handed off the second-to-last tablet showing the same island with shaking hands. *Only one more.*

Nova was having trouble catching her breath. But she would have continued had Zhi not forced her to stop. Her vision was blurred when he spun her around, a detail she was grateful for because it prevented her from seeing his thunderous expression.

"Stop," he hissed, pulling her away from the tables. "I will not allow you to damage yourself to confirm what we already know."

He raised his head, pining the alpha wolf with a glare as he tugged her close. "Do you hear me? She's stopping. She has found enough of them to be sure of the location."

Rafe held up his hands. "Agreed."

"No." Nova blinked to clear her vision. "We need to do every last object."

As Zhi had guessed, she couldn't bear adding another connection, but she didn't have to. Not unless the location of the victim was someplace other than the island. But if any of those little cubs or their protectors were dead, the families deserved to know.

"No, we don't." Zhi cupped her cheek, an arm wrapped around her

waist to support her. "You can't even stand. Even the fool wolf agrees. We have enough to confirm there isn't a second location."

"The body isn't on the island."

"What?" The wolf alpha's blurry face appeared over Zhi's shoulder.

"The woman who died, she's not on the island. She died on the mainland." Nova didn't know where. She would have to reconnect with her to pinpoint the location, something that could very possibly push her over the edge.

Swallowing back a mouthful of bile, she took a deep breath, trying to calm her roiling stomach. "The last one could be somewhere else too."

"Our priority is the living." Zhi shared a harsh truth, but Rafe Hawkins took one look at Nova's trembling countenance and agreed.

He turned to his soldiers. "She's done. Get ready. We move out within the hour."

CHAPTER THIRTY-EIGHT

Zhi exchanged a knowing look with Han as he exited the bedroom of the plane. His cousin was stationed in the chair outside it. *"She's asleep. Keep an eye on the door."*

"Not a problem." Han kept eyeing the shifters, giving them toothy smiles whenever they looked over at him.

"Can you ask him to stop doing that?" Hawkins muttered as Zhi drew level with his seat. "Everyone is on edge enough without having to wonder if your cousin is going to start doing that freaky thing he does."

Zhi glanced at his cousin. "Look less happy...but keep the same air of menace."

Han's expression shifted appropriately, a smug glint in his eye. The man enjoyed being the top predator in the room. And if it served a purpose, Zhi encouraged his posturing.

He dropped into the seat opposite Hawkins, a soda in hand. He wanted to be resting with Nova, but even with Han standing guard he wasn't about to sleep. There were too many other predators on his place.

Hawkins sank deeper into the seat, regarding him with a disgruntled expression. "Not that I don't appreciate the assist, but why did you offer to come along?"

Zhi raised an eyebrow, but the alpha wasn't intimidated.

"Don't get me wrong. The ride is appreciated. But the pack has its own planes." Rafe jerked his thumb at one of the soldiers across from Han, one who didn't seem perturbed to find himself so close to such a notorious member of the Seven. "Nathan flew in on one of them. It's not as fancy as this one, but it gets us from A to B. He's also an able pilot."

He leaned forward when Zhi didn't reply. "Your girl has gone above and beyond with those tablets. We have the location of our people now." He waved at the closed bedroom door at the back of the plane. "I'm surprised you haven't bundled her off to your mansion. You're obviously itching to get her away from all of this."

"True. But Nova has to maintain the connection for the tablets to work. And she won't cut any of those threads until she knows your cubs are safe. That's why Han will accompany you on that raid."

He tapped his skull to indicate his telepathic connection to his cousin. "The minute he tells me your children are secure, I'm going to have Nova cut the threads."

Zhi paused, taking a sip of his soda before continuing. "I'm sorry, but you'll have to find the rest of your people on your own."

They both knew those others would be dead.

Hawkins inclined his head, all feral energy carefully contained. "Understood. And what you've done—it's more than I expected. You have my thanks."

They sat in silence. But shifters were impatient, and soon the alpha was breaking it.

Rafe gestured behind him to the closed bedroom door. "I didn't realize touching things would be that hard on her. I always thought witches using their magic was natural, like a wolf's heightened strength or sense of smell."

"For the weak perhaps. But the more advanced the magic, the higher the cost." Zhi harrumphed, passing a weary hand over his face. "Had you read Nova's employment contract and its millions of stipulations, you would have gotten the picture. Almost every aspect of Nova's magic is self-destructive on some level."

She had been cursed with too much of the bloody stuff.

The alpha considered that. He sighed heavily. "I would have avoided her involvement if I could have."

Zhi knew Hawkins believed that, but he didn't. Had Nova been alone, an employee of some auction house unaffiliated with a major house, he doubted the alpha would have hesitated to involve her.

Even knowing it hurt her, he would have done it for his pack. And then he would have made a pass at her, hoping a mate bond would twist her magic in his favor.

But he was too late. Nova was his. "All I want to know is this—who identified this aspect of her talent to you?"

Rafe shook his head.

His voice froze over. "I said that is my price."

"I can't tell you that because I don't know. Given that look in your eye, I'm glad I don't."

Hawkins picked up the tablet lying on the table next to him, as if reassuring himself that the pin was still present on the map application. "Our boats will be waiting at the harbor to take us to the island. Will you stay on the mainland with your mate?"

It was a little jarring to hear Nova referred to that way. Odd but satisfying. Not that he'd use that word on his own after this. In his daily life, he would use the word "wife."

"We'll stay on the boat."

The wolf raised his brows. "Our boat?"

"Hell no. I've already chartered one of our own."

The wolf said nothing, just rolled his eyes. "There is no tree cover on the island, so we head in under cover of dark—not that we have choice at this time of the year. How good is your cousin's night vision?"

"Better than yours."

Hawkins snorted.

"I'm serious. It's part of his magic."

The alpha wrinkled his nose. "Fine. Just make sure he gives my people a wide berth. I don't need him accidentally doing that thing to one of us."

"Don't worry," Zhi said, unable to resist teasing. "If he does, you'll be fairly compensated."

Zhi lifted his piece of chalk and examined the complicated nest of circles he'd drawn on the deck in front of him. The incense he'd lit was starting to make his eyes water. Expending a little magic, he encouraged the smoke to stream the other way. *I'm almost done here. What about you?*

"Five more minutes," Han said from the other boat.

Zhi nodded, updating the alpha next to him as he tweaked the runes around his circle.

He, Nova, and half the shifters were on the Spinner Queen, a sleek, mid-sized cruiser that typically operated as a charter vessel along the west coast. His people had secured it on extremely short notice, paying a premium and staffing it with his own crew.

The rest of the wolves were with Han on one of their own vessels, where his cousin was laying down his half of the spell, one they had all agreed was necessary after getting the surveillance satellite photos of their target.

The shifters were being held on the south side of the island in a multi-story bunker originally built by the Russians as a research facility. Abandoned over three decades ago on a tiny unimportant island, the online maps had no record of it.

However, the newer military-grade satellite images Douglas Maitland had acquired for them showed clear evidence of new construction. There were half a dozen outbuildings, one large main facility, a mid-sized garage, and smaller storage units as well as an observation tower. This last was set behind the buildings to give their enemy a mile-long three-hundred-and-sixty-degree view of their surroundings.

The wolves had brought drones equipped with infrared as part of the soldier's arsenal, but getting them close enough without being spotted was going to be an issue with that tower.

There was also an unknown number of magic-capable mercenaries among the perpetrators. That meant there would be spell traps and motion detectors seeded into the terrain all around the compound.

That was why he and Nova were on one boat and Han was on another. The fishing vessel commandeered by the wolves was twenty miles off the coast of the island, directly opposite the Spinner Queen. Han had been preparing the magic-detection and obfuscation spell on his side for over two hours.

The wolves were champing at the bit, pacing and cleaning their weapons, but they hadn't objected to the wait. They knew their people would be safer going in as informed as they could.

"The spell would work better with three points," Nova whispered in his mind. *"The wolves have another boat. I could have been on it, doing this there."*

He looked up to meet her eyes. *"Not going to happen, love."* Zhi wasn't about to leave Nova in the care of anyone else if he could avoid it—something she was well aware of.

"Two sides are enough with an island of this size," he said aloud for Hawkins's benefit. "Holding onto those strands is work enough for you."

That was the understatement of the year.

Despite sleeping for the majority of the flight, Nova was visibly exhausted. The strain of holding onto what she called the heart-bonds was written in her pinched features and the paleness of her normally gold-tinted skin. She was also moving slower, carefully, the way people did when they had a bad headache.

"But my magic is structured to detect curses and spells," she argued. "I don't have to expend a lot of energy to do it."

Nova waved her hand at the complicated series of circles, runes, and burning incense he'd constructed. "With a little alteration, I can use this same magnification spell and spread it more easily than you."

Rising to his feet he cupped her cheek. "That might be true, but I'm no novice and neither is Han. Let us deal with this. This is what we've been trained to do from the cradle. Keeping hold of the bonds is work enough."

Despite being disgruntled, Nova leaned into his hand, her lashes fluttering closed. Even when she was arguing with him, she couldn't help savoring his touch.

God, he loved that.

"I know you have way more training than I do," she acknowledged. "But this is my wheelhouse. I can't help thinking I should be helping given the nature of my talent."

"You're doing more than enough."

"Agreed," Hawkins chimed in from behind them. "And we're grateful."

Nova turned to give him a wry smile. "But you'd be even more grateful if I stopped interrupting Zhi so he could get back to work."

"We're fine." But Hawkins's calm demeanor was belied by the way he kept checking his watch.

Zhi gave Nova a final squeeze, using his hold to usher her back down into a nearby chair before her legs collapsed out from under her. A moment later, he finished the final flourish on the last sigil. The complex circle at his feet flared a bright neon yellow before fading to a pale glimmer.

"It's ready," he told the wolf, contacting Han to tell him the same.

It took his cousin a few more minutes to get ready on his end. Synchronizing with the ease of two people who'd been working together since childhood, they each triggered the circle at the same time. A drop of his blood, imbued with power, and it luminesced again, this time with a blue-green glow.

As he watched, the lines of the circle separated and began to float above like a three-dimensional rendering that contracted in on itself. The light coalesced into a ball before twisting and spreading out. It flew out of the boat like a high-powered searchlight as it coasted over the terrain.

Nova gasped, leaning forward to peek out of the windows.

He turned back to her with a grin. The glowing threads of the spell should have been invisible to all but the practitioners who cast it, but then Nova was exceptional. "Can you see that?"

She nodded, her eyes glowing in awe. "It's amazing."

Basking in her admiration, he turned to the wolf. "The spell is working." He pointed to the shore, spreading out his fingers. "The two branches of the casting will meet in the middle right over the compound."

The wolves' brows drew together. "But if we're right and they have one or two witches among their number, won't they be able to see it too?"

Zhi lifted a shoulder. "This spell is designed to be visible only to the practitioner who cast it, but Nova's magic is tuned to read such vibrations. The result is that she can detect magic and curses, even in small amounts. That's why she can see it. The likelihood they have someone of a similar caliber on their team is small. But I can't make any guarantees. In any case, I think we have to chance it. It's better to go in knowing what lies ahead."

The wolves were waiting to disembark in inflatable zodiacs with ultra-quiet motors. Some would shift into wolves the moment they hit the shore while others would stay human, using the guns they brought to give their four-legged packmates cover.

Zhi looked back down at the tablet occupying the front whorl of his interlocking circles. Inspired by Nova's use of the device, he'd integrated one into this spell. On the screen was a series of rectangles and squares that represented the buildings of the compound. A translucent swath of pale yellow overlayed them, two acute triangles—the wings of his and Han's spell coming together. They weren't quite interlocking, so Zhi had the captain adjust the heading until they lined up just right.

Sparks in different hues began to flicker in the highlighted section. Blue for shifters, orange for humans. The magic capable would show up in green.

They didn't stabilize right away, continuing to flash on and off like a channel with poor reception. "We have to get closer," he told them.

When they did, he swore. There were way too many green dots.

CHAPTER THIRTY-NINE

Nova bit her lip. She looked up at him, unsuccessfully masking her anxiety. "Can you tell how powerful they are?"

"No." Zhi's face was grim as they examined the small swarms of shifting dots. "The spell only identifies the nature and number of individuals. Not their relative strength."

With greater effort and more ingredients, they could have layered a second spell to the first one to do just that, but there was no time now. "There are still triple the number of humans."

He didn't have to point out that those humans were in charge. It was obvious in the distribution of the signals. The magic capable individuals were separated, a cluster of them milling around in what was either the same large room or suite of rooms with two more near the group of shifters. The blue dots representing the wolves didn't move, indicating they were immobile or sequestered in some way, while the orange dots were swirling all over the place.

Some were stationary across the different buildings. But others were moving in a regular circuit—guards rotating around the property. His money said they would be heavily armed.

A coven would never surround themselves with so many humans by choice. Even the lowliest practitioner considered mundane humans beneath them. However, power and magic did not necessarily go hand in hand. The Seven families were the exception, not the rule. As for the rest of his brethren, there were many mercenary enough to ally with someone they saw as lesser for cash. Whether they stabbed their client in the back afterward was a risk for those foolish enough to play on this field.

"You have to go." He looked up. Nova's green eyes appeared to glow in the reflected luminescence of the spell, brightly enough to appear as if they were lit from within like the wolves they were with.

"This many magic-capable unknowns on the field changes things," she continued. "I know Han is your head of security and more than capable of handling himself. But we have no way of knowing how dangerous these practitioners are. If it's the worst case..."

The wolf alpha was watching him. He would sooner chew off his own arm than ask for help, but he was savvy enough to keep his mouth shut, relying on Nova's softness to give his pack the best chance of success.

"What will happen to you if one of the heart-bonded dies while you're still connected to them?" Zhi asked.

Nova blinked, sucking in a breath as if this hadn't occurred to her. "I don't know. It's never happened before."

Given the strain she was already under, the consequences could be catastrophic. He couldn't risk her this way. "I'll go."

<hr>

ZHI LOOKED DOWN at the winter fatigues he'd borrowed, adjusting the thigh holster holding a Mark 3 tactical knife as they slipped over the black waves. The cold spray coated their clothes and was seeping in because they hadn't been able to source tactical wetsuits fast enough.

That wasn't going to be a problem for the wolves, since most intended on stripping down and shifting before they hit the compound perimeter. Even in human form they were fairly cold tolerant. But Zhi wasn't looking forward to splashing through the icy water on shore and crossing the terrain with wet pants. In this cold it would turn to ice, despite the waterproof combat pants, field shirt, and jacket his people had sourced for him.

One of the larger idiots was eyeballing him, giving him a skeptical look. "Do you have any fighting experience?"

A snort filtered down the open channel from his cousin. Zhi was maintaining an open line with both Han and Nova, who would also be watching through the cameras of several small drones. But Nova was maintaining her silence. She was determined not to distract him or Han.

His cousin's amusement was understandable. Han had been his constant companion in the brutal war-games, trials, and tests his father's diabolical mind had conjured as he was growing up. Not even Jinx escaped unscathed, although his father had been sexist enough to steer her away from any wet work.

Little had Bao known how much his sister enjoyed getting her hands dirty. Han's body count may have been higher, but Jinx was the most bloodthirsty.

"Don't worry about me. I can handle myself."

"Sure about that?" The wolf lifted a bushy supercilious brow as he secreted blades on his own body in special fitted sheaths that wouldn't get in the way once he shifted to his animal form. "It's not too late to ask for a gun."

Only a handful of the wolves were carrying firearms. The plan was to take out their adversaries using stealth. The guns would be a last resort, because once the armed guards were alerted to their presence they would open fire.

He was tempted to whip the blade out with a flourish and use it to carve something creative on the wolf's oversized pecs, but he just flicked a look at the alpha, who gave him an amused smile. "I won't need one," he repeated.

Unlike the incident on the bridge, he wasn't going to hold back this time.

Anyone not a captive shifter was fair game. The knife was on the off chance one of the witches or shifters had enough immunity to his talent to get within striking distance. Neither was likely with Han on the field, but Zhi was almost hopeful one would slip through the net. He didn't mind getting his hands dirty either.

If he had a problem with killing, there was no way he would survive among the Seven. And if the practitioners on site were tied to one of the other Seven, this would be an excellent reminder that house Zheng was no easy mark.

The only problem was Nova's reaction. He didn't want to kill in front of her, even if she had acknowledged the possibility when she had put him on this boat, resting her forehead against his for one poignant moment.

"You do whatever you have to do to come home to me," she'd ordered.

And so he would. It didn't matter to him if the setting was the cabin, the family's eighty-eight room mansion, or a hovel somewhere. Home was anywhere Nova was.

The Kodiak had almost reached the shore. *"How close are you?"* he asked Han. Given the number of opponents, they had to reach the compound concurrently, the timing critical.

"Almost there. ETA two minutes."

"Acknowledged."

When they reached the shore, Zhi slipped into the shallows water as quietly as any of the wolves, getting a surprised glance from the one called Nathan. But Hawkins didn't even blink as he kept pace with the shifters.

Zhi couldn't outrun them. They would always be faster. But they were aiming for stealth, not speed, and in that his training was every bit as good as theirs, if not better.

As agreed, Zhi coordinated the two strike teams through Han so the shifters could maintain radio silence. They flowed over the unforgiving terrain like ghosts, shielded by a thick sound-muffling fog he and Han generated from charms they carried with them.

They were inside the perimeter when all hell broke loose. A shift in his awareness warned him to move just before bullets sliced through the air. Zhi dove behind as small rise.

"What happened?" he asked his cousin.

"One of these total chǔnhuòs ran over a spell trap I had specifically told him

to avoid." Han sounded like he was seconds away from strangling someone.

"Shift and get out there," he sighed, relaying the events to the soldiers pinned down around him.

Hawkins rolled his eyes as if he knew the idiot responsible. "Nate, can you circle around and get behind that observation tower?"

"Don't bother," Zhi said, gathering his magic for a burst, enough for it to leak out of the target's eyes. "I have it." His voice resonated a touch with a preternatural timbre.

From Hawkins's double take, Zhi knew his eyes were luminescing the way they did when he expended a lot of magic.

Ignoring the way the wolves sidled farther from him, Zhi focused on the turret, finding and seizing the mind inside. He didn't let go until after the sniper had jumped out of his crow's nest, giving the man enough time to scream before the panicked sound abruptly cut off with a teeth-rattling thud.

Two more swear-filled cries, one apiece from the gunmen stationed on the building roof, followed soon after. Hawkins scowled as more screams followed. These new ones had a hysterical panic-filled edge few things on this world could cause.

Zhi grinned. Han had entered the field.

"What the hell is that noise?" one of the wolves asked, his face ashen. Zhi knew he wasn't talking about the roars Han's second form made.

"Coins." Zhi couldn't hear the distant but distinctive clink-clink of gold coins hitting the ground, but the shifters could.

The werewolf named Nathan turned to him, his eyes as round as saucers. "What the hell, man?"

Zhi twisted to see Han mid-leap. His massive leaning body was topped with a dragon head, small wings in his back, and a long tail he used to grab his victims.

The small wings beat once before he came down behind two assailants in green camouflage gear. As they watched, he stepped on one man, pinning him down while using his thick muscular tail to grab the other, drawing him to his mouth with that strong muscular tail.

Bright-red light sparked. Han glowed from within, the light

measuring his victim's worth. In a blink the man was gone, and coins clattered to the ground.

Nova was startled enough to break her silence in his head. *"What is he?"* she whispered in his head.

"Han is a Pixiu—a fortune beast," Zhi said aloud for both the shifters and her benefit. "In legends, Pixiu protect Heaven from demons, turning their essence and power into gold. Well, it turns out we all have a little demon in us. The more you have, the less you're worth, and fewer coins fall."

He squinted at the field, ignoring the circle of shocked and stunned expressions. "Not much of a haul here. These guys were bottom feeders. Just stay out of his way. There's no coming back from being turned into spare change."

"Just kidding," he added silently. *"It's never accidental. Han has to will the consumption."*

What he would explain later, when there was time, was that the truly righteous were immune. But the transmogrification was only one aspect of his cousin's might. With the Pixiu's strength and speed, even the righteous would get their ass handed to them in a fight.

A gasp turned his attention to the field where a camouflaged mercenary was unloading an entire four-stack magazine clip at Han. His cousin roared, stepped on the bastard, then continued jumping and stomping on him repeatedly for good measure.

The man became a puddle of bone meal and blood. The Pixiu was a heavy bastard.

"Is he bulletproof?" Nova asked in disbelief.

"Yes," he assured her. The Pixiu's thick hide turned away all high-velocity projectiles. Slower swords and knives were another story.

"Better get out there." Hawkins was staring at the soup-de-merc with a queasy expression, but his voice was its normal steady growl as he waved his men forward. "Or Han won't leave any bad guys for you."

Their stupor broken, they ran sleek and fast like quicksilver streaks of night. Each gave Han a wide berth.

"He won't be able to fit into the door without crushing the walls and compromising the structure," he called after them, broadcasting on a wide

band only their two teams would hear. *"The extraction of your people is still on you."*

Hawkins acknowledged that with a grunt before running to join the fight, faster than normal human could. Saluting his cousin across the field Zhi followed.

ZHI HUNG BACK until after the wolves had flushed the main building and the coven ran out.

Han beat him to the marks, taking out two of the coven with his tail and swipe of his paw. One managed to lob a particularly nasty curse at the Pixiu's flank, but it slid right off.

"Yeah, asshole, he's impervious to those too," he murmured as Han knocked the offender unconscious by slamming his head against the wall two or three times. But he didn't finish them off.

They had tacitly agreed not to execute the witches on sight. Not until they knew who was paying the bills and just how far the bastards had gone.

It wasn't ideal. Zhi preferred to neutralize threats before they became a problem. But in the short time he'd been head of the family, he'd learned it was sometimes expedient to figure out who was connected to who. There was no need to start a war with one of their families when trussing up the offenders and shipping them back to their allies was an option.

Of course, if the shifters decided to execute the idiots, that was their prerogative. The coven had messed with shifter cubs. Zhi wasn't about to get in the pack's way if they decided there was only one suitable punishment. And knowing wolves it wouldn't be quiet or secret. Hawkins would want others in their world to know—targeting his people, especially their young, meant getting your throat torn open with claws and teeth.

He was still thinking about that when an unexpected spell ball narrowly missed his head. Angling his head to the side in a fluid motion borne from years of training, Zhi let it whistle by him. He incapacitated his opponent with a mental blow that would take weeks to heal.

The witch, a tall and thin female, crumpled where she stood. The subsequent bellow of rage and pain caught him off guard.

Just behind the fallen witch was another the size of a monolith. At least six and a half feet tall, the male had to be over three hundred pounds of bulging muscle. And he was hurtling straight at Zhi, screaming in rage, spittle flying from his mouth.

A quick scan for Han showed his cousin was busy up field. *Okay, then.* This was on him—just the way he liked it.

Zhi lobbed another mental strike, scowling when it hit and slid off. The guy kept coming, his mental shields freakishly strong. Maybe more than the shifters'.

He hit him again, hard enough to ring his bell. The guy stumbled but kept his footing, continuing to run at him like a freight train.

"Screw this," he muttered, tensing before taking off like a track star.

A wail in his mind indicated he'd taken Nova by surprise. She had expected him to run *away* from cut-rate Lou Ferrigno, not toward him.

Zhi surprised his opponent too. The human mountain stopped when he was a few yards away, letting Zhi close the distance. Taking a running leap, Zhi's foot connected with the man's thigh. Using the boost to spring up, he climbed the mountain and spun around. Twisting, he enclosed the man's neck—what little there was of it—in a classic jiu jitsu triangle choke.

The behemoth tried to bat him off, but Zhi kept squeezing, all the while hammering with blunt but viciously strong mental strikes. He didn't stop until the mountain began to crumble.

Zhi leapt off as he landed on his knees. Bruised from a lucky hit to ribs, he added a savage fouetté kick to the head to finish him off. The male witch toppled over with a grunt.

He didn't get back up.

All around him the sounds of battle began to fade, the spitting guns falling quiet. That was when he heard the high-pitched tears and cries that couldn't be made by mature mouths.

The wolves had found their young.

CHAPTER FORTY

Zhi patted Han's mane as his cousin preened for the circle of murmuring and yipping children. The initial trauma lingered on their little faces, but it was slowly melting away into acceptance and hope. They had finally been rescued.

"See, he's very nice," Zhi said, scratching behind Han's ear. "He only turns bad guys into gold."

The kids, whose ages appeared from three to sixteen stared, wide-eyed.

Han snorted in his head. *"There's barely enough gold to buy a cup of coffee out here. There's no way these guys were affiliated with a major family. The Seven can afford better."*

Zhi ignored this, focusing on the kids. "You can pet him. He likes it."

"I really do, but only from the babies, so stop stroking me like I'm a damn cat. It's weird from a grown man."

Smirking, Zhi broke off to see a nearby shifter, Nathan, jerk in their direction as the children approached the big cat. The big werewolf looked as if he wanted to intercept the kids. But Hawkins, who was holding the rescued infant, murmured something that checked his progress.

A small blonde girl with messy pigtails toddled over to pat and stroke the Pixiu's velvety coat. "*Kitty*," she cooed, hugging one tree-trunk-sized leg.

As if they'd been waiting for a sign or the chief's tacit permission, the others surged forward, swarming Han.

A little boy in a dirty green vest and ripped jeans tugged on Han's fur. "Are you a person too sometimes?"

"Can you make silver or platinum or is it just gold?" a preteen girl asked.

"Yes and no, it's only gold," Zhi answered for Han. He tapped his temple. "And unless you have telepathy, he can't talk in this form."

He scanned the field to check if all was clear. There were more scattered bunches of coins than actual prisoners, but every one of the bastards had been secured.

Still, the wolves were tense as hell. Although that might have had more to do with the bodies that were being discreetly collected and stacked out of sight of the little ones.

"Why don't you all go out and try to gather all the gold into one big pile," he suggested once that field was corpse-free. "You guys can keep whatever you collect as long you promise to split it evenly among you."

The kids scattered like he'd thrown a firecracker into their midst, the older ones taking the little ones by the hand as they whooped, forgetting their trauma in a burst of joy both macabre and innocent.

At his suggestion, Han took off with a shake of his leonine head to do another circuit around the perimeter.

"That was generous of you," Hawkins muttered as he handed off the baby to one of the female soldiers. "Letting them keep the money."

Zhi shrugged. "We don't need it. Put it toward their college funds."

Those poor kids deserved to get something out of this mess.

They turned as one to watch the impromptu treasure hunt. "I'm not counting wrong, am I?" Zhi asked. "There's more kids here than there should be."

You could have used Hawkins's jaw to smash a geode open. It was that hard and sharp. "Too many and not enough."

Zhi swore under his breath. He knew with that extra sense of his that not all these kids were wolves. There were a couple of cats and something that might have been a juvenile polar bear in the mix.

"How many cubs are you missing?" he asked. The surviving adults were accounted for. The ones who'd made it to the island were still alive, although one needed medical attention—his problems stemming from malnutrition. Their captors had starved him, kept him too weak to help the children.

"Just one," Hawkins said. "Jason. He is the oldest of the kids, seventeen. Myalin, the next oldest over there told me the children were kept together in two cells away from the adults. Every other day or so someone would come for one of them to make them do tests or obstacle courses. Jason kept volunteering to be taken...to spare the others."

Rafe passed a clawed hand over his face. "The last time he didn't come back. That was three days ago. Do you think you can try and scan for him?"

Zhi fought to keep his face impassive. "Aside from the prisoners, there are no other unaccounted minds. And juvenile shifter minds are distinctive. But I'll keep trying."

Casting his mind out, he expanded the geographical search area with every sweep. "I'm pretty sure I'm scanning the whole island. Unless—"

He broke off with a scowl. "The ground is dense but I'm sensing openings beneath the main building. Does the building have a basement?"

Hawkins frowned. "Let's check."

They ran together to the main building. Nathan had taken charge of clearing the rooms. He was the one who showed them the tunnels he'd found in the basement, leading out to a twisting corridor with no light.

"What the hell is this?" Hawkins asked, touching the rough circular walls of the opening.

"Looks like a lava tube," Zhi muttered. He'd visited a park with lava tubes in Oahu. "These are the biggest I've ever seen though."

It was as if the molten rock had been guided by a higher intelligence, one with a very specific purpose—to design a warren of catacombs.

"The lab was upstairs. Why the hell would we be scenting Jason down here?"

"Are you?" Zhi asked, his misgivings intensifying.

"Yeah," Nathan volunteered. "Him and one other, an unknown juvenile female. But the scent trail dies off because we get swamped with sulfur. Somewhere in these lava tube tunnels, there's a gas vent or pools of lava. The smell is strong enough to mess with scent-based tracking."

There was an unspoken request at the end of that sentence.

"The unknown female is younger than Jason," Hawkins added when Zhi didn't run into the cave. "Prepubescent—she doesn't have that reek of teen hormones. No scent of hormones at all. Just a little zing that might mean magic. We can't always tell when they're very young, but there might be a prepubescent witch somewhere in there with Jason."

"That so?" Scanning, Zhi went in a few hundred yards.

"Shit," he said, turning around "It appears the walls are saturated with silica and other minerals. I may not pick up a mind until I'm on top of them."

Nova stirred in his mind. *"We have to go down there for them. Wait for me, Zhi!"*

He took a deep breath, holding up a finger when Hawkins began to speak. *"Nova, I want you to stay put."*

"If the missing girl is a witch, my ability can find her."

He shook his head. *"You haven't seen this place. Not to mention I'm one of the strongest telepaths around—if I can't find them, maybe they're not here. We're just guessing that they are. Those two could have been taken off the island days ago. We have no way of knowing."*

"Together, Zhi." Her voice held a plaintive note now. *"We have to at least try, and we have the best chance as a team..."*

"Fine," he growled under his breath. He turned to the alpha, who was wearing an amused expression and shrugged. "This does not bode well for my ability to win arguments against my future wife."

The damn wolf started laughing.

CHAPTER FORTY-ONE

It took Nova and her lupine escort almost half an hour to get to them. When she did, she threw her arms around him, making him feel like a conquering hero. That lasted two whole minutes, which was when she began to remove her shoes.

"What the devil are you doing?" he asked.

She gestured to the dark mouth of the tunnel. "If there's crusted over lava down there, this is the safest way to cross. You can detect the heat better without shoes. If it gets too hot, we go back or find another way."

Zhi looked ready to pull his hair out. "Put those back on," he snapped, before stroking her cheek in apology. He undid his laces and toed off his boots. "Only one of us needs to go barefoot, and it's not going to be you."

"Don't bother," Hawkins said, beginning to take his own shoes off. "I'll come with you."

"That's not—"

"I said I'm coming," the alpha growled, throwing a boot aside. "And *I'll* take the lead, so you may as well cover those delicate tootsies back up. Of all of us, I'm willing to bet I'm the only one who runs around barefoot on a daily basis."

"He's got us there," Nova said, taking his hand.

Shaking his head, Zhi shoved his foot back into his boot, getting up to press her to the side of the tunnel, standing between her and the alpha when the wolf squeezed past them. "Let's go."

One of the shifters brought them a spool of string he'd dug up from somewhere. They tied the free end to a desk and began to move down the lava tube, the black enveloping mere meters from the threshold.

THIS WAS the kind of dark that used to visit her in her dreams, the ones where she was still small and alone in her room at Greenfield.

Sensing her distress, Zhi squeezed her hand as they trailed Rafe Hawkins down into the suffocating blackness.

"This is not Greenfield," he said. *"But it might be worse. Stay behind me."*

"I will," she promised, part of her still amazed he'd let her come down here, because this had to be the route to Hell. Hot, dark, the smell of sulfur. All it was missing was an ominous red flow at the end of the tunnel. But the twists and turns of the lava-formed channel didn't allow for even a glimmer of light, which was why they were relying on old-fashioned flashlights.

Even magic light did not work down here. Zhi had lit several spell balls designed to illuminate their surroundings. These were doused immediately, as if magic couldn't live here. Except in people. Or in this case a little girl and a teenage boy.

Nova couldn't feel the shifter boy, perhaps because his magic was too integrated to his body. In this atmosphere she might only be able to feel him if he was changing from one form to another. At least that was what she kept telling herself. She didn't want to believe him dead.

The little girl was another story. She was the pale beacon Nova clung to. Her light was smothered, the tiny pulse she caught here and there difficult to pinpoint, but it *was* present.

Nova did her best to pinpoint its direction, but this subterranean space was a warren with no way to get to it without walking a twisted and circuitous path.

Zhi also felt the echo of an immature mind, but it was faint and haphazard, as if the child's thought waves were bouncing off these strange walls from a long way away. But in her opinion that shouldn't have diminished their power. There was something about these damn tunnels, a suppressive shroud they had to actively push through.

They came to a branch, the sense of open space leading in two different directions. Nova waited for the alpha to turn to raise her arms and point left. "I think I feel something going this way."

The sound of her voice didn't fade in the normal way. It died off suddenly, abruptly smothered as if it'd been eaten.

"Well, that's unnerving." Even their voices were subject to the freakish oppression.

Zhi tugged her a little closer. "Agreed. But if anything comes for you out of this dark, it will have to go through me. Just stay behind me."

Warmed by the proof of his concern, she felt almost buoyant as they continued further down the rabbit hole. But the feeling didn't last long.

The heat kept accumulating like a tide rising. As long as they could breathe, they would keep going. And if they couldn't, they'd come back with special equipment.

"My ears are starting to clog." Hawkins was shouting now, but it was a lot fainter than it should have been. "Are yours?"

"No, but it's more work to breathe." Zhi broadcast that into her mind as he said it aloud, a precaution to losing the ability to hear each other in this hungry place.

"How could they send children down here? How?" Nova was furious. There was no rational reason, no explicable purpose other than torture to send anyone into this pit.

"I have no idea." Zhi's voice was grim in her head. *"But they didn't get away with it."*

He was right of course. That big pile of coins the children had collected was testament to that.

She'd seen it on the way in, had been struck by the sheer absurdity of it all that she'd stopped and stared until Han had snuck up on her, blowing his hot breath on the back of her neck. Startled, she had turned only to find herself eye level with his smug, monster-sized smile.

Her heart had done a loop-de-loop in her chest before she was able to remember that this was her friend, and he was messing with her. Aware that she had to set an example for the children, she stopped short before she flipped him off, settling for wagging her finger at him in a warning scold.

She would have felt better if Han had been able to accompany them, but he'd only be able to do so if he shifted back. He couldn't go back and forth as easily as the wolves, so it made sense for him to stay a Pixiu. That fearsome form was a very effective deterrent to the prisoners. More than one had wet themselves when he bent over and breathed on them, especially after some of the wolves pelted them with coins.

Nova didn't condone terrorizing anyone under normal circumstances, but she didn't mind turning the tables on these kidnappers, not after what they had done.

She didn't know if any of the bad guys would make it off the island alive, but after seeing these tunnels, felt the way they wanted to consume her, she would not have a problem with that.

And just like that it was easier to pump her chest in and out as if a weight had been lifted. Nova knew it was her anger pushing back at whatever force was working in these caves, but it also made her wonder. Perhaps it was innocence that could not survive down here.

Spurred by that, she kept straining for those elusive hints of magic. Turn by turn, they got closer until Zhi could pick up two minds.

"I can't identify the second mind, so it might not be your boy," he warned the alpha.

They realized why he couldn't be certain when the stark white beam of his flashlight landed on an arm lying very still on the floor of the tunnel. The boy's mind was compromised, barely hanging on.

Rafe swore. "Jason!"

Tossing their torches to Nova, he and Zhi ran to the body half-buried in a pile of shiny black boulders. They began to toss them away, revealing the form of a lanky teen.

Keeping one flashlight on them, Nova swept the space with the other one. The boy couldn't have been alone. She could feel—*there.*

Swinging one of the flashlights to the right, she illuminated a pair of wide green eyes set in a pale face. This was surrounded by a cloud of tangled brown hair that was so pale it looked tan.

The little girl couldn't have been more than five or six. Dressed in a dirty t-shirt and shorts, she sat huddled against the wall six or seven meters down from the boy.

"Zhi, it's her."

Shoving the last heavy boulder away, Zhi straightened.

"Do you have him?" he asked the alpha. The boy was free of the rubble but still not moving. Quickly checking for broken bones, the alpha hauled the boy up. He was too tall for a fireman's carry, so the alpha slung one of Jason's arms over his shoulders.

"Should you move him?" Nova asked.

"Wolves are tough. At this age they heal up fast since they break bones more often. Go get the girl."

Handing Zhi one of the torches, she crouched in front of the child, who shied away, terror in her clear, peridot eyes.

Heart aching in sympathy, she knelt. "Hi, I'm Nova. What's your name?"

The little one didn't respond. She stared at them vacantly as if she didn't think they were real.

"I came with friends of Jason's," Nova continued, inching closer. "All the bad guys have been taken care of. We're going to leave this place together."

The child finally stirred. She raised her little hand tentatively.

"Don't let her touch you," Zhi warned, pulling her back.

Stricken, Nova twisted to look at him.

His face was set, a carefully blank mask that concealed his rage. He was beyond furious with the people who had done this. Had he been able to telepath outside these walls, she strongly suspected those last remaining captives wouldn't be breathing by the time they reached the surface.

Zhi crouched beside her and held out his arms to the little girl, murmuring in a soothing tone. But the child jerked away, flattening herself against the rough wall.

A mix of Russian and Chinese swear words filled her head. Whoever hurt this child had been male.

Her pulse thickened with urgency. *"How do we do this? We have to get out of here."*

Jason could be severely injured. Shifters could take a lot of damage, but judging from the fallen stones hundreds of pounds of rock had fallen on him. He could be bleeding internally, have fractures that Rafe's quick check missed.

"Sweetie, I can't touch you, but Zhi is my best friend in the world, and you can trust him. Please come with us."

The child looked at Zhi's offered hand like it was a snake. Rafe offered to switch, to hand Jason to Zhi, but the little girl reacted worse to him.

Nova's eyes were burning. She was holding back her tears through vicious effort. The little girl would have taken her hand. She knew that as clearly as she knew Zhi loved her. But Nova couldn't offer this child what she needed.

Zhi's hand came down on her shoulder. "I'll shield you."

Surreptitiously wiping away a tear she turned to frown at Zhi. "What?"

"I can try and shield you."

"How?"

"Like the touch in the car but everywhere," he said in her head, not wanting to relate something so personal before the alpha's sharp ears. "There's still a risk to you, but I can layer it on thick. It should protect you long enough to get out of here."

Not willing to waste another second, she waved him on. His grip on her tightened, but he hesitated.

"Magic makes exception for mates," she said urging him on. "We have to believe that your magic won't hurt me no matter how you choose to use it."

There was a short pause as he considered that, then suddenly Zhi's magic inundated her, the wave starting at his hand and running to the crown of her head and the tips of her toes simultaneously.

It was as if a blanket had been thrown over her. She could still see, but her vision was hazy, her hearing muffled.

Heart racing, she reached out to the little girl. The last time she had touched anyone but Zhi, she'd ended up in the hospital, but there was no choice. "Come on, sweetie. It's time to leave this terrible place."

A very long hesitation. "I have a friend who turns into a lion as big as an elephant," Nova added. "He's outside. Would you like to meet him?"

A tiny damp hand reached for her gloved one. She barely felt the contact. Then skinny arms wrapped around her neck. There was a buzz like an electric shock, but it dissipated as her vision faded more. Zhi was pumping so much magic over her she could taste it on her tongue.

"It's okay. I'm okay," she said, trying to reassure him as she picked up the little girl and tried to walk, following Rafe as he turned back the way they came with his charge. But it was trying to move through molasses. Nevertheless, she kept going. She wasn't about to leave the little girl or put her down.

Zhi's willpower lasted about a minute before he swept her up in his arms, the child in hers. Murmuring soothing words, she did her best to calm and comfort her small charge, trying to get her to respond. But the little girl remained mute, her eyes scrunched tight as they made their way out of the maze.

With her senses dampened, she had no way of knowing how close they were to exiting the tunnels until the fluorescent lights blazed around them.

Her impressions were hazy after that. A female shifter came to take the little girl, letting Zhi release her, but she wasn't able to stand on her own. Even after Zhi withdrew his magic, she couldn't keep her body from shutting down, too drained.

The last thing she remembered was a tiny figure swathed in a foil blanket standing on her tiptoes to pet a creature of legend logic said shouldn't exist.

CHAPTER FORTY-TWO

Nova woke in the crowded bunk area of the shipping boat. Zhi was sitting in the bunk opposite hers, his hands templed under his chin as he watched her sleep.

"Hey." He straightened when she shifted to look at him, the tight line of his shoulders easing.

Nova blinked to clear the cobwebs from her mind, pushing up on her elbows. "Hi."

"Before you ask, the little girl is fine. Jason, the shifter boy is still out, but his vitals are steady. Most of the kids are in the other ship, but those two are here with Hawkins. Han is watching over the witch."

"I'm glad your shielding game is so on point. Thank you for letting me carry her."

"You're welcome. Also, it's not happening again. Not until we work on some things. But I'm grateful nonetheless."

He could have forced the issue and insisted on carrying out the girl himself. Traumatizing her was secondary to saving her. But he hadn't done that and instead took the child's feelings into consideration, despite the cost. And in that hellish place, the price could have been very high indeed.

"What the hell was up with those weird-ass tunnels?"

Zhi snickered, his shoulders shaking. But there was a brittleness to his expression. He had let her walk into danger. Even though everything had turned out well, it would take him a long time to forgive himself.

"I have no clue. They are not man-made. Or even witch made."

She shifted her legs over the edge to sit opposite him. "Then it's a naturally evil place, one affiliated with the dark side?"

A hint of amusement, this one genuine flickered across his face. "Or a place of power that has been twisted intentionally."

Nova's stomach swirled unpleasantly imagining the effort such a transformation had required. If that theory was correct, what had happened there to make such a place so hungry and desperate?

"I'm ordering every tunnel opening dynamited shut. We'll use C4 if we have to. I'd nuke the entire island if it wasn't bad for the environment."

She shuddered, grateful Zhi had the power to back that statement up. If he said it would be done, it would happen. "Good. I still don't understand why they would force the children to go in there. If they wanted to kill them, they had more effective means."

"Agreed. Shifter children are stronger and faster than human children, but they are still children."

"Did the kids think the tunnels were a way to escape?" she asked. Had they gone in hoping to leave and gotten turned around, not noticing the oppressive atmosphere because of their own fear?

"No. They were forced to go in. Jason hasn't regained consciousness, and the little witch isn't speaking yet, but a few of the older kids told Hawkins they have been down there too, although not as deep. It was a test."

He leaned against the bunk support, shaking his head. "We caught them by surprise, else they would have burned their records, but the wolves found detailed files. This group's aim was to take children with abilities. Shifters...witches—it didn't matter. The plan was to raise and educate them to suit their purposes. It was meant to be their own private pool of super-soldiers. Enhanced abilities and strength without the black-budget-funded science labs. What's more, this operation is decades old."

Nova's lips parted, the air freezing in her lungs. "*What?*"

Zhi's face was so remote and emotionless you would have thought he was unaffected—if you missed the vein throbbing at his temple. "This is a government-sanctioned trafficking ring. One so secret I doubt more than half a dozen politicians and generals know about it, excluding the soldiers and mercenaries they hire to do the kidnapping and training."

Bile rose in her throat. "*Our* government did this?"

He lifted an eyebrow. "Are you surprised?"

"I suppose I shouldn't be." Nova had seen many terrible things. It was unavoidable when you handled weapons of war. But this was so... inhuman.

"Jason and the girl witch weren't supposed to die in the tunnels. Our attack just interrupted their latest run through it. As I said, some of the other older kids did the 'tunnel trial' too," he said, putting air quotes around the words. "Apparently Jason would volunteer to go down into the tunnels so the smaller kids wouldn't have to. The trainers let him because they thought it meant they would have an operative to field that much sooner."

"He's a hero," she said softly.

Zhi nodded. "His father was the alpha of the first pack targeted. He died trying to stop the first kidnapping. Those protective instincts must be heritable. But the tunnels were just one of many trials and tests they forced on the children. You didn't see it because you were rushed inside, but the kids were housed in a secured dormitory, not cells. There was a classroom where they went to learn everyday subjects like reading and math as well as things like tactics and military strategy, albeit in a rudimentary way."

It made sense in an awful way. "Because ignorant soldiers wouldn't have done them much good. But education or not they also made a little girl go into those hellish tunnels. She's just a baby!"

"A baby with strong magic. They must have assumed she would figure out a way through based purely on her potential." He leaned forward, bracing himself on his forearms. "She may have a family looking for her. We'll have to go through the records, see what we can find of her background."

Except there was another possibility, a terrible one. "That's assuming they weren't killed when they took her."

"Maybe, maybe not," Zhi said. "Too many bodies means a lot more questions asked by the local authorities. They would have wanted to keep things quiet."

She thought about that. "What happened to the other adults who were with the children during the kidnapping?"

"The ones who fought back were killed. The rest saw the writing on the wall. They were allowed to stay with the children, to take care of them. They slept in the same dormitory, did all the cooking and cleaning. Some of the soldiers must have done the teaching. That was the purpose of the witches on site too. They were instructing them how to use their magic for infiltration and defense. Or they were working toward that anyway."

Nova rose, crossed the narrow space between the bunks, and sat next to him, pressing against his side. She leaned into him as his arm wrapped around her. They stayed like that for a long moment, taking comfort in each other's warmth.

"Will you help the wolves deal with the politicians and military ringleaders in charge?"

"If they need it." He ran his fingers through her hair, pressing a kiss to her temple. "But whoever was calling the shots for this round of kidnappings didn't do it with all the facts. They overplayed their hand taking so many at once. Thanks to the coalition the shifters formed decades ago, if you hit one pack they *all* come after you."

Well, that was certainly comforting news. "What about the little girl?"

"Han is going through the records the wolves confiscated, but so far there's nothing on her. None of the survivors know where she came from. She just appeared one day, was brought in alone."

"Have you done a *sanguis narrabo* against the surviving witches to eliminate them as her parents?" she asked.

Literally called "blood will tell," the spell compared two or more samples—ideally drops of blood, or in a pinch a bit of hair, to determine relatedness. It was the practitioner's version of a DNA test, only it was instant.

The idea that one of the enemy witches was the child's parent was repugnant, but Nova had seen too much ugliness in the world to give them the benefit of the doubt. The question needed to be asked.

She was relieved when Zhi shook his head. "No matches. But Han has a library of major and minor players to compare to. He'll take some hair and go straight home, starting with the other Seven."

Her eyes widened. She thought she had been shocked before, but it was nothing compared to this. "You have exemplars from the other families?"

Zhi put his finger to his lips and made a shushing sound. "Let's just say we have a better network for finding the girl's family than the wolves. She'll be coming back with us. But Han and I agree it may be a bad idea to separate her from the other kids too soon. We're going to give her a couple of days with them in Hawkins's territory. Maybe a week."

"That's a good idea. We don't want to traumatize her any more than she has been."

He nudged her. "I'm sorry we're not going home straight away. I know you must be devastated that we won't be seeing my mother for days yet."

Nova blinked then burst into laughter.

Wrapping his arm around her, Zhi started laughing too. They were still laughing about it when Han found them, telling them they were about to dock in Alaska, where they would be guests of the Hawkins pack.

CHAPTER FORTY-THREE

Zhi ran his hand over the polished bridle joint on the balcony, his nose wrinkling in annoyance. Like the rest of Rafe Hawkins's house, the structure was solid, the craftsmanship obvious in every expertly joined beam.

Ever since Hawkins had told them he'd built the whole damn thing by himself, Zhi had been looking for a flaw. Annoyingly enough he hadn't really found one—unless you counted the size of the windows. They were smaller than he was used to, but he couldn't really fault those either. The choice was practical. It was so cold up here that even double-paned windows bled too much heat.

Even the view was choice. The pristine ocean of snow-dusted pines and rugged mountains was framed to perfection.

"*You up?*" Han asked in his head.

"It's only an hour time difference," he replied testily. It was almost ten.

"*What crawled up your butt?*" Han snorted. "*Let me guess, the alpha is being his ruggedly charming self around your girl, and it's getting on your nerves.*"

"*I don't have nerves. I have absolutely no problem with Hawkins,*" Zhi said. "*I'm just eager to get home.*"

Han was generous enough to ignore the obvious lie. *"Does that look likely anytime soon?"*

"The little girl is still non-verbal, but she's bonding with Nova. I think we'll be able to leave soon. A day or two at most."

The child was doing loads better, eating and interacting more and more every time he saw her. Zhi expected her to start talking any day now.

"You're not going to believe which family came up as a match."

There was a push, and Zhi reached out to catch the mental image his cousin had sent him. He whistled, instantly recognizing the man it identified, Gerald, head of the Burgess family. One of the Seven.

In his younger days, Gerald had been known to be an arrogant viper, quick to anger and difficult to defeat. He was old now, but that didn't mean his bite was any less dangerous.

"What's the relationship?"

"Most likely a great-granddaughter or grand-niece. Hard to say for sure because there's no alert or evidence that the family is out looking—not that they would let something like that leak."

No, they wouldn't. Amber alerts were a human thing. Putting out an alert like that for one of their children was slapping a target on their back. Small and full of magic, the children of the Seven were prey in a world full of predators.

"We should reach out sooner rather than later."

"I'll do it now," Zhi said, twisting when Nova joined him on the porch.

He bid Han goodbye and turned to her with a speculative look at her timing. "Did you know I was talking to Han?"

He'd never thought to ask if that buzzing sensation she experienced extended to his telepathic communication with others.

But she shook her head, wrapping her Angora-clad arms around his back. "I just couldn't wait to see you," she said, disarming him in two seconds flat.

Pressing her arms tighter against him for a second, he soon turned the tables, spinning her until she was wrapped in his arms. "We still don't have a name for the little witch, but we traced her back to the Burgess clan."

He could feel her surprise along their private connection. "So she *is* part of the Seven?"

He lifted a shoulder. "It's not all that surprising given her strength. My guess is she's illegitimate and unrecognized. The head of the family probably doesn't know about her, or she wouldn't be untrained."

When you were part of the Seven, even the illegitimate children were part of the fold. Letting a child with that kind of power in their blood run around without training was a recipe for disaster, a scenario to be avoided at all costs.

Nova didn't look happy. "I've never heard anything bad about the Burgess clan, but are you sure informing Gerald Burgess is the best thing for her? Shouldn't we try to find her mother?"

He suppressed a wince. He trusted her feelings for him, but this might be the moment where Nova learned what it truly meant to be a family head.

"I'm afraid that it's not permissible for me to go searching for the mother without informing Gerald. The only exception might be if we had proof the child would be endangered by letting the family know, which we don't have."

She nodded, her dismay clear. "I understand. It's a political issue."

He kissed her cheek, grateful she understood the realities of his life. She didn't have to like them. Neither did he. But in this case, he didn't foresee a bad end. "Don't worry. Gerald isn't the type to allow mistreatment of a child. She'll be safe in his care. He'll also be able to dig into his clan members' lives with impunity. He'll find her parents."

He reached into his pocket for his cell phone. "I was about to call him. Want to sit in?"

"Actually, I thought I'd go down and grab a bite." Her stomach rumbled as if on cue.

His grin was slow and edged in a hunger that never went away. "We did work up an appetite last night."

Nova blushed as red as her hair, caught in the same memories he was.

"Hawkins left about an hour ago, so the coast is clear downstairs."

"Okay." She hesitated. "Did you know he was a carpenter before we met him?"

"Nope." He flipped through his contacts, searching for a number he'd found in his father's phone after his death. He'd recorded it in his own but had never used it. "Why do you ask?"

"Well, it turns out he didn't just build the house. He made all the furniture."

Zhi raised a brow. The furniture in the cabin was all handmade and unique, with flairs reminiscent of both the Craftsman and Mission schools of design. "Really? I complimented him on the pieces, and he didn't say a word."

"I think he's modest."

Zhi snorted. "Sure, he is."

"He sells his pieces online. I think I'd like to order a few, maybe introduce them to some of my former clients."

Zhi rose and took her hand, pressing his lips to the center of her palm, which deepened the color in her cheeks further. Oh, to love a redhead... "He's lucky to have met you. But I'm even more lucky... because I met you first."

Nova's pleasure was like a sunburst in his mind. She wrapped her arms around him, kissing and escaping before he could drag her back to bed.

Sighing, Zhi let her go. "Next time," he promised himself. He and Nova were going to marry and take a proper honeymoon—at least a month in the cabin by themselves.

He checked the time in the U.K., mentally bracing himself for the potentially difficult call ahead.

CHAPTER FORTY-FOUR

Nova adjusted her gloves, making sure they were secure before bending over to stroke the mirror-like satin finish of the dining room table. Made from large slabs of whorled wood that must have come from a massive walnut burl, the table was seamlessly fitted with other pieces of darker wood wherever the cancerous growth had left a gap.

The result was a rectangular table large enough to seat a dozen people comfortably. It was a work of art that Rafe could have sold for a hundred thousand dollars to the right buyer, minimum.

She walked around it, touching the chairs with a devil-may-care abandon she would not have allowed herself before meeting Zhi. But the events of these last few weeks had her reevaluating her strengths and her weaknesses.

Until Zhi, she had never touched a human being without pain. Now she had not only been close to him but she'd also held a little girl in her arms, something she had never thought possible.

Nova would never forget the sensation of holding that warm little body, giving comfort. *She* had done that. Well, with Zhi's help. But even with her senses muffled by his magic it had been one of the most poignant experiences of her life.

What if Elizaveta was right? What if her magic was more malleable than she believed? What would happen if she stopped trying to protect herself constantly and began to try and manipulate it? If she could replicate what Zhi did, or better still figure out a way to draw her magic deeper into herself perhaps, she could get to the point where her magic didn't coat her skin. Then she wouldn't be a prisoner of her talent.

What if Zhi wasn't the exception to the rule? What if he had merely been showing her the way?

Nova was still lost in these thoughts, trying to think of how to begin when there was a knock at the door. She opened it with difficulty—her silk gloves offered the most protection, but she had a hell of a time gripping things. It was worth it when she did.

"Jason! I had no idea you were out of the hospital."

The teenager's head drew back in confusion. A full head taller than her, Jason was still pale and skinnier than he'd been in the tunnel. His muscles were like jerky stretched over bone. If she knew how to cook, she would have offered to fix him a meal.

"Uh, hi." He scratched his head looking as seventeen as a seventeen year old could look. "I was looking for Rafe."

"He's not here but should be back soon." She grinned at him and stepped back to open the door wider. "Come on in. I'm Nova."

THE PHONE RANG seven times before the person on the other end deigned to answer. Rolling his eyes at the evidence of such overt superstition Zhi didn't waste any time getting down to business. "Gerald Burgess?"

A beat of silence. "Who is this? How did you get this number?"

"This is Zhi Zheng."

A longer pause. "I see."

Tellingly, Gerald did not repeat his questions. Though he didn't socialize or even leave his Somerset estate these days, the other man knew exactly who Zhi was.

"I have recently come across a young witch of your bloodline in unfortunate circumstances."

"How unfortunate?" There was an implication that Zhi might be behind it.

Zhi ignored the implied insult. These were extenuating circumstances. "She was liberated from a government-run facility on one of the Aleutian Islands, along with over a dozen juvenile shifters. She was the only witch. Her captors have been...dealt with."

The pack had taken charge of the prisoners. Zhi hadn't asked what was being done with them. They were not his problem. He proceeded to describe the girl, including the fact that she hadn't really spoken since her rescue.

When he got to her height and approximate age, Gerald made a small noise, as if he was smacking his lips. "I'm not missing an heir of that description."

Interesting. But in this case the evidence was overwhelming. "The *sanguis narrabo* does not lie."

He could almost hear Gerald thinking. "How do I know this isn't some kind of ruse-an attempt to draw me out? Or are you hoping to curry favor?"

Zhi snorted. "House Zheng does not require any favors at this time. Nor am I interested in engaging in pointless hostilities. I have my own empire to run. So, consider this what it is—a courtesy from one family head to another. The girl we found was on her own. Her fellow prisoners knew nothing about her. She is strong but untrained, and the spell indicates she is a direct descendent of yours.

"So you didn't know about her before. Now you do. Your grandniece or granddaughter—whichever she ends up being—would benefit from your family's resources and education."

Gerald grunted, the rough sound managing to convey his skepticism. "And what will you want in return? I heard you are looking for a bride. Are you going to demand the hand of one of my granddaughters in return?"

The words were edged in condescension, but Zhi smiled, suddenly certain that despite his bluster Gerald would welcome such an outcome.

Gerald's mind was a steel trap, and he was hale and hearty for someone his age, but the man was solidly in his mid-eighties. And it was a poorly kept secret that he found his children disappointing. Since Zhi had heard little of them, he assumed that to be the case. But it was also no secret that he had higher hopes for his grandchildren. Han had several of them on his watch list.

"You've been misinformed. I have already found my bride-to-be, and she has asked, that whatever your relationship to the child, you seek out her parent or parents without delay. The girl hasn't spoken, so we know very little aside from the general location she was taken—a suburb of the city of Escondido in southern California. Does that ring any bells?"

"No."

The answer was short, but Zhi knew it for a lie. Gerald had some idea of the child's origins and wasn't about to share it. Hardly surprising. Zhi wouldn't air his family's dirty laundry either.

"Do you agree to that stipulation?"

"Which one?" Gerald's attention was elsewhere, likely contemplating which child had sired the girl.

He rolled his eyes. "The one where you find the kid's mom."

Gerald would have known if one of his granddaughter's had fallen pregnant. It was far more likely the girl belonged to one of his sons, who had a history of siring children out of wedlock.

"Yes, obviously the child will need her mother," Gerald said distantly. "If she's still alive."

"I hope so. For her sake," he said before beginning to nail down arrangements for the exchange.

CHAPTER FORTY-FIVE

Despite her inroads with the young witch, Nova had no experience with kids. A teenager was a completely foreign creature.

Jason had accepted her invitation to wait for Rafe inside, but then he just stood there looking around as if he'd never seen the place.

Because he hasn't. Rafe had said something in the tunnel. Jason was the son of the alpha who died, the first pack to be attacked. This was not his home pack. His father had died trying to prevent his kidnapping, and when he was finally rescued from that ordeal he'd been taken out of his own territory to recover in an unfamiliar environment.

Heart aching for the boy, she tried to engage him in small talk. Her first impulse was to feed him. Weren't boys this age supposed to have bottomless stomachs? That was what every movie and TV show that touched on the subject had taught her, but Jason didn't seem interested in food.

Nevertheless, she tried again. "I'm a terrible cook, but I can fix a decent omelet now. Well, an above-average omelet," she tacked on honestly.

"I'm okay," the boy mumbled, his eyes on everything but her.

"All right." Nova rubbed her fingertips together, wondering what else she should do.

The boy didn't know Rafe any better than he knew her, she reminded herself. It wouldn't be the same, coming from a witch and not a werewolf, but she could try to comfort him.

"I, um, I was sorry to hear about your father."

Jason's head jerked, his eyes fixing on her, a flicker of wolf-yellow coming and going so fast she could almost imagine she hadn't seen it. But there was no mistaking the way he was staring. It made the small hairs on the back of her neck stand on end.

Nova took an inadvertent step back. The boy's eyes remained their normal brown shade, one so dark it was hard to distinguish his pupils. But that wasn't the disturbing part about them.

No, that was how empty they were.

She was already running when he lunged for her.

CHAPTER FORTY-SIX

Zhi hung up with Gerald and decided to wash up before joining Nova downstairs.

It had nothing to do with the fact she'd showered off the scent of their lovemaking and he hadn't. Because who the hell cared that their host had a sensitive nose or that he lived alone in this large family-sized home? It was because Zhi liked to smell good for Nova. And hygiene was important. That was all.

Stripping to the waist, he turned on the shower. It was just starting to get warm when he heard a thump. It was followed by a crash of something heavy. A pulse of fear shot through him, and he bolted to the door.

Because the panic wasn't his.

NOVA DIDN'T KNOW if she was screaming aloud or in her head. Either way, it didn't matter. Zhi would have heard her.

But the shifter boy was so fast. Despite the fact he must have just left the hospital or healer's home, Jason moved like a predator approaching his peak. And despite the fact she sometimes ran for her health, Nova couldn't match his speed.

Zhi would never reach her before Jason caught her.

She tried to evade him, keeping furniture between them, grabbing anything she could to throw at him, but he didn't stop. Nova pounded into the kitchen, thinking to go for a knife to defend herself, but there wasn't enough time.

The boy knocked a chair over, inadvertently pushing it in front of him. Desperately to keep him away, she grabbed the back of it, hoisting it up and holding him at bay the way a lion tamer would when faced with a big cat intent on eating them.

The world slowed down as Jason effortlessly yanked the chair away. Then his bare hands were reaching for her.

Those red, gangly hands were all she could see. The body and head behind them were a blur.

"It shouldn't be you who hurts when someone touches you. It's everyone else who should fucking seize up and convulse as punishment for having the balls, the sheer effrontery, to touch the divine."

For a split second, she thought Zhi was speaking to her, but the voice in her head was a memory.

For the first time in her life, Nova got mad. Really mad. *Furious.*

Knocking Jason's hands out of her way, she grabbed his face and *pushed.* All her anger, all her frustration, and all her magic flowed out of her hands. Because of the gall of this kid. How dare he come here and try to hurt her?

Nova was no longer just a useful employee. She had a life now. A partner. She was valued for more than her skills and her magic. She had been seen and was *loved.*

No one was going to take that from her.

CHAPTER FORTY-SEVEN

Zhi ran down the stairs so fast he lost his footing at the landing and crashed into the wall. Swearing, he righted himself, jumping over the railing and running toward the blazing star that was Nova's mind. He was in time to see the wolf boy Jason lunge at her.

Nova tried to hold him off with a chair, but he knocked it away.

The agony of failure exploded in his chest. He was too far. The boy was seconds away from touching Nova's arms, looming over her like a praying mantis. If Zhi struck out, hammering the kid unconscious with his telepathy, his body would fall on her.

A silent scream tore through his mind and his heart. It was everywhere.

Nova was dying. She was crying out for him.

And then the kid jolted, his body spasming and jerking as if he was holding a downed power cable. That was when Zhi realized Nova was still on her feet. The shout had been *him*, yelling on both the physical and mental planes.

He reached the kid and yanked him away from Nova, throwing him so far he sailed clear over that shiny wooden dining table she was so in love with.

Nova was on her feet staring at him with her mouth open. She looked as shocked as he felt.

"You're okay!" He clutched her to him, his hands running over her body over and over in disbelief. But the kid had laid hands on her. Zhi had seen it with his own eyes. But here she was, hugging him back.

"Oh God, *Zhi*." She broke off and tugged him over to the body, her hand refusing to let go of his. "Is he dead?"

She bent as if to check if he was breathing, but Zhi blocked her. "What the hell happened?"

Right then the kid was his lowest priority.

A snarl. "That's what I want to know."

Zhi spun to find him Rafe staring at them, claws out—eyes amber-yellow. It wasn't the alpha in the room with them. It was the wolf. And he wasn't alone.

CHAPTER FORTY-EIGHT

There was a very tense moment when Zhi seriously thought he was going to have to liquefy the alpha's brains. Especially when the room filled with shifters who'd been alerted by his mental shout.

Fortunately for everyone, Nova had earned the benefit of the doubt from these people, enough for them not to be attacked straight-away when she related her startling report.

"I don't understand why he would attack you," Nathan said after the boy had been taken away by an ambulance.

They were sitting at Nova's favorite table with him, Hawkins, and a few others.

"I have no idea." Nova appeared calm, but her hands were shaking, spilling the tea Hawkins had made her after he calmed down. He helped her steady it long enough to sip, before setting it down on a coaster. Nova wouldn't forgive herself if she damaged the table.

"He came to see Rafe. I offered to fix him something to eat and then he just went blank." She waved a gloved hand over her eyes. "There was just nothing there. The next thing I knew, he was leaping at me."

She shuddered. Zhi pulled her tight against him, offering silent comfort while managing to broadcast his hostile intentions should the group turn on her.

"I avoided him as long as I could, but he was so fast. Then he was touching me and I...I pushed."

Nathan frowned. "With your hands?"

Nova shook her head. "I remembered something Zhi told me recently. That I shouldn't be the one who was hurt if someone touched me. He said it should be the other way around."

"I believe I told you no one was worthy enough to touch you," Zhi told her privately. *"I'm simply grateful you make an exception for me."*

She gave him a wan smile, but it faded quickly. "I didn't mean to hurt him," she said, turning to the shifters. "But I couldn't allow him to touch me. So, I pushed my magic out, away from me."

She twisted in her seat, looking down at the spot on the floor where the boy had fallen as if she could still see him there, jerking as if he was having an epileptic fit. "It was instinct. I swear I didn't know it would do that to him."

Rafe rubbed a hand over his face. He had aged five years in the last hour and a half. "I believe you. I just don't get why Jason did that. I spoke to him before they released him from the hospital last night. He was shaken up but seemed stable. Nathan was going to fly him home tomorrow."

"Does he know the role Nova played in his rescue?" Zhi asked. "About her issues with touch?"

Rafe scowled. He and Nathan exchanged a look. "He knew of her role, but I didn't mention the touch thing. However, our clinic is small and staffed by two pack members. It's not unlikely he learned about your issue with skin contact there."

The alpha turned to Nova. "None of the medics know the details of how you found the kids—they think it was traditional psychometry. That secret is safe."

"As safe as it can be with you, Nathan, and I assume Douglas Maitland's aware of it," Zhi griped.

"You forgot the person who told them about Felix in the first place," Nova added.

He snapped his fingers and pointed at her. "You're right. I forgot that asshole."

"We had Jason medevac'd to Anchorage," Nathan said after a beat of silence. "It's the closest hospital with a neurology department. We know people there. Despite the shock you gave him, his chances of recovery are fair. He's young and our kind heals fast."

Nova nodded, looking marginally less miserable.

Zhi rubbed her back. "I know this has been difficult for you. It's the first time you've used your magic defensively. I'm just relieved that you *can* defend yourself, otherwise it would be you in the hospital and not him."

She turned to him with those big green eyes. "But what if Jason wasn't doing it of his own volition? What if those witches implanted some sort of compulsion?"

Rafe sat up in his chair, hope growing in his eyes. Zhi could tell he was ready to latch onto this explanation. He felt like crap for squashing it, but it had to be done.

"He wasn't," Zhi said gently but firmly. "Jason was unconscious in the cave and injured. His shields were down. I scanned him for brain damage as we were climbing out. If there had been a compulsion built into his mind, something that would have activated later, it would have been done with a spell. I would have detected its presence then and there."

"But you can't always detect magic and curses," she said. "That's why you hired me."

He put his hand on her back, rubbing comfortingly. "It's the mind. That's my specialty."

Nathan held up a finger.

"I'm *sure*," Zhi insisted when the man opened his mouth to argue. "A spell of the complexity required to compel Jason to lash out and attack would have glowed like neon. It would have been unmistakable to someone with my training."

The shifter rumbled something under his breath. It sounded like "*shit*."

Rafe rose. "Jason's alpha is dead, so I'm taking responsibility for this."

He looked at Zhi expectantly. So did Nova.

Zhi sighed. "I'm not going to demand you punish a kid who's already been through so much. However, if I ever see him anywhere near Nova, I will not be so generous."

He took his future bride's hand. "I know we had decided to stay until Gerald arrived so the girl can stay with the other kids, but I'm having Han reroute him to our place. The wolves must get their house in order, and we've overstayed our welcome."

Rafe winced but didn't argue. He just thanked Nova again and promised to get to the bottom of things.

Secure in the knowledge that he and Nathan wouldn't allow Nova to come to harm from this quarter again, Zhi ushered Nova upstairs. He wanted to be gone within the hour, and they had to pack their belongings.

CHAPTER FORTY-NINE

Nova went into full-blown anxiety mode as they collected the little girl. The reason why was agonizing to Zhi.

"What if she's afraid of flying?" Nova asked, wringing her gloved hands together in the back of the car. "I won't be able to hold her hand."

"I can hold her hand."

Nova's brow creased. "But she doesn't like you."

He started laughing.

"I'm so sorry." Nova said, stricken. "I didn't mean it like that. Please don't take it personally."

"Why would I take that personally?" he said, choking back laughter.

"You know she's still traumatized of men."

He subsided and reached out for her. She came into his arms with gratifying immediacy. "Of course I know that. And I'll shield you again if necessary. But I think I know a man she'll make an exception for."

And he was right. Because even the woman who rescued you from a hell-tunnel pales in comparison to a man who shifts into gold-spitting lion.

Han had come back on the family jet to pick them up. He greeted the girl with hearty, "Ready to go on another adventure pumpkin?"

He received an enthusiastic "Yes!"

It was the first word she'd spoken to any of them. Grinning smugly, Han swept the little one up into his arms where the formerly mute child transformed into a grade-A chatterbox. One whose name was Cora, who apparently lived in a one-bedroom apartment with her mother Daniela and a beta fish named Simon.

He texted that information to Gerald as soon as they boarded the jet.

Han spent the first few minutes getting the little one settled, explaining Nova's issues with touch and how it would be best if Cora avoided making contact.

"That's okay," Cora said, having already accepted Han's offer to watch the latest Pixar movie together. She wrinkled her small nose in their direction from the other side of the plane. "I'm sorry the only person you can touch all the time is a boy...although he seems okay."

"Thank you for that ringing endorsement." Zhi grabbed her a juice box and offered it to her. "It's almost lunchtime. I had the pilot stock chicken nuggets, fish sticks, and mozzarella sticks."

"Oh, I want chicken nuggets!" Cora chirped enthusiastically.

Han tapped his lips contemplatively. "Mmm, I'll have all three," he said, making Cora giggle.

Zhi turned to Nova, who had sagged into his side to hide her muffled laughter when Cora had so delightfully and effectively snubbed him. "And you, what would you like?"

"I'll start with the chicken nuggets too."

"And after that?"

"After that I'll take everything."

A line appeared between his brows. "You mean the other kid food? Because I have some excellent Alaskan salmon and sushi rice stocked for us. I can prep some quick nigiri."

"That sounds delicious, but what I meant was everything else." Nova rested her hand over his heart. "You. Me. Jinx and Han. Even Elizaveta. I want it all."

Zhi's eyes went to the back of the plane, where is cousin was making walrus teeth out of the straws the flight attendant had just given them. "Kids too?"

Nova looked at Han and Cora. "Yes. If my magic is as mutable as these last few days have indicate it is, then I can shape it. I won't let it define and confine me the way I have been."

She stroked her hand over the hard planes of his chest. "A child is something I never considered, and honestly I still need time to get used to the idea. But in the future I can see it." She laughed suddenly. "Nothing is what I thought. Not your family. Not you. Not even my magic—the one constant in my life."

Zhi held up, his expression of a man about to burst. "None of that was your fault. The way you were brought up—"

"Oh, I know you have a lot of opinions on that. And a great many of them are valid. But I share some of the blame. I could have tried a little harder to free myself."

She stopped him with a finger to his lips when he began to interrupt. "I'm not saying I could have done it on my own. Without your telepathy as a catalyst, I might have failed. The only reason I can take the leap now is because I have you for a safety net now. I'm just kicking myself for not trying a hop or two on my own."

Zhi leaned over, nuzzling her forehead. "I understand. And while I firmly believe you can do anything you set your mind to, I'm not going to lie—the idea of your running touch tests without me is the stuff of nightmares."

"You're right. Luckily, I do have you. And I'm determined. I know I have a lot of work ahead of me. But I *will* do it. Because I need that control. Not just to be with you, but for myself...and for the family we can and should make together."

He took her gloved hand. "Of course. Some things are meant to be."

CHAPTER FIFTY

They arrived home without incident. Cora, having found her voice, now had a hard time not using it.

"This is not a house," she told Han. "It's a hotel!"

"Would I lie to you, peanut? Sure, it's big, but it's still a house. Your grandfather has one *almost* as big," Han added, throwing Nova a smug wink.

Zhi should shut him down for bragging, but it was true. The Burgess estate was large by English standards, but everything was bigger in America.

Cora had been told about her grandfather on the plane, when they explained how Gerald was going to help her find her mother. But Nova knew Han was looking as well—a precautionary measure in case Gerald was conveniently unable to find her mother, named Daniela.

It wouldn't be the first time a powerful member of the Seven cut out a less well-connected family member to claim a powerful child. They saw the action as benevolent because gifted children needed training. It was why they got away with pushing the parent out more often than not.

Neither he nor Nova wanted that to happen here. From what

they'd heard on the plane, Cora worshipped her mom. The father didn't appear to be in the picture.

Fortunately for the little girl, it turned out their fears were unfounded. Shortly after breakfast the following morning, a large stretch limousine pulled into the drive, two brilliant minds glowing with the tell-tale signature of strong magic.

The car hadn't come to a complete stop when a petite woman with honey-brown curls, a darker echo of her daughter's, ran out of it.

"Cora!" she shouted.

Cora ran out of the house as fast as her little legs could carry her, crying out, "Mama! Mama!"

Gerald followed at a sedate pace, joining him at the front steps as he studied the great-granddaughter he hadn't known he had until yesterday.

"She favors her father," he said quietly

"She does," Zhi agreed, having narrowed down which one of the Burgess males sired the child as soon as he saw Daniela. There was only one who could have realistically landed a woman like that.

Gerald had been taller than Zhi in his day, but his spine had compressed with age, so he was an inch or two shorter than him now. Nevertheless, those icy blue eyes were filled with power when he swung them Zhi's way. "You know about Michael?"

Michael, Gerald's youngest and favorite grandson had been Han's pick as Cora's father too. Blonde, handsome, and feckless, Michael had traveled in elite magical circles, a fast set that had overlapped somewhat with Han's. They hadn't been friends. More like nodding acquaintances. But that had been enough for Han to send condolences on the family's behalf when Michael died in a boating accident, his body lost at sea.

Zhi had never met Michael, although he knew his face...and his reputation as a player. As for Daniela, the mother, she was *very* young and nearly as strong as her daughter.

The whole thing was a little sordid. Daniela would have been barely legal at the time of Cora's conception. That didn't sit right with Zhi, but he didn't say anything to Gerald. Michael was gone. And his first impression of Daniela was that she had the strength and grit to handle the Burgess clan. At least he hoped so. For her sake.

Their guests stayed overnight, honoring Daniela's request to put her and Cora in the same room. They put Gerald in a different part of the house without asking.

Nova, who had befriended the woman, was worried for them when she left.

"I don't think Daniela knows very much about our world," she said, sitting on what was now their bed in the master suite. "She has limited training as a healer because it's part of her family tradition, but she hadn't even heard of the Seven before I mentioned it."

He frowned, pausing as he dressed for dinner. Nova was already ready. She was always a step ahead of him. "Did she not know who Michael was?"

Nova's expression soured. "Oh, he told her his name but never explained the significance of it. Daniela met him when she was seventeen and fell pregnant by him at eighteen. He was twenty-five."

He understood what she was getting at—the power imbalance—but he couldn't help but point out the obvious. "We're separated by seven years as well."

And until very recently she had been his employee.

Nova rose from the bed, leaning into his side in that way that made everything in him unclench. "That's different, and you know it. I was a fully-grown woman when we met. Daniela was an impressionable teenager with a rough home life."

He wrapped an arm around her. "You learned a lot about her in a short time."

"I think she was desperate for a confidante. And for information." Nova stroked his butt absently. A touch that would have been verboten such a short time ago was now an unconscious act. It made him want to smile despite the seriousness of the subject matter.

"Do you really think they're better off with Gerald?" she asked.

Daniela had tentatively agreed to travel back to England with her daughter's grandfather, giving up her job after asking Zhi and Han for their advice.

"I do," he said and meant it. "He'll make sure Cora gets the training she needs. Otherwise, there's a very real chance she'll end up hurting herself or someone else."

That was exactly what he'd told the struggling mother, along with a quick crash course on the Burgess family.

Nova sighed. "I hope it works out for them. Daniela said that her own grandmother passed last year—she has no family left. After Michael died, she and Cora were on their own."

"That's about to change in a very significant way." Zhi stroked her arm, glorying in the privilege of touching her bare skin. "Don't worry. I know Gerald seems pompous and inflexible, but family is important to him. And Cora is his blood."

According to Han, Cora was stronger than Michael, something that would no doubt ease her path with Gerald. The Pixiu was never wrong about that. And as long as the old man lived, mother and child would have an ally, even if Daniela didn't realize it yet.

"Family," Nova repeated, her eyes fixed on the horizon out the window. "Family can let you down."

Zhi drew himself up, his brow puckering. "Am I missing something?"

Nova bit her lip and looked down at her shoes. "Yes. I lied to you. Although if it makes a difference, I didn't realize I was lying at the time. I thought the memory was false, part of a dream."

Zhi's confusion was genuine. A telepath didn't get lied to as a rule. "Care to clarify?"

Nova sucked in a breath and let it out slowly. "I do remember my mother. I remember the day she left me at Greenfield."

"Do you want to know what Han discovered about your parents?" he asked softly.

Nova didn't answer for a long while. Then she shook her head. "You're my family now. You and Han. I'm also looking forward to building relationships with the rest of your relatives."

His lip twitched. "Even my mother?"

"Yes," she laughed. "I already said as much. But I do want to know one thing. It's important."

He took her hands in his and waited.

Nova took a deep breath. "Did my parents have any other children?"

He knew without asking that Nova had wondered about this more times than he could count—whether she had siblings and if they were cursed as well. Or had she been the only one with problems too profound to deal with?

Zhi squeezed her to him, his heat and magic enveloping her as solidly as the arm around her. "No. They had no other children."

He had expected tears. But though her eyes shined a little too bright, Nova didn't cry. Instead she inhaled and gave him a bracing smile. "Good. That's good."

EPILOGUE

Zhi took one look at Nova starting to descend the grand staircase and ran up to offer his arm. "Darling, *please*. You know I'd like you to call me to help when you come down the steps."

"I have a touch of the flu," she protested half-heartedly. "That doesn't make me an invalid. I don't even have a fever."

That much was true. He knew because Zhi kept checking her temperature, at least half a dozen times since breakfast this morning. Nova sighed. She loved her husband to bits, but his overprotective tendencies had been thrown into overdrive after their recent visitors.

"You don't have a fever yet," he acknowledged, "but you've had two fainting spells in as many days."

"Those were not fainting spells. I simply got a little lightheaded."

Adult witches normally didn't fall ill from common diseases the way humans did. It was only as children that they were susceptible to viruses and other infections, until their magic matured after puberty and their bodies learned to deal with them. However, Nova had been forced to maintain a strict distance from others most of her life. This recent familial visit had shown them that her immunity was not as well-developed as it should have been, something they were taking steps to correct.

Realizing that she was not about to let him carry her down the stairs, Zhi offered her his arm. "It was more than light-headedness this morning. I warned you not to hug that snot-nosed child."

Nova laughed. "That snot-nosed child is your cousin once removed," she said, wrapping her gloveless fingers around his upper arm.

His beloved bride hadn't worn gloves for almost four months—not in the house anyway. But she always kept a pair tucked in her pockets as a precaution in case guests dropped by or she had to accept a delivery.

"I should have kicked them all out the second that kid sneezed on me." Zhi didn't care that Ekaterina, Alonso, and their kid were his favorite cousins. The city had some lovely five-star hotels. Next time he'd shunt his germ-ridden relatives there.

"And yet you didn't get sick."

Zhi puffed out his chest. "I have an iron constitution." Whereas Nova was only now allowing people within touching distance.

"My own immunity will improve," she assured him. "You and Gallardo have made sure of that. But it must be tested. I can't live in a bubble."

He paused at the bottom of the stairs. "Of course not, but you're already working yourself so hard in shield practice. But there's no need to overextend yourself on two fronts."

After the events in Alaska, building a barrier between herself and the world was Nova's priority. It was slow going at first, but after a few months of diligent practice she had learned to manage her own psychometry to the point where she was no longer at risk of serious harm when touched. It still wasn't comfortable, but she was refining her technique and building new mental firewalls every day.

Zhi covered her hand with his, pressing a quick kiss to her temple. "Humor me."

Nova leaned against him, her smile so brilliant and beautiful it made his heart swell. "I'm not sure I should. You get your way entirely too often."

"Oh, but you love to indulge me." His eyes lit with a wicked light. "The benefits you reap are...substantial."

A lovely blush stained her cheeks. It reminded him of last night. "If you want me to stop being light-headed, you have to stop looking at me that way. My knees are melting."

The predator in him rose, ready to pounce. "In that case, why don't I escort you back upstairs?"

She looked torn. But Nova put a finger to his lips. "Hold that thought. First, I need to get in touch with Rafe. He's expecting my call."

Zhi's expression soured. "You spoke to him last week."

"That was about work," she protested. "We had to add two more chairs to the table he's making for my client. But I want to know if he received the card, I sent him. It's his birthday today!"

Nova had, as promised, introduced Rafe's work to her exclusive client list. The alpha had gained a reputation as a bespoke carpenter to the witching world's elite.

She poked his side when he rolled his eyes. "Do I have to remind you that he's a friend now?"

"He's *your* friend." Zhi tugged her toward his office. "But despite that you should make the call from my couch."

His mother chose that moment to sweep by. "What was the point of redecorating her office if you always make her work in yours?"

"She doesn't mind," Zhi grumbled.

Nova beamed. "I really don't."

Elizaveta tsked. "What did I tell you about always making yourself agreeable to your husband?"

Unbelievable. "Mother, whose side are you on?"

Elizaveta smiled and patted him on the cheek, ignoring him. "

His mother walked away, waving behind her airily. "Oh, and I'd like a refill of that eye cream you found."

"You have an assistant for that now, Mother." Zhi shook his head as she ignored him. "Nova, love, you have to set boundaries with her."

"That's what I was trying to do with you," she pointed out, pretending to be exasperated.

"I didn't mean boundaries with *me*. Just for that, you don't get to walk at all."

Zhi swept her up into his arms, effortlessly carrying her squealing self up the stairs to his office.

"Yes, this is healthy," she said with a giggle. "We have an elevator now, you know."

He'd had one installed as soon as the rainy season began in case she slipped again.

Zhi looked down at her, his eyes luminescing with the force of his emotions. "Then I couldn't touch you as much."

Nova put her hand over his heart, her love a pulse he could feel traveling down their mental channel like a beam of sunshine.

That communication channel almost never shut down. The only time he closed it was if it was distracting Nova from her work. But it usually wasn't necessary. They'd grown accustomed to being quiet observers of each other's lives, although they were happiest when they were together. Which was why they rarely left one another's side.

Even when discussing prematurely crotchety wolves. "So how old is the alpha?" he asked waspishly.

"I have no idea," she said, wrapping her arms around his neck as he kicked his office door open. "But he's looking forward to our visit with Andrei next month. That was brilliant idea by the way. The Hawkins pack is isolated enough and so shifter heavy it's the ideal place to test his new shields."

It would be Andrei's first attempt at mixing with people since he left the mental institution. With luck, the harder-to-read shifter minds would add a layer of protection should Andrei's new mental shields fail.

His cousin was excited about the trip. He kept asking if he could bring Nadia. "I'm glad you still like the idea because I hate it. But I haven't thought of a better one, so I suppose I should be grateful Rafe is willing to host us. Did he mention Jason?"

"Doing much better, thanks for asking," she said as he set her down on the plush leather couch in his office.

Thanks to the shifter's accelerated healing, the teenage shifter had recovered much more quickly than Nova had after Larissa had touched her. It helped that Nova hadn't hit him as hard as she could have. She'd been too shocked, but they had been assessing her true strength since then.

Eight months later, after several hundred failed attempts, Nova had finally succeeded in taking down Han in human form, which meant she could defend herself against almost any adversary.

"He was in no shape to even be out of bed at the time, so it didn't take much to take him down," the alpha guessed when he called to report the boy's recovery a few weeks after they left Alaska.

He also shared the boy's poor reason for attacking Nova.

Jason had heard about the miraculous witch who'd used psychometric powers to find them. Assuming his belongings had been those read, Jason had come to Rafe's house to confess his sins. But he hadn't found the alpha. He'd found the witch he thought knew his secret. And he'd attacked her to stop her from revealing it.

Approximately six months before the kidnappings Jason had met a young woman two or three years his senior. Frankie, as she had called herself, started popping up at the parties he went to. Then she showed up at the local restaurants and movie theaters he frequented. Finally, he'd found her stranded on the side of the road with a flat tire, which the earnest boy had helped her change. Before he knew it, Jason was head over heels in love.

And then Frankie had revealed she was a witch.

Jason had assured her that his father wouldn't care, but she had told him her family hated shifters. She persuaded him to keep their relationship a secret. Before Jason knew it, he was telling her everything about his pack and more. That information had been used against them. Several adult shifters, including Jason's father, died as a result, the children targeted.

Frankie had disappeared a week before the first kidnapping. There was no sign of a witch of that age or description from the POWs at the island, and Han hadn't changed any similar-looking females into coins during the rescue. Of course, "Frankie" could have been using a glamour spell when she was with Jason, but somehow Zhi doubted she'd gone down during the fight. She was still out there somewhere. He was sure of it.

When Rafe asked Nova if she'd seen any of this in her reading of Jason's object, she reminded him that she *hadn't* been able to read his item. Nova had relied on the reading she took of the other children's belongings to find them.

Zhi wasn't thrilled that Jason had made a miraculous recovery, but Nova had been so relieved she hadn't done any permanent damage that he was willing to let it go.

He was, however, determined to hold Hawkins to the promise he'd made on Jason's behalf. The boy wasn't allowed to come apologize in person. Zhi wouldn't even let him call.

Instead, Jason wrote a ten-page apology letter. After reading it Nova called Rafe, suggesting the boy stay with his pack for a while. She also suggested he do community service, recognizing that Jason needed to make amends in a tangible way. The exact details were left to Rafe, as was retribution for the kidnappings. But Zhi had never been concerned those responsible would escape punishment.

Wolves were not prey. The political ringleaders of the kidnapping cabal had forgotten that. But the claws and teeth that had torn apart their bodies and ripped out their necks reminded them. For the brief time they had lived anyway.

Zhi sat at his desk while Nova made her call. She talked to the alpha for a whole ten minutes while he bided his time impatiently, occasionally touching her mind to stroke her, just because he could.

Nova shot him a warning glance when the touch began to wander down her body, but she didn't stop talking. Unrepentant, he kept going, scowling when an unfamiliar spark of consciousness interrupted him.

He shot to his feet, scanning the entire house and the lands around it. But there were no strange minds in the vicinity. Alert and battle ready he scanned again, deeper this time. What he'd caught wasn't a stray thought, rather an awareness, as if a stranger were listening in on Nova's conversation.

But the second scan revealed nothing, not even a hint of magic that would have indicated a masked mind hiding beneath a spell. That would have been impossible with the wards around the house.

His wife hadn't noticed his distraction. Calming, he sat back down, chalking the weird incident up to his preoccupation with Nova's flu and his ongoing irritation with her and the alpha's friendship.

Then she laughed and warmth bubbled around him, innocent and bright.

Zhi froze. The emotion had lasted a fraction of a second, but it had been too pure, too elemental to be a human mind. At least not a mature one.

Everything stopped. Slowly, he turned to study Nova. He waited until she laughed again. And then that golden intangible something returned, streaking across his mind like a comet before fading away.

He rose on autopilot, coming around the desk to the couch, sitting next to Nova. He put his arm around her, and she cuddled against him, continuing her conversation. Zhi took his free hand and stroked her waist before settling it over her flat belly. He closed his eyes as the spark filled his mind, a dancing glow whose attention suddenly turned to him.

His breath caught. It wasn't an intruder. What he sensed was the first stirrings of consciousness of his unborn child.

He stayed there, pushing air in and out of his lungs. It was harder than it should have been.

Zhi had stopped taking the contraceptive potion a little over a month ago. Five weeks at the most. As far as he knew, no telepath had ever detected a mind so early in development. It wasn't usually till after the mother began to show that a telepath was able to pick up any kind of brain activity.

Then again, telepaths as strong as him were exceptionally rare. The few he'd heard about had lived like monks. He doubted there had been one as connected to his partner before.

Nova finished her call and turned to him with a puzzle expression. "What's wrong?"

He stared at her for a moment, his mind utterly blank.

Alarmed she pulled away, sitting up straight. "Zhi, what is it?"

"Uh..." He wracked his brain, searching for the right words. "Do you remember when we agreed I'd stop taking the contraceptive potion because you were getting so good at shielding?

Her lips parted. She looked down at his hand, a bewildered expression on her face. "But you said it would take months for the effects to wear off, maybe as much as half a year."

His brow creased. "I know. It should have taken at least that long for the potion to work itself out of my system."

Her big green eyes met his, and she huffed as if all the air was escaping her lungs. "It's *you*. You're too magical. It started to burn out of your system the moment you stopped taking it."

She collapsed back on the couch, sucking in a deep breath. "We were supposed to have time. We're not ready."

"*Hey*." Zhi tugged her up until she was sitting in his lap. "I know this is a bit of a shock, but we decided to live our lives to the fullest, as if nothing is out of our reach. That included a family."

He remembered the exact expression in her eyes during the conversation. They'd been in bed, the moonlight providing the room's only illumination. But that look in her eyes, half hope and half determination had taken root in his soul.

Zhi moved his hand up, covering her heart. It was still beating too fast, but it began to slow at his touch. "I know we thought we had time, but from the moment you came into my life I've seen you handle everything life has thrown at you, at us, and you kicked its ass."

He pressed a line of kisses along her hairline. "You are going to be an amazing mother."

Her face regained some of the color it had lost. She contemplated him for a minute. Then her face cleared. "I am, aren't I?"

He squeezed her tight. "Damn straight."

The smile disappeared. "But what if pregnancy erases the progress I've made? What if I can't hold the baby when it comes?"

He put his hand over hers. "Even if you couldn't shield, which you can now, magic makes exceptions for mates. Don't you think it will make an exception for our kid?"

She bolted up, pacing up and down the length of the Oriental carpet. "If it doesn't, we'll bend it till it does. We'll break it if we have to."

His grin was slow and satisfied. "That's my girl."

Almost vibrating with pent-up energy, she shook out her arms and jumped up and down, letting out a muted, closed mouth scream.

When she was done, her perfect posture sagged, the tension melting away. She took a step forward and held out her hand. "I know we just came downstairs, but if you're free I'd like to go back to the bedroom."

He sat up. Zhi knew pregnancy could be draining, but he didn't think she'd ask to be carried straight off the bat. Not that he was complaining. Like he'd said, any excuse to hold her was good with him. "Are you tired? Do you need a nap?"

She giggled, bending to take his hand. "No."

His concern evaporated. Heat, love, and so much more filled him to the brim, spilling over all around them, literally brightening the room. Love among the Seven had its perks—or quirks—depending on your point of view.

Zhi leapt to his feet, sweeping her up into his arms for the second time that day. But she didn't complain this time. She simply curled against him, enjoying the ride up the stairs and laughing the entire way.

The End

ABOUT THE AUTHOR

A 7-time Readers' Favorite Medal Winner. USA Today Bestselling Author. Mom to a half-feral princess. WOC. Former scientist. Recovering geek.

Lucy Leroux is the steamy pen name for author L.B. Gilbert. Ten years ago Lucy moved to France for a one-year research contract. Six months later she was living with a handsome Frenchman and is now married with an adorable half-french 5yo who won't go to bed on time

When her last contract ended Lucy turned to writing. Frustrated by a particularly bad romance novel she decided to write her own. Her family lives in Southern California.

Lucy loves all genres of romance and intends to write as many of them as possible. To date, she has published twenty novels and novellas. These include paranormal, urban fantasy, gothic regency, and contemporary romances with more on the way.

Subscribe to the Lucy Leroux Newsletter for a free full-length book!
www.authorlucyleroux.com/newsletter

facebook.com/lucythenovelist

x.com/lucythenovelist

instagram.com/lucythenovelist

tiktok.com/@lucythenovelist

bookbub.com/authors/lucy-leroux